Also available from Unsung Stories
Déjà Vu by Ian Hocking
The Beauty by Aliya Whiteley
Dark Star by Oliver Langmead
The Arrival of Missives by Aliya Whiteley
Winter by Dan Grace
The Bearer of Grievances by Joseph McKinley
The Speckled God by Marc Joan
The Dancer by Rab Ferguson
Pseudotooth by Verity Holloway
You Will Grow Into Them by Malcolm Devlin

METRONOME

OLIVER LANGMEAD

**UNSUNG
STORIES**

Published by Unsung Stories, an imprint of Red Squirrel Publishing
"Red Squirrel" is a registered trademark of Shoreditch Media Limited.

Red Squirrel Publishing Suite 235, 15 Ingestre Place, London W1F 0DU,
United Kingdom

www.unsungstories.co.uk

First edition published in 2017

Cover Artwork © 2017 Alex Andreyev
Interior Illustrations © 2017 Darren Kerrigan

Paperback ISBN: 978-1-907389-39-9
ePub ISBN: 978-1-907389-40-5

Editors: George Sandison & Gary Budden
Copy Editor: Robert Clark
Proofreader: Katherine Stephen
Designer: www.coxdesign.co.uk
Publisher: Henry Dillon

Printed in the UK by Clays

For Dad

PART ONE

THE DOORS BETWEEN DREAMS

AWAKE

There is a painting of a fishing boat at sea on the common room wall, and if I stand close enough, I can just about make out the sailors. The artist put a lot of effort into things like the froth of the waves, and the billowing sails, and even the texture of the clouds, all so vividly captured that sometimes I imagine I can smell the salt coming off the canvas. But the sailors bother me. They are lazy matchstick lines, with black blobs for heads, and no sailor I ever knew was so two-dimensional. It is as if the artist has missed the entire point of the piece.

'Dreaming again, Manderlay?'

Valentine is proud of his new slippers. They let him sneak up on people.

I turn to see him. 'One day, you're going to give me a heart attack.'

Though bent-backed to the point of being crooked, and made squinting by the fact of his glass eye, Valentine is still a proud military man. Something in the curl of his bushy grey moustache, perhaps, and the way I know he insists on wearing green. I am aware that, on more than one occasion, he has been made to remove medals from the front of his dressing gown. Valentine grins a grin made simultaneously ugly and silly by his false teeth. 'Missing the waves, eh?'

'Something like that.'

He draws in closer beside me, as if he is admiring the painting as well.

'Meet you out back,' he mutters, out of the corner of his mouth. 'Got some contraband.'

The two of us shuffle towards the back door.

Right now, the common room is full of broken folk like us, who have been deemed by higher powers – our families, mostly – of being incapable of living without carers. There is an almost funereal air to the place, as if mortality is something tangible here. There is the clatter of Connect 4 pieces, and the shuffle of cards, and the murmur of idle recollection as a dozen pensioners slowly fade from the world.

However... Once a week, on Fridays, this room takes on a different atmosphere. At precisely half past eleven at night, a small group of us sneak down from our rooms and gamble in the light of a lamp stolen from the storage room. We play poker, and bet whatever it is that we have to bet: coins, and stationery, and all manner of marbles and trinkets. I once saw Valentine try to bet his glass eye.

The game is run by one of our fellow pensioners, lovingly dubbed Island Pete because he insists that he once owned an island. He also insists that he lost it to a wealthy baron playing blackjack on a steamboat docked in Glasgow.

'So… where is this island of yours?' I ask, sometimes.

Island Pete will waft his hand of cards vaguely around. 'Tropical,' he replies, as if that is an answer.

Valentine and I have a side bet going about whether or not he is telling the truth about his island. And being the sentimental old fool that I am, I have wagered that one day Island Pete will arrive at our weekly poker game waving some kind of deed, or an ancient photograph of him on his island, and prove all the sceptics wrong.

Today is Wednesday and the home is already suffering from its weekly paper-clip drought, as we few gamblers seek out tokens with which to place bets. I am looking forward to Friday. Of course, because of my hands I am unable to hold my cards steady when we play, so Valentine lifts them up for me, and I know that the crafty old fool uses this opportunity to cheat whenever he is able, but this does nothing to deter me from playing. Indeed, I rather think that without Valentine, and Island Pete, and all the rest, I would have run away from this place by now.

There is a nurse on duty at the back door, absorbed in a well-thumbed novel, and Valentine loudly proclaims that he wishes to stretch his legs outside as we pass her by. 'Oh, how they ache!' he moans, theatrically.

There are quite a few folk in the garden, enjoying the late summer. Some sit nattering and knitting in that way which makes them look like caricatures of the elderly – balls of wool at their feet – and others kneel at the edge of the grass, digging with trowels and planting bulbs. Valentine navigates us a route around all this outdoor industry to the very back of the place, where there is a hidden veranda half in shadow. There, he quickly patrols the perimeter to make certain that we are alone.

I settle down on a bench. 'What have you done?' I ask him.

Valentine raises his storm-cloud eyebrows mischievously, before drawing a pair of lollipops out from beneath his robe. 'Strictly between you and me,' he says. 'Nearly half an hour of reconnaissance for these. That chap at the front desk is a stickler, and I was running out of excuses to be there.' Licking his lips, he unwraps the first. 'A dashing shame to waste these on the kids, eh?'

I raise my hand to accept the contraband, but my fingers refuse to grip.

Seeing my struggle, Valentine is kind enough to simply pop the sweet straight into my mouth. Then, he lowers his bones onto the bench beside me, sucking industriously at his own lollipop and eyeing me up. 'What's that, then?' He jabs his lollipop in the direction of the letter sticking out of my shirt pocket. I am quite certain that Valentine has the sharpest eye in our home – as if, when he lost one, the other became twice as powerful.

I lift my aching hand to pat the folded paper there. 'A cheque,' I tell him.

The letter from my old record label genuinely surprised me when it arrived this morning. I am quite used to mail from my daughter, and the occasional bit of mail from the bank, as well as news of another death among those I used to sail with. But mail from my record label is quite unheard of. After all, I have not released anything new in nearly a decade now.

'Won the lottery, have you?' asks Valentine.

'Not quite,' I tell him, rolling the lollipop around in my mouth. In fact, the cheque is for 40 pence, and by my calculations, this means that over the past six months I have sold a grand total of one album. Still, the cheque is cause for celebration, because someone out there is actually still listening to my music. I do not think that I will ever cash the cheque. Instead, I will save it, and place it upon the mantelpiece in my small apartment upstairs, beside the picture of my daughter, Samantha, and my grandson, George, from the last time they came to visit.

'I sold a CD,' I tell Valentine.

'Well I'll be damned,' says the old soldier, chuckling, 'that's bloody marvellous. Well done, Manderlay, you old codger.' He raises his lollipop into the air. 'A toast! To whichever fool out there stumbled across your album and actually bothered to pick it up. May their ears survive the onslaught of your terrible songs!' He laughs loud, but so do I, and we two share a long moment of peaceful reflection at the bottom of the garden, sucking on our illicit sweets and watching the trails of planes as they fly through the blue sky.

Eventually, there is a change in the direction of the wind, and a chill in the air. I pull my old threadbare dressing gown closer around my shoulders. And perhaps it is the chatter I can hear from the garden beyond, or perhaps some wisp of smoke from somewhere outside the garden, which reminds me. But it is then that I remember my dream.

I turn to Valentine, rolling the lollipop around in my mouth.

'I had the most peculiar dream last night,' I tell him.

>•<

I dreamed of the time I wandered the shipyards of Gothenburg.

It was midway through a voyage I remember well, because we were under the command of Captain Radley, who was a good man when he was drunk and a tyrant when he was sober. That whole journey through Europe, delivering cargo from port to distant port, was an unforgettable experience. Thankfully, as we pulled into Gothenburg, Radley was as drunk as a lord, and gave everyone on deck a day's shore leave.

I had taken it upon myself to leave the rest of the crew to their drinking and explore the port-side. I remember that afternoon clearly, because of the peculiar taste of the tobacco I was smoking: a fresh blend from Indonesia with a sharp kick to it, which I have never been able to find again.

It felt good, being so young. It felt great. I could flex my hands as easily as a man without swollen joints, and the tattoos on my arms looked close to fresh. There was the serpent and rope coiled around my shoulder, still clear, and the dozen white sails of the galleon over my heart, still seaworthy, and the small heart on my wrist for Lily, the clearest of all.

With the sun about to drop behind the hills of Gothenburg, everyone at the docks was working harder than ever. I walked through the ribbed shells of gigantic housings, dappled with lowlight, beneath which floundered the hollowed-out structures of huge vessels being taken apart and put back together again. The ships were all lit up in patches around me, aglow in the light of dusk and scattered with the burning ends of engineers' cigarettes. There were great gouts of black smoke rising into the orange sky above, where stars were starting to show themselves.

Halting, I recharged my pipe, admiring the view. And in that moment, my dream diverged from my memory. I did not continue along to join my fellows at the bar just as I did that day more than fifty years ago, because something caught my eye. Something out of place.

I am not sure what to call them. Nightmares, maybe. I saw the first standing beside the bright light of an open coal burner, and I could see that his feet were blackened from standing there. He looked as if he was damaged, on account of the bandages wrapped all around him. Except, I realised that they were not bandages: they were strips of soiled sheeting. Where his skin was visible, it was scarred with illness, and I thought: *That man is a leper.*

I moved swiftly along – feeling my heart quicken – well aware that the eyes of the man were upon me, until I rounded a corner beside the hollow hull of a tanker.

I noticed a second leper striding with a peculiar gait past the steps of a distant cruise-liner, and I could see that his limbs were too thin, to the point of emaciation. And further along, I could see another still – hairless, with a broad chest, standing among the sparse crowds along the street like a rock among the tide of people.

Then he caught sight of me, and started to move.

They were coming for me.

I emptied my pipe, pocketed it, and started to jog towards the nearest pier, where I thought I might be able to lose them.

Coming close to the pier, where a freighter was unloading its cargo, I emerged into the last orange light of dusk.

Turning, I saw the first leper as he reached the edge of that glowing, and stepped beyond it, reaching out with heavily wrapped hands towards me.

Skirting the rusted remains of an anchor, I dashed quickly up the nearest gangplank and onto the freighter, pulling myself through the low doorway. I thought I might lose my devilish pursuers by leading them into the maze of the place.

My feet clanging off the metal corridor, I rushed past glowing lights until I came to the cargo deck. There, I could see the crates that would be my labyrinth. I rushed down, among the heavy boxes, which formed corrugated metal corridors for me to hide among.

At the place where three crates formed a crude arch, I turned again, to see two lepers in the doorway. It looked as if they were in conversation; I could hear a scratchy whispering beneath all the dockside noise.

They surveyed the deck with their hollow, watery eyes.

'Manderlay!' I heard one cry.

They knew my name.

I made a left, and a right, and another left, hoping that by getting myself lost, they would not be able to find me. I continued on, glancing up at the last ebbing rays of the sun, and the stars gathering in the dark behind them, and I knew that if I spent much longer running through the maze of cargo, I would not be able to see. So, instead, I started to make my way towards the stern, hoping that there were some officers on board, and that they would be armed.

Vaulting from the top of a tower of crates, I grabbed hold of a railing and pulled myself up. The upper decks were dark, and empty, and when I turned back to the maze of cargo, I could see the shadowy figures of maybe six or seven nightmarish lepers as they hunted for me.

I pulled myself up two steps at a time to the freighter's bridge, and was glad to find the door there unlocked. I knew that by turning on the power to that section of the ship, it would be a beacon to my pursuers, but I also knew that I had no other choice. By turning on the power, I would be able to use the radio to call for help.

The floodlights burst on at the flick of a switch, and I grabbed the handset.

'Mayday, Mayday!' I called, but there was no answer, only the crackle of static.

Still, I stood, crying out for help, until I could hear the rattle of the steps below the bridge, as nightmarish figures clambered up after me. I am not sure if I was frightened, then. I had the fearless immortality of my youth on my side, or enough foolish confidence to consider my options instead of giving in to fright. And it was in that manner that I decided to take my chances with the river Gothia.

Abandoning the bridge, I rushed out to where there was a balcony overlooking the freighter. I leaned over the edge, just to see, and saw the mismatched silhouettes of a dozen lepers following me. Their bony fingers reached out as they paused at the sight of me, foul and toothless maws opening up in a hideous serenade of wordless noise.

I climbed the ladder up to the highest part of the ship.

And when I reached the apex, where there was a flashing red light, I could see all of the shipyards, and all of Gothenburg, spread out before me. The sky was encrusted with so many stars that they seemed to outnumber the black. And even though I was being pursued, and even though I was scared, I knew that my dream was wonderful, and remarkable.

Then, as the first of my dark pursuers found the ladder below, I dived into the river.

I remember the way the warm air flowed across me, as if for a moment I might be flying instead of diving. And I remember the way the waters rushed up to meet me, and the way the stars reflected from the river's surface, as if I was diving into the sky. I remember the impact of the waters as I parted them, hands together, smashing that sky. And then I remember nothing more.

I woke.

Remembering my dream casts a gloom over the rest of my day. I follow Valentine around restlessly, considering the intensity of it.

'What do you think?' I ask him, in the queue for dinner.

He turns, and squints at me. 'What do I think about what?'

What I lack in dexterity, Valentine makes up for, as he takes both his plate of food and mine. I follow him through the dining room to our usual table, near the back. Outside, Edinburgh has darkened, and there is even a small smattering of rain rolling down the windows.

Twice a week, this room is used for bingo. I tried it once, and absolutely loathed the experience: the clatter of the balls, the monotone drone of the announcer, and the collective groans of the elderly. It was definitely not my kind of gambling. Unfortunately for most of the home's occupants, bingo afternoons are also mandatory, in some feeble attempt at getting the home's more reclusive pensioners out of their flats and doing something social.

Thankfully for me and Valentine, there is a sympathetic

receptionist, who signs us onto the bingo register as attendees, and lets us slip out through reception. As such, not only do the two of us manage to avoid mandatory bingo, but we also head to the local cinema twice a week, where we have become regulars. Indeed, I have become rather attached to modern cinema in all its peculiar flashy glory. And Valentine makes for a wonderful companion, in that he is happy to hold the popcorn, will inevitably fall asleep halfway through most films, and is superb comic relief when he insists on seeing 3D films despite only having one eye.

'A bit blurry, wasn't it?' he will grumble, afterwards.

Sitting at our table in the dining area – and occasional bingo hall – is a lovely woman by the name of Aggie, who I know for a fact used to be a boxer. She does not talk much about her boxing days, or about anything, because her lungs are on the way out, and she wheezes even when she breathes. But even though she often struggles with her breathing, all the hallmarks still remain: the nose broken too many times to count, and her huge hands, knuckles scarred.

'Hullo Aggie,' I say, and she moves her breathing apparatus out of the way for me.

Aggie smiles her scarred smile at us both.

When we are seated, Valentine sorts my plate out for me; he gets both of our soups, and I get his portion of mashed potato. Then, he helps me get my fingers arranged around my fork, before settling down and tucking his napkin into his dressing gown, as if he has arrived at a formal dinner wearing the clothes he sleeps in.

The arthritis in both my hands means that I should really have someone feeding me, but I will be damned if I am going to suffer the indignity. I will take my time with my meal, and avoid messy foods, and even endure the discomfort in my hands. I will be the last man in the dining room, when everyone else has finished. But I refuse to be fed.

'About my dream,' I say to Valentine, continuing our conversation.

The old soldier seems to consider what I have told him as he slurps at his soup.

'I think you need to remember the name of that tobacco,' he says. 'Sounds grand.'

'You know what I mean.'

Glancing at Aggie, who is frowning at our conversation, Valentine sighs. 'Manderlay here,' he says, 'has a head full of nightmares. And if you ask me, he rather needs to stop yammering on about them. They're just something you ate, you silly old codger. A bit of indigestion.' He rotates his spoon around, so that it makes a circle in the air, as if he is making a circumference of the planet. 'Everybody gets bad dreams every now and then.'

'It was so vivid, though.'

'Nonsense,' grumbles Valentine. 'You and I, we get vivid dreams every night. It just so happens that you remember yours, that's all. Dreams are just...' He sips at another spoonful of soup. 'Dreams are just bits of memories, muddled up with bits of imagination. And if you ask me, which you have, you've just been watching too many movies. Filled your head up with all manner of ghouls. Remember that gory film we watched last week? About the shark monsters? I'm surprised you're not going on about sharks.'

I smile. 'You fell asleep before it started.'

'And it's a good job I did. From what you told me, it was rubbish.'

There is a comfortable quiet between us, filled with the clinking of plates being emptied by the elderly, and the gentle wheezing of Aggie, who looks to be deep in thought.

'What do you dream about?' I ask Valentine.

This question seems to sober the old soldier, and I immediately regret asking.

'Guns, mostly,' he mumbles. 'But not the look of them. Every other sense. The feel of the metal, and the wood. The force of the kick. The taste in the air. And the sound. The noise, like fireworks gone to hell. Pop pop pop.' Valentine lowers his eye, to watch his soup.

I feel something on my hand, and notice that it is Aggie's hand. She has reached across the table, and is looking me in the eye. Every one of Aggie's breaths is precious, and when she speaks, it sounds like a parody of speech, full of phlegm and pain. But still she speaks. 'Fight 'em,' she says. 'Put up your fists and give 'em what for, 'til there's no nightmares left.' Then, she squeezes my hand, smiles at me, and goes back to her food.

As foretold, I am the last man to leave the dining room.

In defiance of my age, I skirt the queue for the chair-lift and take the stairs.

Up in my flat, I take the cheque I received this morning, and place it beside the picture of Samantha, just as promised. My whole little mantelpiece is covered in memorabilia, with the most important objects being the closest to my daughter's photograph, so it is quite the honour for that little slip of paper.

As an afterthought, I head across to the trunk in the corner of the room, and open that beaten old trove with the edges of my hands.

Inside, there is a heap of junk from my old house. It takes me a small while to find what I am looking for, but when I do, I take it out – held between my wrists – and close the trunk, heading across to settle into my armchair. I have never used the bed in my humble flat, and nor do I think I ever will. This chair is the place that I sleep, and one day, when the time comes, I hope to die in it.

By the light of the lamp, I open my old notebook.

The album I sold – probably found at the bottom of a bargain bin somewhere – was called *Solomon's Eye*, and it was the most peculiar album I ever released. Mostly, when I used to compose, it would be a slow thing. I would start with the seed of an idea, and let it grow as I played, letting it gradually come to life through my violin.

Solomon's Eye was different.

It is not easy for me flip through my notebook. My fingers keep getting muddled. I skip leaves of pages covered in bars and filled with notes, scrawled in my old neat handwriting. But then, halfway through, I come to the place where I wrote *Solomon's Eye*. Instead of tidy, the notes across these bars are wild, and hastily scrawled. I flip further on, seeing their mad dance across the page. Because I wrote this whole album in one day.

I was very ill indeed, when I was 72. In fact, I nearly died. But I held on, through my terrible fever, and survived. I can remember very little of those two long feverish days, except for the madness that took me: the bizarre hallucinations, the fever dream.

They had me in a small hospital room by myself. And at the height of my delirium, I thought that my wife was with me, her delicate hand in mine, our wedding bands clinking together. And though I could not see her face, I could hear her gentle laughter, and I could smell her perfume - all the things I knew so well of her before she passed away.

Lily spoke to me, in those fevered hours. 'William,' she said, and she tugged at my hand, as if she wanted to lead me somewhere. 'Follow me. Come with me to Solomon's Eye.'

And I remember, at the worst moment, the way the television in the corner, all mad static and hissing, suddenly became very clear. It showed a long black road, going on forever, dividing mountains and crossing seas, like a line drawn around the world. And as the image on the screen followed that road, on and on, as if I was a bird flying above it, Lily sang to me. She held my hand tightly, and sang songs so brilliant and wonderful and strange that they fixed themselves in my head, and I wanted that fever dream to never end. I wanted to watch the black road roll along forever, and hear the strange songs my wife sang to me.

And when I emerged from my hallucinations at last, I still had those songs in my head. Samantha was so worried about me those days that at first she refused to fetch my notebook. But eventually, at my insistence, she did, and I spent the next day recovering and scribbling down all of Lily's songs as quickly as I could, before they vanished from my thoughts. A whole album was born from terrible illness.

I close the notepad, because I can feel my eyelids drooping. There is a blanket beside my chair, and I pull it over my knees. My memories of writing *Solomon's Eye* have awakened a pang of regret: I have not seen my daughter for so long now. Why should it take the threat of my death to reunite us? But then, as I start to drift away, to sleep, to new dreams, my thoughts return to my strange dream of last night. My head is full of nightmarish lepers. And as I close my eyes, and leave the room, I have Aggie's words echoing around in my thoughts to comfort me instead.

'Fight 'em,' she said. 'Put up your fists and give 'em what for.'

>•<

I dream of the lighthouse.

In my late teens, I found my rebellion in riding my motorbike as far north as I could, in some attempt at escaping what I imagined to be the humdrum ordinariness of home threatening to make me boring. And it was on one of those trips that I stumbled across a forgotten cove at the edge of the Highlands, just beyond a set of crumbling low walls that must have been a kind of farming village at some point.

I am back on the pebble beach of that cove.

Behind me looms the set of jagged cliffs that hide this place from everyone, a torn array that look as if some giant has ripped a chunk out of the edge of the land. Before me is the frothing silver sea, washing across the pebbles.

I am wearing my leather jacket, and a nearly-new pair of jeans which are already ripped in one knee. I draw my sleeve back, but the heart tattoo dedicated to Lily is not there yet because this is before I met her. And it would be so easy for me to forget that I am an old man dreaming myself young, were it not for the notebook I am holding, the same notebook I fell asleep reading, filled with songs; a relic from the waking world.

I place the notebook into a jacket pocket and try to forget about it.

The abandoned lighthouse where I used to camp out is further along, but I do not go there yet. Instead, I clamber across pebbles towards where there is a jumbled shape beneath a worn tarpaulin, which I haul back.

Here lies the object that brought me back here every weekend for almost a year. By some convergence of currents, the North Sea brings a lot of detritus to this cove, all manner of driftwood, floating fishing gear and rubbish. Back then, I saw potential in that rubbish. So, I built a boat out of it.

The boat is just about big enough to fit one person, and it looks like it is made of patchwork. In its current state, it is little more than a collection of bits of beaten tin and twists of driftwood, held together with bleached fishing line. The shape is unmistakable though. In the months to come after this moment, I will bring tools and treatments through from Edinburgh, and even some materials to make sails out of. And by the end of my year here, my little patchwork boat will have a mast, and I will sail her out to disaster, to where she will sink roughly half a mile out from shore. It will be my first short voyage, and inspire a great many more.

I run my hands, so unaffected by age and disease, across the rough driftwood of my boat.

Then, I turn and run to the sea, flinging my jacket aside and wading in, feeling the cold water cling to my jeans. I walk out until the water reaches my waist and I can feel the chill of it invigorating my fingers. I take a deep breath of sea air, feeling my lungs shudder, tasting the salt of it.

It was here, in this cove, where I first met Lily. A girl from the nearest village, a few miles down the coast, who grew curious about the lights glowing in the abandoned lighthouse. I first saw her as a silhouette at the top of the cliffs, and then in person, wearing a white dress and a slanted smile as she asked me who I was and what I was doing here.

Of course I fell in love with her. Anyone would have. She was rare and wild, and though not as infected with wanderlust as I was, she still yearned for adventure. Eventually, she would bring more blankets, pillows and even an old mattress down from her village, and set them up in the top room of the ruined lighthouse, which would become our place together. She would share in the magic of my secret cove. I would bring my violin through from Edinburgh, and play songs for her deep into the nights, when her eyes would become wide and dark and her slanted smile would soften and become something sweeter.

'Will,' she would say, 'play me another.'

I learned so many songs for her. And though I knew I had some talent for the violin already, my love for Lily improved my art so much that I would eventually not only audition for the London Philharmonic but get offered a job there. And it was in that way that my year at the cove would come to an end: with the sinking of my patchwork boat and a great bonfire at the top of the lighthouse, where Lily wept all night long at the sight of our hidden nest burning.

I wade back up to the beach and sit, letting myself dry off.

It is cold, so I pull my leather jacket back on. Perhaps now would be a good time to go and explore the ruined lighthouse and find some shelter. I grab a pebble before I go, and skim it across the waves, wondering whether it would be such a bad thing were I to never wake again. I would not mind dreaming of this place forever.

At the end of the pebble beach, out on a ring of concrete,

stands the empty shell of the old lighthouse. Perhaps it was once painted white and red, but it has been so worn by the years that it is a stony grey finger, pointing at the heavens, and pock-marked with holes which whistle when the winds are strong.

There is something horribly wrong with the lighthouse. I stop short.

Clinging onto the side of it is a monstrous shape. It has a body the size of a yacht and eight spindly legs the thickness of masts dug into the stone. From what I can make out, the texture of its limbs, and its bulbous body, are the same as if it has been carved from the trunk of a tremendous tree. The way the light plays across it lends its many eyes a terrible gleam, and I am sure that it is watching me. Right now, it is perfectly still, clutching hold of the very top of the lighthouse, where its eight legs keep it at a terrible angle, defying gravity.

There is a giant wooden spider at the top of my lighthouse.

I take a deep breath, and raise my skinny fists.

MARCH

A moment of stillness before the spider moves.

Pebbles scatter as it lands on the beach and scuttles quickly towards me, rushing with a terrible eight-legged locomotion. I run for the cliffs. The giant wooden spider is more than twice my height and I do not think my fists will have much of an effect.

The path is thin and winding – made mostly of mud – and in places I have to crawl up the side of the cliff. All the while I can hear the spider as it approaches, every leg causing a rocky landslide as it skitters from its lighthouse perch. At the top of the path I turn and see it raise its front legs up at me, mandibles like wooden stakes feeling the air, and I see myself reflected in its many eyes, small and fleeting.

My bike is on the other side of the ruined village and I run like a sprinter through tumbled-down buildings towards it. The ground is uneven, as if it is a piece of paper that someone has crumpled and tried to flatten out again, and I have to take care across the thick purple heather coating everything. I leap across a fallen wall and through the empty shell of a farmhouse, which is now no more than a rocky perimeter.

I catch sight of my bike in the near distance, a thundering old thing that cost me far too much to buy and far too much to maintain. Still, it gleams, a green and silver machine that might mean my salvation. But before I can reach it, I make the mistake of looking back, watching in horror as the spider's front legs emerge at the edge of the cliff behind me.

Too large to use the path, it has navigated the sheer concave cliff-face.

Tripping on a patch of heather, I right myself and pull myself forward using the edge of a wall. Two more ruined houses along, I finally emerge onto the dirt track: a more even surface, where I can run without care. I bound the distance between me and the bike, fumbling through the pockets of my leather jacket for the keys, and finding them beneath my old notepad. Keys in hand, I rush the last few yards, ready to hop on and ride away.

With an almighty crash the spider lands on the building behind me.

I am thrown forward by the force of its landing, among dust and pieces of rock. Ancient bricks clatter and whole walls tear away as the spider rips the ruined farmhouse into pieces with its tree-trunk legs. I spend a few long moments on the ground, dazed by the dexterity of the terrible spider and by the distance it must have leapt to intercept me.

The spider pulls itself free of rubble, and begins to advance on me again, mandibles raised.

Rolling myself around, I leap to my feet and dive for my bike.

Keys in the ignition. Foot on the pedal. The bulky old machine starts first time.

Almost blind with adrenaline, I put my bike into gear and speed away, whirling dirt in my wake. The spider attempts to follow, stake-end legs thumping into the ground, but it is too slow. I see it as I go, waving its legs at the fly that got away. And as I speed beyond the lighthouse, and the ruined village, and the giant wooden spider, I feel the rumbling of the machine beneath me as it roars. I kiss the metal between the handlebars.

'You marvellous beast!' I cry.

My laughter is lost on the wind.

I pull my goggles on to protect my eyes from the wind and dust.

The old track winds on through scrubby, windswept woods, all trees at an angle as if they are bowing towards the sun. There is a spray of dust and moisture in my wake. And though I might be mistaken, I believe that I see the movement of even more malevolent creatures among the trees around me, watching me go.

Where the track forks – one path leading on to the local village, and the other leading up the hill to where an overgrown church overlooks the sea – there is a man standing at the divide. My initial reaction is to speed up, to carry on riding my bike and spend my whole dream running the roads of Britain. But this man does not look like another terrible nightmare. Instead, as I approach, he raises his hand, in the manner of a policeman flagging down a car.

I slow to a halt beside him.

He seems out of place here because he is from the wrong era. The soldiers of this time wore plain green, metal helmets and had rifles that were little more than glorified slingshots. But this man, this boy, has broken-glass greens and sandy browns across his fatigues, and he wears fingerless marksman's gloves, and the helmet hanging at his side looks like some tremendous bowl for the gathering of bullets. He has a complex-looking black rifle slung across his shoulder, and he looks as if he is from one of those modern war movies that Valentine loves so much.

He is crunching on an apple. 'Bitter,' he comments, screwing up his face. He is young, almost too young, for the uniform that he is wearing. Most of all I am struck by the fact that his hair is the colour of fire, with a natural wave to it that only enhances the effect.

'You should get off the road,' I warn him. 'The woods are full of monsters.'

This does not seem to surprise the strange soldier. 'That's why I'm here,' he says.

I turn the engine off, pulling my goggles up to survey the soldier better. Judging by the mud on his boots, it looks as if he has come down the track from the church. He finishes his apple, spits out some seeds and throws the core into a thicket. 'We should head up,' he tells me, swinging his rifle around. 'Better view from the hill.'

'Who are you?' I ask him.

'I'm March,' he says, 'and I hunt nightmares.'

The track continues for a while through trees. I push my bike as far as I feel able, before we come to a steeper incline. There, I pull the keys from the ignition and pocket them. Before us is a tall hill covered in long grasses, and at its apex is the silhouette of the old church standing at the edge of a cliff. Together, we tread through the grasses, moisture staining our trousers dark, until we come to the gravestones, scattered at odd angles like a mouth full of stone teeth grown wrong. The winds are stronger up here.

I notice the nightmare-hunter has raised his rifle, and feel my heart lurch when I see what it is he is aiming at. Standing in the doorway of the church is another one of those diseased and bandaged creatures from my dream of Gothenburg. Lurching from beneath the arch, it raises its arm towards me, pointing with a crooked finger. I take one step back for every step it takes forward, ready to turn and run back to my bike.

Only, when it notices March, it stops and parts its ripped lips, letting forth a word hatefully. *'Sleepwalker!'*

I nearly jump clear out of my skin when March opens fire. The rifle bucks in his hands. The first shot hits the leper in the torso, and its whole body spasms, jerking backwards. But before it can fall into the dark of the church, the second shot hits it clean between the eyes. There is no blood. And instead of landing with a thump, the terrible creature disintegrates as it falls, turning to a black dust that rolls away with the wind, like the last remnants of a bonfire.

I lower my hands from my ears, hearing the crack of those shots still echoing.

'One down,' says March, lowering his rifle.

I pull my jacket closer around me. 'Holy hell,' I say. 'Please give me a bit more warning if you're gonna do that again.'

At the nightmare-hunter's direction, we begin to pile up loose stones in front of the church, like a crude bunker. I heave some from beside the cliff while March pauses to check his equipment. 'You got a name?' he asks, as I roll another stone around.

'William Manderlay,' I tell him.

'Nice to meet you, William,' he says. 'Now. You've got a real bad nightmare problem here. One of the worst I've seen, actually. So what I'm going to do is go ahead and sort it out for you. Clear out the nightmares. But to do that, I think I'd rather have you somewhere out of harm's way.' He glances down at the valley and then back at me. 'I'm going to do something really stupid to get them all up here, I think. So I'm gonna send you somewhere safe.'

'I can help, though.'

He shakes his head, preparing his rifle. 'The problem is that if you get hurt, you might wake up. And that's a bad thing. Because if you wake up, then your dream collapses, and I get woken up as well. So I can't finish the job, and it becomes a bit of a pain trying to find you again.' March aims down the sights of his gun at the grassy hill before us. 'There's a lot of dreams out there,' he says. 'You got lucky I stumbled across this one. Finding a dream is like...' He waves his hand vaguely about. 'It's like finding a needle in a haystack. Except the needle keeps shifting around, and sometimes the needle isn't even in the haystack.'

At last there is a ring of stones in front of March's flattened-out patch of grass.

'Where can I go?' I ask him, because we are at a dead end here. There is only the sea.

The nightmare-hunter nods at the church. 'There's a door in there. That's how I got into your dream. Go through it, and you'll be in somebody else's dream. Keep going through enough doors, and enough dreams, and you'll eventually find your way to the Capital. And that's where I'll come and meet you when I'm done here.' March rearranges a few of the stones in his fort, before reaching satisfaction with his firing range. Then he stands and does some stretches. 'Don't worry about getting lost,' he says. 'Go through enough doors and you'll always get to the Capital. Can't miss it. Bloody great tower, right in the middle. You'll know when you see it. It shouldn't take me too long to finish up here, so just sit tight there and keep yourself busy.' As an afterthought, he adds, 'There's some nice bars at the tower.'

I try and pierce the dark beneath the church's archway with my vision, to see some kind of mysterious door, but there is nothing. Indeed, there is nothing behind the church but a sheer drop: nowhere for a door to lead.

'All right, then,' I tell him, still unsure.

'Here,' he says, and he throws me an item from his belt. I turn it over, and see that it is a compass. At first glance, it looks like standard military issue, green metal, worn at the edges. Except that its face is different. Still white, it has no markings – no North, South, East or West. Instead, it has an excess of needles, all in different colours. There are a couple of blue needles, three red, and, right now, more than two dozen thin black needles. None of them are spinning.

'You can use that,' he says. 'The red needles are doors, and the blue ones are dreamers. If you spot someone and they don't have a blue needle pointing at them, then they're just a figment. Not real. Part of the dream. Got it? Your best bet is to follow the red needles from door to door until you get to the Capital, and avoid the blue needles. There's no point in disturbing any dreamers.' Finished with his stretches, March fishes around in his heavy pack. 'You take real good care of that compass, though, William. There's only twelve of them and I'm screwed if you lose mine.'

I move the device around, watching the needles fixed on me and March.

'What about the black?' I ask him.

At this, the nightmare-hunter grins – a boyish expression. 'Nightmares,' he says.

Drawing a bright red flare gun from his pack, March gets into position behind his fort, lying in a marksman's pose. 'You'd better get going,' he says. 'I'm going to do that stupid thing now.' Lowering the bipod at the front of his rifle, he shuffles around until he's comfortable, with his sights set down the long hill. The gravestones are lined up in shoddy rows to either side of him, and at the tree-line near the bottom of the hill, I can see my bike, gleaming in the half-light leaking through the clouds. Of course I am hesitant. 'Don't worry,' says March, sensing my pause. 'I've got this under control. I'll see you at the Capital.'

One slow step at a time, I make to leave, not sure if I am doing the right thing. Maybe I could stay and at least play the spotter or something. Still, I obey orders and carry on up, and at the archway of the church, I turn and give him a feeble, 'Good luck!'

He gives me a thumbs-up in return, then reaches for the flare gun at his side. Aiming it up at the sky, he pulls the trigger, and a tremendous point of red light streaks from the end of it, with a scream. The flare goes up and up, into the grey and white, until it pauses there like a red star, smoke drifting from its edges. I look back down into the valley and I see them there: nightmares. Dozens of them, running towards that bright beacon, towards the hill, with the red of the flare glinting in all their eyes.

Suddenly, I am very glad that I am leaving.

March brings his rifle to bear.

Inside the church, there is a door that does not belong, set into the far wall. It is painted white, and has a brass claw handle. I approach the alien door with caution, gripping hold of the handle and pausing for a moment. Logic is telling me that on the other side of this door is a sharp drop down to the sea, but I am not so sure any more.

I turn the handle and pull the door wide.

Through the door is a shopping centre.

I can tell that it is somewhere in the USA because of the announcements, and the noisy exchanges between shoppers. I stride aside sparkling fountains, where pretty girls sip from colourful cups and ignore one another, and I carry on past enormous pots filled with flora, drooping in the heat burning down through the windows above.

The shoppers continue and I am ignored. I feel out of place here, with my antique biker goggles around my neck, and my leather jacket, far too warm in the heat. I am a young man from another time.

By the needles of the nightmare-hunter's compass I am led past the dreamer, and he is a child of no more than five years old, standing alone and ignored beside a tall fountain. There is the glistening of snot fallen from his flared nostrils, mingling with the tears rolling awry of his reddened eyes, and gripped tightly in his chubby hand is the string belonging to a perfect round blue balloon, which floats like a buoy above his head. The dreamer is utterly abandoned by his figments, a hundred, or a thousand, men and women striding about their shopping without a care for the wails of the child. They seem like distant bodies, distant planets orbiting a lonely star.

I pause at a coffee shop and watch the boy for a while, wondering whether I should interfere. Every paternal instinct I have is telling me to part the crowds, pick the child up and go in search of his parents. Instead, I carry on, heeding the advice of the nightmare-hunter, until the child's wails fade into the background. I come across a shop selling kitchen supplies, where I take a large kitchen knife and tuck it into the back of my belt, concealed beneath my jacket. Of course I feel a pang of guilt for leaving the child behind, but I tell myself that he will wake soon enough, and be comforted by folk who love him.

Beyond the refrigeration section, I locate the next door, and travel beyond the shopping centre.

The next dream is a festival. The wide street is a sea of bodies, shouting and laughing, and the air is a haze of colours as they throw brilliant neon powders over each other, and they all look like characters from some vividly inked comic book. The faces I see belong to India, and I realise that this is a dream of Holi.

Samantha insisted that I take her to a small celebration of Holi in Glasgow when she was eight, but she was not interested in the importance of the festival in Hinduism. She was only interested in the colours – in becoming neon. It is a dear memory to me, because it is the way that I remember Sammy as a child: as a rainbow girl.

I have to push myself through the street, rubbing up against people and feeling the heat of the stones beneath my shoes, overwhelmed by the mingled odour of flowers and spices and sweat. I am caught up in the laughter and joy despite my inability to understand the language, and find myself stepping to the same rhythm as the drums thumping over the crowd's noise. Upon the balconies of the windows above there are bright depictions of the gods, and more powder streaming down from the laughing figments beyond, showering me and those around me, until I must look as if I am one of them. I move with the flow of the crowd, past folk with water guns and washing-up liquid bottles filled with more colour, spraying everywhere and all across me, and I laugh with them, ducking and weaving like an amateur boxer around the bright streams.

A dreamer is visible on March's compass, the only other blue needle in the dream, but he or she might be anyone here – all people, including me, made anonymous in the colours.

At last, I successfully navigate my way to a thin alley, with the water from the drains streaming across the cobbles a swirling neon, where I catch a glimpse of my reflection. My hair is green and yellow and my face and jacket are stained pink. I have to laugh at myself as I try to remove some of the colour from my skin. What a fool I look.

Through a metal door with a bar handle I go, leaving the festival behind.

To where I stand blinking in the light of a dazzling new dream.

>•<

It is becoming increasingly difficult to remember that I am really an old man, fast asleep in my armchair at home. I stand solitary here, more awed by the sight before me than anything I have seen so far in dreaming.

I have stepped into a ruined and flooded London.

It looks as if the earth has broken open in the wake of an earthquake, shattering the city. There are the shapes of familiar buildings balancing at angles on shards of earth that rise from the high waters. Everything is coated in a layer of life.

I have emerged from a door facing London's twin railway stations. From here the roof of St Pancras station looks like a gargantuan set of ribs, every window smashed, with lengths of vine draped between each curve. And King's Cross station looks like an empty birdcage, its thick net of a roof stained so dark it looks as if it is made of wood.

As I wander forward, I see lily pads among crisp packets and plastic bottles, and in a way it is reminiscent of the London I knew as a young man – wealth and filth, violence and romance, crowds and loneliness – and I am struck by a strong memory of Lily.

She would come to every one of my performances with the London Philharmonic that she could, and I would see her in the audience. I remember Lily in winter, wrapped up warmly and wearing a little tinsel in her hair. I remember Lily in spring, wearing such bright colours that she already seemed ready for the warm months to come. I remember Lily in summer, confident enough to bare her collarbones and wrists, and that sly slip of a smile that always seemed to bloom in June. And I remember Lily in autumn, wearing the knitted cardigans she made herself.

And later on, in the darkness of my small apartment, she would trace the sounds she heard me play across my chest with the tips of her fingers.

I shake my head, to clear it of the memories threatening to slow me down.

The nightmare-hunter's compass is leading me towards St Pancras, where there is another door. For a moment, I entertain the idea that this city is the Capital that March was telling me about, but there is no tower here. He said that the Capital would be obvious, and there is nothing obvious about this place at all. There is not a soul in sight, either.

There are a lot of nightmares showing up on the compass, however, making me nervous.

I keep my head down as I clamber up the fallen steps of the railway station, noticing that there are three blue needles – dreamers – on the compass. There is the needle pointing at me and the needle pointing at the dream's owner, whoever and wherever they may be, but there is also a third needle, twitching along with the nightmares evident all about. I wonder if it perhaps belongs to another nightmare-hunter, emptying this dream of terrors.

Inside, St Pancras station is an acoustic joy. Birds fly from perch to distant perch, calling out and filling the place with vibrant noise. They have made their nests in every crevice available, including the almost unrecognisable statue near the entrance, which I hide behind.

The furthest arch of the station is open to the sky and makes the yellow sun look like a lidded eye. And it is beneath that arch that I see the silhouettes of a great horde of nightmares, shifting as if they are entirely composed of shadows. My breath draws short.

With my back against the statue's base, I draw the kitchen knife and consider my options. The compass is telling me that the next door is beyond the shifting mirage of creatures in the near distance. I could sneak around, perhaps. Or just make my way back to the door I came in by, hoping to come across a different route to the Capital through other dreams. But then, I notice something upon the face of the compass that strikes fear through me.

I am surrounded.

Between the fallen pillars of the great entrance behind me shuffle a collection of terrible figures. More nightmares. I raise my knife and back away, well aware that I am being corralled towards an even greater mass of awful creatures in the station.

Backing up between glass barriers, I hear their collective wails.

None runs at me. They advance steadily, even as I try to back away, desperately seeking some means of escaping the horde. I step across fallen beams to where a great flood of light pours in through a gap in the roof. There I make my stand, concealing March's compass as best I can and gripping hold of the kitchen knife with both hands. I turn on the spot, brandishing my knife, the nightmares reaching out towards me with their horrible hands, limbs stretched too long, shadows too dark, eyes like a pack of demonic wolves.

And yet they stop, having formed a great circle around me.

'What do you want?' I cry, and my voice echoes.

'William Manderlay!' calls a voice.

Stepping out from between the mass of nightmares comes a girl who looks like a burst of sunlight. She is small, and wearing bright yellow flowing garments lined in gold, including a veil across her dark hair. Her skin is the colour of fertile earth, and she is covered in jewellery and intricate piercings, which flash in the gloom.

The girl is holding a wooden compass.

'You—' I keep my knife aloft. 'You're another nightmare-hunter?'

'We're called Sleepwalkers,' she says, 'and not all of us hunt nightmares.' The girl crosses the distance between us smiling a warm smile, as if I am not brandishing a knife at her. She seems to be examining me as she approaches. 'You were very handsome when you were young,' she says. 'But roguish. A real heart-breaker. I can imagine you running off at the first sign of adventure. Still, it's lovely to meet you at last, William. It's taken me a long time to find you.'

The girl – the Sleepwalker – stops before me, but I keep my knife raised. I can feel a cold breeze across the back of my neck, and all the terrifying eyes of the gathered nightmares upon me.

'Who are you?'

'My name is June.'

'What do you want from me?'

June licks her lips before she replies. 'Your music really is something,' she says. 'I can't tell you how many times I've listened to your album. I know all the songs off by heart, even if they don't have words. One day, I'd love to hear them live. From your own hands. But right now, I'm here because you didn't finish your album. It's incomplete. Or maybe you just didn't use all the songs. I'm not going to ask you where you got hold of them in the first place. I don't really mind, to be honest. But I need the rest of them. I need every single song that leads to Solomon's Eye.'

The knife wavers between us in my unsure grip.

'I don't understand,' I tell her.

'You don't have to,' she says. 'Maybe you don't even know what Solomon's Eye is. It doesn't matter at all. What matters is that you need to give me all the songs. Not just the ones you used on the album. I need the complete map, William.' Her smile fades, becoming something sinister instead. 'And trust me when I tell you that I am willing to do whatever it takes to get them from you. I have a great deal of respect among nightmares. And even if you do something silly here – try and wake yourself, maybe – my nightmares will find you again. They will hound you every night for the rest of your life, until you give me the songs I need. Neither March, nor January, nor any of the other Sleepwalkers can stop me, either. Yes, I know you've met March. But he's just a boy looking for a war.'

I try to back away, but June reaches out and gestures at the knife in my hands. At once, like sorcery, the wooden handle bursts into life – growing leaves and small branches. It clatters to the ground and I stumble, hands thrown wide. June advances.

'Wait!' I cry, and she halts.

Reaching into the pocket of my leather jacket, I grab the old notebook – that remnant from the waking world – and pull it out, flicking through. Because June was correct about the album I put out. There were something like eighteen songs in total before I trimmed it down, and though only eleven eventually made it onto the finished piece, they are all still scrawled down here: the complete set of songs from my fever dream.

I locate the right page and hold the notepad out. The

nightmares surrounding us raise their broken voices in a terrible crescendo, echoing wildly around the flooded station. But I am not giving June the songs she wants to preserve my own health. Rather, I am giving her the notebook so that she will not search me and find March's compass – a device, I am sure, which is far more important than a mere set of songs.

'Here,' I tell her. 'They're all here.'

The small Sleepwalker takes the notepad and flicks through. Then, she smiles broadly – a genuine, attractive, youthful smile, and she turns on the spot, her arms outstretched, dancing in celebration. Her nightmares howl louder and stamp their feet, and the whole station rattles as it fills with the noise. I cringe back. 'Oh, William,' she says, laughing, golden-star earring glittering as it turns. 'You have no idea how important this is. What a wonderful thing it is you've done here. With this… with this, I'm going to see God.' She rushes across to me, grabbing the back of my neck with her free hand and kissing me deeply.

'I'll see you again, I hope,' she says afterwards, breathless. 'In another dream.'

Then, she turns to her nightmares, skipping away among them. 'Wake him!' she calls.

And in a calamitous confusion of terror, they rush me all at once, to grab at me, to tear me apart – all those wretched creatures howling in delight. I wake in fright.

THYME

I wake feeling dazed.

Today is Thursday, which means that after I am done with breakfast, I must head to the record shop with a friend of mine called Vinnie. We go slow because Vinnie's legs have seen better days, but despite his disability Vinnie still walks with a rhythm. Vinnie has a weakness for jazz that runs all the way to his bones, as if his years listening have affected his speech – given it a music. 'Hop to it,' says Vinnie, hustling as quickly as he can. He is excited.

At the record store – a wonderful, wood-panelled place just off the Royal Mile – Vinnie settles into the armchair they keep set out for him and listens through headphones to the first of the stack of records he has gathered for himself. He clicks his fingers, bobs his head and scat sings along with the instruments, all with such an enormous smile across his face that it makes the journey, every week, worth while.

With the help of the store's owner – David, who makes a point of coming in on Thursday mornings to help us because

I once taught his son how to play the violin – I gather my own small stack of records and sit down on my wooden chair beside the front door, where I can see people passing by. One by one, David puts the records on for me, and I spend the morning absorbed in the music and the movement of the city – the faces of passers by – and recovering from my dream. I am fond of jazz, but today I am mostly listening to quartets dug up from the dusty corners of the record shop: forgotten records by forgotten musicians.

'You all right, Will?' asks David, before we leave. 'You're very quiet today.'

Vinnie pats me on the back. 'Chin up, Will. Life ain't so bad.'

In the afternoon I take a train with Valentine across the Forth Bridge to Queensferry, to where there is a Deep Sea World. It is unusual to see Valentine this far away from our home, because he struggles with long distances. The home keep asking him whether he would like a frame or a walking stick to support him, but Valentine always refuses, and uses me to lean against when the going gets tough. 'Why on earth would I need a lump of wood,' he says when offered a cane, 'when I have Manderlay?'

The two of us make the rounds of Deep Sea World, walking through the glass tunnels, with all manner of pretty fish swimming about above us. I used to take Samantha here, when the glass was still shiny and new, and I remember the way she pressed her nose so close to it that she left little marks wherever she went. Sammy was always fascinated by the creatures of the sea.

'What's that?' asks Valentine, pointing at a fish.

'That's a barracuda,' I tell him.

And further along, 'What on earth is that?'

'That's a stingray.'

'And what about that, then?'

'That's a diver, Valentine.'

He squints through the glass. 'So it is.'

By the time we are done perambulating through the tunnels we are both too tired to take the train back, so Valentine orders us a taxi at the front desk. I have to gently nudge him awake when we arrive, and when he pays for the absurdly large taxi fare using my wallet I barely put up a fight. We join the others in the hall for dinner, and Valentine looks absolutely exhausted, but happy – his cheeks ruddy.

'What's bothering you, Manderlay?' asks Valentine, over his soup. 'You've been stomping about all day, head full of storm clouds.' He aims his spoon at my shirt pocket. 'Got something to do with that old notebook of yours? Barely had your hands away.'

I place an aching hand over the pocket, again surprised to find the notebook there.

'I had a bad dream,' I tell him. 'Someone took it.'

Valentine stops eating his soup, and puts his spoon down, his mirth fading. 'The problem with you,' he says, tapping his temple, 'head in the clouds. Always dreaming about this or that. Running off to sea. Now, I don't know anything about any bad dreams, but you just keep a close eye on yourself, eh? Keep that noggin of yours healthy. Remember what happened to Donaldson? Don't think I could go through all that again.' He goes back to slurping at his soup and glances up at me from time to time, as if I am some kind of firework that might go off at any moment and startle him.

'I'm not losing my mind,' I say, with a sigh.

But I do remember what happened to Donaldson, and the memory is still tender. Donaldson was a windswept aviator, always with a bit of white hair sticking out at an angle as if he'd just dropped out of the sky. He was a good friend of ours, all the way up to the end. The problem was that Donaldson started forgetting things. Only small things at first, like names and places, and his befuddlement was nothing serious, as if he had simply misplaced his memories somewhere about his person. But by the end, there was not very much of poor Donaldson left. Just a frightened and confused old man.

Once I am done with dinner I head upstairs to my room and try to get some sleep. And I wonder if I will be afflicted by further strange dreams. It is beginning to feel rather like a storm gathering in my head.

As I drift away, beset by memories, I feel the frown across my forehead, creasing up my brow with worry.

>•<

Tonight, I dream of Donaldson.

He is close to death. His family – a kindly collection of farmers – took him from our care home and deposited him in his old room at their farmhouse. The room was small, but it overlooked the hills of the farm, and there was always a beam of sunlight lying across some part of him.

Right now, as I am dreaming him, he looks lost among his excessive pillows, and fragile, as if he has become the sketch of a man instead of a full portrait. Donaldson's eyes are closed and he does not look out of the window – as he was often found doing – at the open skies he liked to fly in his little planes and gliders.

This was the last day I saw him before he passed away. I had taken it upon myself to flee the care home and go in search of him. Somewhere out there, a gathering of worried nurses and a frantic old soldier named Valentine are trying to hunt me down, but I have a while yet.

I had the idea that I would bring my violin along with me. Donaldson always used to love me playing it and I thought it might evoke some memory in him. The instrument is on my lap and I am attempting to tune it, but my arthritis is making it difficult and painful. The first three strings are at their correct tensions – their sounds filling the box room with song remnants – and though my hands are sore beyond belief, and though I can barely see any more for all my tears, I am now trying to tune my violin's most fragile string, plucking at it as I turn the last peg.

There is a new sound, a voice calling out in distress, a wrong note, as the string snaps. I open my eyes to see the blood rolling from the mark the broken string has left across my hand. But worse is the nakedness, the absence, along the neck of the violin – a black void where once a line was drawn. I bow my head, and let my useless hands drop, giving in to my sorrow completely.

'Will?' A voice. Donaldson's voice. He has awoken and is sitting up.

I wipe at my face with the back of my sleeve. He says, 'When did you get so wrinkly? You look like an old leather boot.'

He was never a handsome man, chin so flat it might be mistaken for a second throat. 'Oh yeah? Well you look like a prune,' I tell him.

'Are those meant to be tattoos?' he says. 'They look more like ink stains to me.'

'Didn't your hair used to have colour? Looks like you've had a terrible fright.'

His Adam's apple yo-yos as he laughs, until his smile fades and he grows serious.

'You should be out there,' he says, nodding at the open window, at the sky. 'Sailing away to distant seas. What are you doing here? This is no place for you.' He frowns. 'I should be out there. Wings like a bird.' And with that, all expression fades from his face until his jaw is slack and his eyes are glassy. I help him as best I can to lie down again, and not soon after, he has returned to sleep.

I pack my violin away and shuffle the case across my shoulder.

Pottering downstairs one step at a time, I find the rest of the farmhouse empty. In the living room there is a set of china laid out upon the coffee table. And, inexplicably, as if it has been set out with the rest, there sits March's compass, in stark contrast to the doilies and varnished wood it lies upon. The compass confirms what I already knew. I am alone here. This is my memory of the death of Donaldson and he is not real.

Just a figment.

'You silly old fool of a man,' I tell myself.

I stamp my feet, and shake my head to clear it. The last time I held this compass I was being set upon by a horde of nightmares. And the girl... that girl, June, who took my notepad and called it a map. I feel angry at myself, that I just gave my notepad to her with no idea why it was so important. And I am angry that I still have March's compass, leaving him without the means to navigate dreams and hunt the nightmares of others.

'Well, enough of that,' I say to myself. 'Pull yourself together, Manderlay.'

I pick up March's compass, fumbling and clumsy because of my arthritis, but managing to find a comfortable place to make it sit, wedged in between my fingers and palm. And with that I go in search of a door through to another dream. I will find March – go all the way to the Capital where he said he would meet me, if I have to – and return his compass. And I will ask him what June meant by using my notepad to see God, as well.

Beyond the first door, I come to a school.

Japanese characters are inscribed above each doorway. Through the windows I pass I can see children playing outside, and behind them is a backdrop of moss-covered rooftops and strange soft mountains. I am reminded of picking Samantha up from school almost every weekday, at precisely 3.15, for nearly six years back in Edinburgh.

A bell would ring, a distant tolling, and children would rush out in a stream. They would fling themselves with abandon towards us. I would stand with my hands tight around the black bars of the fence, my forehead against them, and wait for her there. Always the same conversation between the bars, as if I was a prisoner and she was visiting. How was school today? All right, Pa. Did you learn anything new? No, Pa. Always the same smile as well, a sly slanted line angled beneath shy eyes. She took after Lily, that way.

The compass is leading me through the school.

At an open doorway I pause and see the dreamer. She is a girl of around six or seven, sat at her desk in complete solitude. The desks of the other pupils sit empty around her, and through the far window those figments are visible at play. Her head is bowed over a set of loose papers and she clutches her pencil in a fist. She keeps glancing over at the window in longing.

I make to go on, but something stops me. My memory of Samantha, perhaps.

In what I know is a grave breach of March's instructions, I head across to the dreamer and crouch down beside her desk. 'Hullo,' I say. 'I'm William. How are you?'

She says soft words in a language I never learned, despite how many times I visited this country.

It takes her a while to realise what it is that I am trying to teach her, but when she does, her uncertainty fades and her eyes grow wide in fascination instead. There is no way that I can fold paper myself; my old hands refuse to work properly in the best of situations these days. But through a series of gentle motions – palms brought together, shaking fingertips pressed along lines – I instruct her in the art of origami. Nothing special, of course, and her first plane leaves a lot to be desired, but by the time she has folded the third we have at least two little aeroplanes to race.

My throw is clumsy, and so is hers. The paper planes barely fly.

'Still the best use of maths papers,' I tell her. She grabs her plane and leads me to the cloakroom. From her coat, she pulls out a clutch of coloured pencils, and then she waits at the back door, paper crumpling in her grip. I smile and open the door for her. The light from the sun is bright and brilliant. And with a skip, she rushes out to join her classmates, and show them her plane. I am forgotten instantly.

At the other end of the school, I walk out through the open gates and step across a stream that runs through the middle of the street, where large carp swim and shimmer in reds and golds.

I pass through more doors, through a dusty desert village, where the sun bakes the back of my neck, and through a huge prison complex, where the inmates reach through the bars and leer at me, and the dreamer is the only guard. And further still, through a wedding, with guests dancing and laughing, and on past that, through a ranch, where I stop and watch the horses on the ridge of the far hill dance, their manes coiling and uncoiling in the wind like the long grasses that swish across their hooves. The nightmare-hunter's compass leads me on and on, through so many doors, and so many wonderful dreams, and I wish that I was young again – young enough to have a compass of my own and tread the dreams of others every night.

Until at last, I come to a dream like no other. March was correct in telling me that I would know it when I saw it; I have no doubt that this is his Capital.

I find myself paralysed by the view that greets me, awed in its presence. The new city is laid out before me, but its gem, its centrepiece, its crowning glory, stretches out above me. There is a tower here, at the heart of this tremendous city, and try as I might, I cannot see its end. It is the tallest tower I have ever seen, vanishing into the heights and clouds above.

The tower here dominates the city. It is more than a landmark.

Tall houses and teeming streets seem to have tumbled from its edges, as if they are fallen pieces of masonry, shadows made long by the golden sun. They sweep away on every visible side, made in all manner of different designs. The roads I can see are arranged haphazardly, as if spun by a careless spider, but in such a way that all of them seem to lead to the tower. There is no telling where the tower begins and the city ends, however, because the tower rises from the city gradually.

There are long slopes to every side of the city, some of which lead to distant plains and mountains, and some of which lead to crowded docks beside a glittering sea. I can see the black silhouettes of dozens of sailing ships, steam ships, tankers and all kinds of seafaring vessels.

The tower itself is impossible; it should not be able to support its own weight. It seems to be made up of the same amalgamation of different designs and architecture as the rest of the city, with parts of it resembling castles and forts from various periods of history. And there are more improbable sections, as well: an enormous statue of Buddha embedded in the side, and, further up, I can see the many arms of Vishnu supporting a length of stained-glass windows. I can see workers and scaffolding and cranes all along it, labouring at making it taller by supporting its lower length. There are balloons rising alongside carrying huge girders, but they are lost to sight when they reach a certain height. They become dots beside the needle-point tip.

I stand and stare and lose track of time in awe of the tower, before carrying on.

I come to a tangled network of streets. They are filled with people and movement and sound. The crowds here are as much an assortment as the city they inhabit, treading the cobbles of the incline on heavy boots, sandals and even bare feet. I can hear conversations in European languages, and African, and Asian, with accents so varied that I struggle to even recognise English.

Where the streets open up and become roads, I travel past vehicles as well. Vans and cars rumble past, and so do tuk-tuks, bicycles and horse-drawn carriages. I am reminded of the chaos of the streets of Mumbai; with so many different vehicles the sight becomes confusing and dazzling.

The compass held loosely in my grip has become useless – almost everyone I pass is a dreamer, and the doors to dreams encrust the streets. The face of the compass is so full of blue needles and red needles and even black needles that I realise that I am about to become lost.

I turn about at the crossroads, and wonder how I am meant to find March, or anyone, in all this chaos. I need help.

I catch sight of a small building squatting between two others, as if it is hiding between them. Written in stone above the door of the small building is the word INFORMAYTION. As badly spelt as it might be, I waste no more time in striking across. If someone is offering information then perhaps they will be able to help me find March, at least.

I push the door open and step through.

Inside, there is a deep gloom. The oily windows look as if they have not been cleaned in decades. It is a cramped space, made tighter by the amount of literature crammed into every corner. For a moment I believe that I have stumbled upon a kind of tomb for words.

There is a sound I recognise filling the air. It is the static crackle of the space between radio stations, but amplified. On the other side of the room, I can just about see the thin aerials of dozens of radio sets, sticking out at angles. Every single set is playing static, making so much sound it feels as if I stand before a waterfall.

I was mistaken about trying to find information here.

Except, before I turn to leave, I notice that there is a human figure draped over one of the far tables. I wander a little closer, turning scrolls aside with my feet.

There is a body there, face down on the hard wood.

The man is obviously dead. Spiders have woven webs across his fallen head. Beside his ears are two ancient-looking radio sets, covered in the same dusty cobwebs, still emanating that obnoxious white noise.

Yet, as I stare, there is a stirring. With a great heaving the body moves. Webs tear from the table as the man rights himself, blinking with sad and watering eyes, and pulling white strands from his face with weak hands.

He is wearing a stained white tabard over a rusted chain-mail coat, and he looks like a shabby Arthurian knight. He has a pointed beard, and the skin of his face looks as if it has been pulled down to his chin, giving him a drawn and aged expression. I quickly pop March's compass into the top pocket of my mackintosh coat to keep it out of sight, just in case.

When the dusty man finally catches sight of me, his face erupts into a wolfish grin. I am unable to tell if it is a grimace or a genuine sign of joy. 'Name thyself, welcome stranger!' he wheezes, barely audible over the radios that surround him. His voice is a strained hiss, and I am struck by the idea that this is no noble knight, but a parody of one.

'I'm William,' I tell him. 'William Manderlay. Who are you?'

With a great cracking of bones, as if his body is a forest in high winds, the dusty knight stands. The last of the cobwebs fall from him. When he bows, I am not certain if it is a mocking gesture or a genuine one. 'They call me Thyme, for the flavour of my lies,' he says. His accent feels ancient, given a Shakespearean quality. 'Seekest thou information?'

I feel as if I should be backing up, towards the door.

'I'm looking for someone,' I tell him.

'Thou art lost,' he tells me. 'The rumours speak of thee. Thou art the bard come to Babel from the doors.' I notice a sword at the knight's side, wrapped in black leather. He leans forward across the table, sending scrolls tumbling. 'Speak thou hence the cause of thy quest and I shall furnish thee with my aid, Manderlay the Bard.'

I remain hesitant.

'I need to find a nightmare-hunter called March.'

Thyme lowers his gaze, looking thoughtful. 'This realm is not blessed with seasons. The months that plague these lands are flesh and bone. Speak ye of the Sleepwalker?' The same word that June used. I suppose he must be right.

'March the Sleepwalker, yes.'

The knight narrows his eyes.

'Seekest thou conflict? Trouble thyself not with the Lord of War, Manderlay the Bard. Must it be the March Soldier? Wouldst thou settle not for the gentle curiosity of May, or the wisdom of October? March burns brightly, yes, but fiercely. There exist tamer Sleepwalkers that might tend to thine ailment.'

'I need to find March,' I insist.

Thyme sighs. 'Justly,' he says, 'I shall aid thee. By the fates, thou art in luck. Just as the rumours whisper of thee, they speak of thy Sleepwalker. I shall take thee hence to him.' The wolfish grin across Thyme's face has vanished, replaced with a kind of sorrow visible in his dark and sunken eyes. The old knight rounds his table, and I can see that he is wearing metal plate across his legs and feet.

'This way, Manderlay the Bard.' He heaves open the front door.

'I don't have any money,' I tell him. 'To pay you.'

At this, Thyme's pointed grin returns. 'I shall not accept currency,' he tells me, 'but only the presence of thy company. It has been many an age since the others of my kind passed beyond this realm. It has been many an age more since the crowds called for a liar. Mine is a lost art, and I shall be grateful to share it with thee.' He turns aside, and lets me pass. We stand back out in the busy street.

'You're a liar?'

'The last liar,' he says, slowly, sadly, observing the tower. In the light of day Thyme looks like an artefact recovered from some lost tomb. 'Once, dreams were built of my tales. Quests formed by the skill of my words. But now there are only the whispers and the rumours, and little room for a liar. Dreams are built on dull facts. Mine,' he repeats, 'is a lost art. Follow me, Manderlay, and we shall locate thy Sleepwalker.' Reluctantly I do as I am told, wondering whether I have made a grave mistake.

>•<

Closer to the tower the streets of Babel become a tangle, filled with dozens of improbable sets of stairs and archways, and I am reminded of the paintings of Escher.

As we approach the tower, the folk we pass begin to look almost fantastic in nature. We stride alongside a set of men with pointed boots, lengthy moustaches, and gilded turbans upon their heads, and we travel through a marketplace filled with ugly vegetables and slabs of meat turning on spits, where everybody calls out to us in languages I do not understand.

'What is this place?' I ask Thyme, who is leading the way.

''Tis a market,' he replies, humourlessly.

'No, I mean the City. The tower.'

As we move I notice that Thyme is slowly shedding his dust and walking more upright, as if new life is being breathed into him. 'Babel? Thou art asking the question of a philosopher, and I am no creature of philosophy. Perhaps thou wouldst prefer an artful lie? The philosopher would tell thee that thou seest before thee the heart of dreaming, where the dreams of men come together and reveal their true communal desire – an unfulfilled longing for the divine. But I – ah, I would tell thee that the tower is a mystery waiting to be solved, an artefact from ages past, which men do not understand, but which they continue to build out of some long-lost primal instinct left unsatisfied from the first dreams. Indeed, I meditate often upon the true nature of the tower, for it is my strong belief that to understand the tower would be to understand dreams themselves. Every night, the tower grows taller, and every night, the heavens seem so much further away.'

'Thanks,' I say, still mystified.

Beyond the marketplace, we come to a crossroads, and the tower is revealed fully before us. I find that if I stare up at it for any length of time I am struck by the fear that it will collapse. I glance across at Thyme.

'A crossroads,' he comments, 'not only in Babel, but in our quest.'

I shift my violin case into a more comfortable position over my shoulder. 'Which way?'

'Ah,' he says, 'but this is a question for thee to answer. I shall furnish thee with the choice. One route should take us to thy Sleepwalker safely, but it is a slow route, and there is no guarantee that he shall be at our destination once we reach it. But there lies before us a second route, a perilous alternative which might lead thee to harm shouldst thou tread uncertainly along the path, but which would speed us through to thy quest's end.'

'Why would the second route be dangerous?'

Thyme raises a knobbly finger and points to a part of the network of streets before us. 'The shadow of the tower,' he says, in such a solemn manner that it becomes comedic. He is correct that the tower's enormous shadow sweeps out before us. It is difficult to see what lies beneath that shadow, but it looks like more of the city, more of the same bustle and sound.

'It can't be that bad, surely?'

Thyme shakes his head, and dust fills the air. 'Thou art perhaps misunderstanding. The sun here is no celestial body, but a fixed point unblemished by clouds: a nightless day eternal. And while the city we stride is baked, there is a slender portion,' he squints his watery eyes, 'which remains... in the dark. And it is this slender portion where the city takes on a different countenance. Its streets no longer simple. Its doors leading to little hells. Its inhabitants often less than human.' He lays his hand on the hilt of his surprisingly well-kept sword, still wrapped up in leathers. 'I can keep thee safe, if thou hast trust for a liar.'

'What's the alternative?'

'The tower itself,' he says. 'By which we might avoid the shadow.'

It is at this point that I dearly wish I trusted Thyme. Or, at least, trusted him enough to reveal the nightmare-hunter's compass. I am not sure the device would be much use in navigating the city, but it would bring me a lot of comfort to know whether Thyme is a dreamer or something else. Still, he seems earnest enough, patiently waiting for me to come to a decision. And there is something endearing in the way that everything about Thyme is at odds with everything else; he is a liar who announces his lies, and he is a knight in not-so-shining armour.

I give him the benefit of the doubt.

'All right. Let's try the quick way through.'

At this, Thyme grins his wolfish grin. 'Splendid,' he says. 'Stay close, Manderlay the Bard, and I shall guide thee through the labyrinth hence.' And with that, he strides across the street, causing an immediate collision somewhere further down the road as cars and bikes slam on their brakes to avoid hitting him. I quickly follow in his wake.

Without further pause Thyme steps into the shadow of the tower.

I go in after him, and I am immediately struck by the gloom. Blinking, I wait for my eyes to adjust, but they do not. I find I am clumsy along the cobbled pavement, stumbling after my guide as he navigates through the dark without the aid of a torch or lamp. Trying not to pay too much attention to the black alleyways and side-streets we pass, I follow the clinking of Thyme's greaves.

'Stay near,' says Thyme, but his voice sounds far away.

Though the sky is still blue, the rooftops of the buildings around us have enclosed it, like the jaws of some enormous beast. The tower itself has become a black monolith, blocking out the sun, and there is a layer of slippery frost across everything in the cold.

I raise my aching hands to my mouth, to breathe some warmth across them, and when I lower them again, Thyme seems distant. I can see the gangly shape of him ahead, but I am falling behind. 'Further!' he says, and his voice sounds distorted somehow. 'Deeper still we must go.' And then, 'Keep thy wits about thee, Manderlay the Bard, and do not stray from the path.'

'Wait!' I call, but my voice sounds small. I lose sight of him.

Rushing across the icy road to try and catch up, I come to a warren of streets leading off in almost every direction. Thyme could have gone down any of them. I pause, rubbing at my eyes as if I might clear the gloom away. There is no traffic here, but there are shifting figures shuffling along the paths and bulkier shadows moving vaguely behind blackened doorways.

I have no idea where Thyme has gone.

I feel a cold air lift the hairs across the back of my neck. Shivering, I attempt to retrace my steps, to find my way free of the tower's shadow, but the streets I walk seem different, as if they have somehow changed since I moved through them.

Turning about, I make my way to the nearest source of light, and find that it is one in a small series of low-glowing street lamps, arranged around a dark park filled with black and leafless trees. I stop, bathing in the yellow glow, and try to get my bearings.

Perhaps it would be best if I just try and make my way towards the tower itself. It is the most obvious landmark, after all.

I strike out, hunching my shoulders against the gloom and trying to make myself seem small and insignificant. I make my way up a brief incline and come to a long dark bridge lined with bent-backed street lamps, where a swathe of mist is swirling in. And as I cross that bridge I lose sight of the tower.

I wonder if this was Thyme's plan all along: to lead me here, to trap me here. To take the nightmare-hunter's compass from me, perhaps.

Halfway across the bridge, I stop and peer over the edge. There is nothing but black below. Beneath one of the bridge's pale lamps I draw out March's compass. There is no comfort on its face. There is a blue needle pointing at me, and a handful of red needles pointing here and there. But there are so many black needles encrusting the face of the compass that I can no longer see any white. With a sharp intake of breath, I squirrel the compass away.

'Damn you, Thyme,' I say, quietly. Something howls in the distance.

I rush as fast as I am able to leave the bridge. On the other side, there is nothing but thin and winding streets, buried in mist. I go from dark doorway to dark doorway, feeling the ache in my legs. The shadowy figures here have started to take notice of me. Some are shrouded in great black cloaks, and others have odd, white skin. Their eyes are sullen hollows, staring with hunger.

Completely lost, I stumble on.

Through cold alleyways I pass, and from time to time I will catch sight of an open door, beyond which is a frightening dream: a meat factory, or a war-zone, or one of countless dark and stormy nights with lightning flashing and thunder booming. I try to keep myself calm, tell myself that soon these terrible streets must end, but I find that I am walking quicker and quicker, in defiance of my aged legs, desperately seeking the edge of the tower's shadow.

I jog up another cobbled incline, slipping through the mist. I keep glancing behind myself, catching glimpses of cloaked figures, some with arms outstretched, stumbling after me. There is a rushing sound now, like a frenzied whispering from a hundred mouths unused to speaking. My violin case thumps against my hip, and I find a railing by which I am able to pull myself up the hill.

I have somehow returned to the bridge. Or is this a different bridge? Breathing heavily, I part the mists, pausing beneath the glow of a white lamp. I see a whole crowd of terrible cloaked figures moving in the mist behind me, visible only in snatches. Beginning to panic, I draw another rattling breath and force myself onwards.

Almost at once, I am confronted by a bright light as it emerges from an alleyway at the end of the bridge. I have to shield my eyes from the sudden brightness, stumbling as if the sun itself has come to burn me. And there is a voice with the light, a somehow noble voice, belonging to the silhouette standing beneath it: an upright silhouette looking like something from a tale of mighty heroes.

'Hark!' cries Thyme, holding his burning torch aloft.

He advances through the mists until he is beside me. The crowd of terrible figures on the bridge halt and raise their hands to protect their eyes from the sudden beacon. They fall about themselves, but they do not retreat. *'Liar!'* calls one, and that word ripples out among them. *'Liar!'* comes the cry, and, *'Liar!'* goes the echo.

'Hark!' repeats the dusty knight, except that he is dusty no longer. His hair is now silver instead of grey, and the stains across his tabard are battle-wear instead of rot, and the dark patches across his armour are blood instead of rust. His hand rests on the hilt of his sword, still wrapped in leathers. 'This,' he calls, 'is the sword that once guarded the gates of Eden! Mark ye well: should I choose to draw this blade, ye shall see before ye a righteous conflagration, for the blade burns eternal still! I give ye the choice! Disperse now, and begone back to your shadows, or face the wrath of the heavens themselves!'

Though that same hateful word is passed among them – *'Liar! Liar!'* – the nightmares on the bridge rush away, to be devoured by the mists almost all at once. Thyme keeps his torch aloft, his watery eyes glinting.

'Art thou well, Manderlay the Bard?' he asks.

My heart thumps heavily in my chest.

'I'm fine,' I tell him. 'Can we… can we leave here, please?'

Thyme inclines his head. 'This way yonder,' he says, and this time it is easy for me to follow him. There is no mistaking his torch in the gloom. And while by myself, the streets beneath the shadow of the tower seemed like an impenetrable labyrinth, Thyme strides with purpose through them, until I gladly catch sight of a bright street before us.

'Thyme?' I say to him, as his torch begins to burn low.

'How may I aid thee?' he asks, and in the light of day he seems himself again – all rust and dust and old pointed features – and I wonder why he seemed so formidable before.

'Is your sword really the Sword of Eden?'

Thyme grins his wolfish grin. 'Perhaps,' he says. 'Give her enough belief, and she will burn brightly. For that is the nature of lies, and that is the nature of dreams.' Almost as an afterthought, he says, 'Have faith!' and we step back into the light of the sun.

METRONOME

We descend towards Babel's sparkling waterfront.

'Not much further hence,' Thyme repeats, 'to thy Sleepwalker.'

At a gated river crossing the dusty knight elbows us through the crowds, and for the first time I get a good glimpse of Babel's river. The waters swirling below are a rainbow mess, simultaneously oily and clear, and the whole thing looks so polluted with colour that it takes me a while to realise why I am so delighted by the sight.

There are doors lined up haphazardly on both walled banks, all open, and it is from them that streams are running and filling the river. From one door a lovely crystal waterfall drops and informs the flow, and from another, a slow-moving oily mess sloops and swirls into the main body of water. I realise that there must be hundreds, thousands, of doors like these, feeding the river from dreams, stretching all the way up to the tower itself.

'Sammy would love this,' I say, reminded of her art. All

those ridiculous, formless colourful messes she would paint with her hands so that she could feel what she was making. I remember how I ran out of space on the fridge back in our house in Edinburgh, and then the notice board I set up beside it, and then even the walls and cupboards, until the whole kitchen was a rainbow explosion.

'An unfamiliar name,' says Thyme, who must have heard me speak.

I smile at him. 'My daughter. I was saying she would love this place.'

Through a couple of flaps of canvas, the self-professed liar brings us to a busy bazaar, and continues on between the tents. 'Babel is no place for the young,' says Thyme, 'or the unwary. There are plenty here who would take advantage of those without guides to lead them, for there is profit to be found in the dreams of fools. Dream of solid stones, or great forests, and thy dream might be sold to the tower.' Thyme ushers away a boy trying to sell tiny copper replicas of the tower. 'Or worse yet, dream of gold, and thy dream might be sold to the Golden Gate: a distant outpost, where gold is always in demand.'

Through a sandstone archway at the edge of the bazaar we come to a wide and sunny courtyard with a fountain at its centre. Doors line the walls, and Thyme gestures towards a closed one in the corner in the manner of a magician revealing his finest finale.

'Thy Sleepwalker's dream,' he says.

I give him a grateful nod. 'Thank you. For bringing me here. I'm in your debt.'

'Thou art,' he says, and he grins his wolfish grin. 'Take care, Manderlay the Bard. And remember: have faith!'

And as if to highlight his advice, Thyme unbuckles his sword belt, pulls himself onto the fountain's rim and sits cross-legged there. Eyes closed, he raises his hands to the blue sky, lost in prayer.

I head across to the metal door at the corner of the courtyard, and as I go, I wonder who it is that Thyme is praying to. Some god of lies, maybe.

Dry lightning reveals the silhouettes of distant mountains. I hunch my shoulders against the overwhelming screeching of jets as they fly overhead in formation, and stumble uncertainly past a congregation of tanks and transports.

Endless dust. A dry cough that refuses to leave my throat.

March's compass directs me up to where there is a packed-earth compound. The soldiers at the entrance, who are all figments, peer at me through their dusty goggles but let me pass. Inside they loiter around the terrible bulky shapes of heavy ordnance, and when there is the boom of a shell hitting home, none of them wince like I do.

Through an opening in a bunker, I enter a clinical hallway where nets hang from the white ceiling dividing up beds. I traipse a long trail of dust across the clean ground, and glimpse wounded soldiers being tended to by serious-looking medics. As I progress the wounds get worse: a head so swathed in bandages that it might be a white and brown turban, skin so burned that it looks as if it has been boiled.

Through plastic sheeting curtains, I push open an emergency exit and find the dreamer.

March stands tall at a bullet-scarred balcony where he

can survey the whole valley before him. The white of his vest is in contrast against the endless gloom. He turns to see me, but does not seem to recognise me.

'Don't suppose you've got any fruit on you?' he asks. 'Trying to eat something healthy every time I feel the need to light up.' The boy soldier takes the cigarette from behind his ear and flicks it over the wall. 'I'm gonna end up eating too much acid at this rate; burn a hole right through my stomach.'

'I don't. I'm sorry.'

He frowns at me. 'Wait. Who are you?'

Of course he does not recognise me. Before I dreamed that I was young; now I am old. 'I'm Manderlay,' I tell him. 'William Manderlay. You helped me with my dream last night. The dream of the valley and the church on the hill. You gave me your compass.' I hold it out to him. 'I came to return it. To say thank you. There aren't any nightmares left in my dream now.'

A pause. 'Manderlay? But you're—'

'Old. I know. This is me. The real me, I mean.' The compass in my hand shakes as I struggle to keep a grip on it. I feel embarrassed by how feeble I am.

March takes his compass and watches the needles turn there. He runs his free hand through his bright hair. 'Hell,' he says. 'Didn't think I'd ever see this again. Thanks for this. Seriously. I'd be pretty much lost without it.' He pockets it, and folds his arms, leaning against the balcony wall. 'I owe you one, Mister Manderlay.'

I join him at the wall and rest my weary legs. 'I met another nightmare-hunter last night. Or Sleepwalker. Whatever you call yourselves. But her name was June.' At the mention of her name March screws up his face as if he has tasted something sour. 'She took something from me. Something important. So I thought I'd ask you what you knew about her. Maybe where I can find her, to try and get it back.'

March squints up at the desert sun, and at the helicopters hovering in between, and then leans to pull his camouflaged jacket on. 'I never get good news,' he says. 'Always gotta be something to balance it out. You know like in the movies, where the guy gets the girl, or wins the lottery? For me, it's always – you get the girl! But she's pregnant with another guy's kid. Or, you win the lottery! But you've gotta have your arm chopped off.' He sighs. 'June's trouble,' he says. 'Got some odd ideas in her head. What did she take?'

'An old notebook of mine.'

'All right,' he says, grabbing his rifle. 'Then let's go get it back.'

March leads us through Babel, and where he goes the folk we pass treat him with nods of respect or gushing greetings, as if he is some kind of local hero. The young soldier takes it all in his stride, and continues on with me – the funny old man pottering along in his wake – to a long set of gardens and orchards. People kneel in prayer on the grass, or picnic on the multitude of fruits and vegetables, or tend to the endless greenery.

At an orange tree, March slings his rifle over his shoulder, grabs a particularly ripe-looking specimen and peels it. 'June's door usually shows up around here somewhere,' he tells me.

Popping a segment into his mouth, he nods at my violin case.

'What's that?'

'My violin.'

'You a musician?'

'Not so much these days.' I smile, and show him my hands: blue veins protruding, the shudder I am unable to shake.

'Arthritis?' March flicks orange peel into the bushes we pass. 'My uncle got it in his knees. Real shame. He was a hill-walker, you see. Every weekend he'd be up in the hills and mountains. Walked the earth as if he meant to see every corner of it. Damn near killed him when he got the diagnosis.' He glances at the trees we pass as we head into the dappled shade of their canopies.

'It's a cruel disease.'

'Sure is,' he says. 'Your best bet is to think young.'

'I'm sorry?'

'Think young.' March stops, then, 'Ah. There we go.' He points at a yellow door, embedded into a tree nearby. 'Always yellow,' he says. 'Like she owns the bloody sun.' He finishes off the last segment of his orange and swings his rifle around, before knocking at the worn wood and listening for a few moments. The birds in the trees around us sing their songs.

'Doesn't sound like she's in,' I say.

'Ah, hell. I've always been curious anyway.' He grabs the handle, and opens the door.

We step out onto a forest plateau. Ahead of us is an awesome sight. Between two thickly forested expanses rests a great grey dam, dividing a silvery reservoir from a set of sparkling falls. The sun is powerful here and the air is close and muggy, filled with the buzzing of insects. I feel overdressed, and I observe March as he wipes sweat away from his brow. The nightmare-hunter grabs his compass and watches the needles turn. 'Ah,' he says. 'She's not in. There's a nightmare here, but no June.'

'What about that?' I point to a station set up at the very centre of the tall dam. Something is reflecting or glowing in there.

'Could be anything.'

'Maybe she left it here,' I say. 'My notebook, I mean.'

March seems uneasy. 'Maybe. I don't really like the idea of messing around in June's dream, though. Don't get me wrong, I'm not her biggest fan. She's... uh, not very good at her job if you ask me. But I wouldn't like it if one of the others was in my dream without my permission. Seems a bit disrespectful, maybe. I dunno.' He shrugs. 'I guess we could pop down and have a look. Might save us having to hunt her down, wherever she is. Just... tread careful, yeah?'

'I'll follow in your footsteps.'

'Sure,' he says, and he ducks into the forest path, leading down to the dam.

By the time we reach the edge of the concrete it becomes apparent just how big June's dream is. We are both out of breath and there are great dark patches around March's throat and beneath his arms.

'Her real name is Kareena,' March tells me, 'and she lives somewhere in India. I don't know her last name, or anything else about her really. Just that she's got this real hang-up about nightmares. Some hippy rubbish about befriending them or something. That they're a "natural" part of dreaming. Whole line of Junes always been that way.

It's a pain in the arse.' At the edge of the dam, he glances over the edge, and then steps back from it. 'Christ, that's a long way down.'

'So your name isn't really March?'

'Nah.' He grins at me. 'You're best off calling me March, though. Some nightmares can do some nasty things if they find out your real name. You ever hear about random killings – folk claiming it was the voices in their head telling them to do it? Yeah. I guess some Sleepwalker a while back came up with the bright idea of giving us all code-names to stop that from happening. Twelve months for twelve Sleepwalkers.' March's hair is so drenched with sweat now that it looks as if his fire has been put out. 'It might sound a bit stupid,' he says, 'but a lot of stuff in dreaming is stupid, and sometimes you've gotta fight stupid with stupid.'

All at once an enormous shape leaps over the edge of the dam from behind us.

March is thrown back with a surprised yell, and his rifle clatters to the ground. I stumble back, panicking, and try to work out what is happening.

The massive, multi-legged creature scuttling towards the fallen soldier is familiar, and I feel my heart lurch when I recognise it. It is the wooden spider from my dream – legs the thickness of tree-trunks and a body like two yachts stapled together.

March has drawn his side-arm and rolls towards the edge of the dam. He fires twice, but the spider does not slow down. It raises its legs, mandibles waving, and makes to spear him in place.

I am frozen, staring at March as he rolls, narrowly avoiding the spider's legs. It leaps around to better pin him down. I take a step forward to where his rifle has fallen, but then a better idea strikes me. Something I can see signposted at the station nearby. Something I know how to use.

At sea, you do not have very many options when it comes to dealing with pirates. Sometimes, you can employ armed guards, but more often than not, whoever's cargo you are shifting is too cheap to afford them. As such, the best pirate-repellent we ever had was the fire-fighting system. Pirates, being pirates, do not tend to have particularly robust boats. More often than not, they are to be found in motorised dinghies, flimsy things that might be turned over by a large wave. So, we would turn the hoses on them. Dodging bullets, certainly, but throwing pirates from their perches through sheer force of water pressure.

I dash across and unhook the hose from the wall.

With my hands tingling I turn on the water and aim the hose. At first there is only a disappointing sprinkle. Then the rubber in my hands turns rigid and my feet slide back, fighting for purchase as the pressure hits. A tremendous sparkling stream hits the spider's flank, and it turns, scrambling, too late to stop me. It tries in vain to bury its stake legs into the hard concrete.

With a monstrous screech it tumbles over the edge.

I drop the hose before it throws me over as well, and rush to turn off the pressure before it whips around. Then, breathless and triumphant, with the beating of my heart causing blood to flow uncertainly through my fingers as it has not done in years, I return to March to see how he is faring.

He is scratched, and drenched from head to toe, but he is laughing. 'You washed it away!' March says, as he regains his feet. 'You washed the damn thing away! Holy hell, Mister Manderlay. That was brilliant. Like a spider in a bath!' The nightmare-hunter wrings out his uniform and shakes himself down, before recovering his rifle.

I am unable to help myself from laughing. 'Fighting stupid with stupid,' I tell him. 'And please, call me William. Or Will. Nobody calls me Mister Manderlay these days.'

The two of us regain our senses. March checks his compass again. 'Alone at last,' he says. 'But I reckon we should get out of here before June comes back. If that was one of her friends, then she's not gonna be very happy.'

'Hold on,' I tell him, because I saw something peculiar when I dashed across to the station at the centre of the dam. 'Just before we go. I need to see.' I lead us both up the steps to the small control station, which commands the ultimate view over the valley below the dam.

And the room, just as I remember, is filled from doorway to doorway with sketches.

They are mostly landscapes. Here, a mountain range, there, a desert. But through all of them, the artist has drawn a great black line, so straight that it must have been done with a ruler. In some of the landscapes, the black line has arches beneath it to support it, and at once I know what it is. 'The black road,' I say, and when I turn to see March, I notice the object hanging from the ceiling at the room's centre, which must have caused the reflection we saw from above. It is a CD, hung up like a child's mobile, and one that I recognise, because it is mine.

'Will...' says March.

He is stood at the far wall, where there is a sketch like no other here. I cross the distance between us and stand before that sketch in awe, because it is like looking into a mirror. June has drawn a detailed portrait of my likeness, just as it was in the booklet that accompanied my last album. Whatever else June might be, she is certainly a great artist.

'Why,' March asks, 'does June have a picture of you in her dream? What's going on here?'

'I think I might know where she's gone,' I tell him.

'What do you mean?'

'She called it a map.'

'She called what a map?'

'March…' I say. 'Have you ever heard of Solomon's Eye?'

After I am done describing my encounter with June, the blood seems to have drained from March's face. 'Jesus Christ. We've wasted enough time,' he says. 'I need you to come with me. Right now. We need to sort this out.'

I struggle to keep up with March as he rushes back through Babel. Somehow, despite the size of his heavy pack, he manages to go at an easy jog.

Beyond the orchards, he leads me through the streets towards an industrial district, where all manner of trucks and carts carry heaped materials – wood and stone in a myriad of different qualities – in a steady stream towards the tower.

'March!' I call after him, pausing to catch my breath at a corner.

The nightmare-hunter glowers back at me, hands wringing at his rifle.

'Not much further,' he says. 'Come on now, Will.'

Beyond the chain-linked fences we come to a quarry. There are the bright yellow trucks on tracks, a spiral of roads in the dark earth and a hundred folk with wheelbarrows, passing back and forth in industry. They do not appear to be mining the ground. Instead, the people here are using all the open doors in the valley walls; they enter with empty wheelbarrows and exit laden with heavy materials. They are mining dreams.

March avoids the valley, heading across to some kind of processing plant, where conveyor belts run beside corrugated metal offices. He halts before a set of three bizarre-looking machines.

The closest contraption looks like a hybrid between a Chinook helicopter and an enormous armoured beetle. It has a hunched back made of slabs of thick metal, and no less than four rotors, positioned at each corner. For the time being, the beetle's earth-stained belly is empty, doors rolled back and awaiting fresh materials.

'Karl!' The nightmare-hunter waves across at a worker approaching through the dust.

Wiping his hands on his overalls, Karl raises his goggles. 'What's up?'

'I need a favour.'

I come alongside March, and the oily man glances at me. 'How can I help?'

'We need to get up to the skydocks.'

'This urgent?' Judging by his accent, Karl is Nordic.

'Really damn urgent, Karl.'

Pausing only for a moment's thought, Karl heads over to a black telephone on a dented pole. He speaks into it. Then he hangs up and turns back to us, pulling on his gloves. 'Hop in the back,' he says, and as the two of us rush over to the helicopter beetle's empty belly, Karl draws his goggles back over his eyes and hauls himself up the side of the machine, to where there is a small open cockpit. I hear the four rotors around us starting up as March slides the enormous metal doors closed.

I feel my stomach lurch as the helicopter takes flight.

'So you know what Solomon's Eye is, then?' I ask, over the sound of the vibrating hull.

For a brief moment, I wonder if March has heard me at all. Then he says, 'It's a prison.'

Shouldering his rifle and searching around in his pockets, the young soldier locates a very beaten-looking packet of cigarettes. He attempts to straighten one out. 'And June is a gods-damned hippy moron who's gonna end up putting us back into the dark ages,' he says, and he places the limp-looking stick in his mouth, lights the end, and takes a deep drag.

'I thought you were giving up.'

'So did I.'

The helicopter transport shudders slightly against a breeze, and both of us make to grab something in order to steady ourselves. We are definitely rising. I catch glimpses of the blue sky and the edge of the tower through the slats above.

'A long, long time ago,' says March, 'before the Sleepwalkers, dreams were ruled over by nightmare kings. The Nightmare Monarchies, they were called. It was a bloody dark time, and people were scared of going to sleep. And it went on for years and decades and centuries, until a guy called Solomon came along and changed everything.

'You've probably heard of Solomon, right? The wise old king. Well, I don't know too much about who he was when he was awake, but in dreaming, he was a great dreamer. Probably the greatest. He single-handedly ended the Nightmare Monarchies by banishing every last nightmare king he could find, and he went on to found the Sleepwalkers: twelve dreamers meant to guard the doors between dreams, and stop nightmare kings from happening. Solomon was the first of us, and the best, and every one of us is taught to do what he did.

'But he was also this great explorer. Solomon went out and explored the far reaches of the wild dreams. One story goes that he went all the way to the very edge of the wild dreams, where he found a vast, nightmarish storm. The kind of storm that makes normal storms look pathetic. And Solomon being Solomon, he braved the storm and passed through it, all the way to the middle, where he found an island in a placid sea. And the story says that on that island, in the middle of that great storm at the edge of dreaming, Solomon built a prison.

'So that's where June's going. To that massive, ancient, perpetual storm, which we call Solomon's Storm, and to the middle of it, where the prison is. The eye of the storm. Or, if you like, Solomon's Eye.' March hisses through his teeth. 'Because she's an idiot.'

'But why?' I ask.

'Hell if I know. To free whatever it is that's locked up there, probably.'

'She told me that she was going to see God.'

March raises an eyebrow. 'Maybe she worships nightmares now? Look. The story I know deliberately doesn't go into detail when it comes to whatever it is Solomon imprisoned there, but it's probably a nightmare king. Do you know how nightmares work?'

'I'm very new to all of this...'

'Okay. So. Nightmares feed on fear. Simple enough, right? The more you fear your nightmare, the stronger it gets. Now, nightmare kings aren't really kings in the usual sense. Not your benevolent, crown-wearing ruler of a kingdom king. They're kings more in the sense of – you know when a bunch of rats get their tails knotted up? But they're still alive. That's called a rat king. And it's big and nasty, and it can still bite and chew and screech like hell on earth. That sort of king. Nightmare kings are what happens when a nightmare finds the door to its own dream, and starts scaring a lot of people. Hundreds, or thousands. Accumulating so much power that it can do some crazy things, and influence countless waking lives for the worse.

'Think of the tower of Babel. Thousands of people build it in dreaming, and it's pretty inspirational. You might wake up after visiting the Capital and feel invigorated, or closer to God, or like you might do something creative – paint a picture, write a book, change the world for the better. Nightmare kings are the opposite of that. When they turn up, thousands of people wake up feeling anxious, or faithless, or like they might just go out and murder someone, because why the hell not, it's all meaningless anyway. You know how you can wake up after a bad dream, and your whole day gets worse? Imagine those bad dreams going on for weeks, or months. When nightmare kings turn up, the worst in people starts to come out. Your friends become your enemies. Wars happen, and people die.'

March takes a long drag of his cigarette and squints at me.

'I've never seen one,' he says. 'But back when I was an apprentice to the last March, the Sleepwalkers went to war against one.' March stares at the glowing end of his cigarette before he continues. 'There used to be a town out in the mountains,' he tells me, 'called Vale. I loved that place. It was like a winter paradise. There were hot springs, slopes you could ski down and this great big permanently frozen lake that was always clear, no matter how much you skated across it, so you could see the fish swimming underneath.

'And then, one night, it just... started to get colder. Or so I'm told. I was away at the time, learning the ropes, how to hunt in dreams. But apparently, the temperature started dropping and dropping and people didn't know what was happening until it was too late.

'People began to see a strange animal in the woods. I guess they didn't think it was a nightmare because it was so pretty. It looked like a glass stag. You know those ornaments old people – sorry – put on their mantelpieces? Sort of like that. Except, instead of glass, it was made out of ice. Antlers like enormous icicles, frozen solid, as sharp as knives. I dunno. Maybe the dreamers out in Vale thought it was a good omen or something.

'But it sure as hell wasn't. Because when people saw it, they found their dreams freezing over. They would wake up numb. And in Vale, the hot springs were freezing, the fires wouldn't light any more and the lake frosted over so thickly and sharply that nobody could go out there and skate without getting stuck to the surface. Then, a name started getting passed around. And when you heard that name, you'd feel cold. And maybe you'd wake up with feet like blocks of ice, no matter how warm it was.'

All at once, the helicopter shudders into the shadow of the tower and the cabin is plunged into darkness. 'Thawn,' says March. A chill runs down my back.

'They couldn't kill it,' he continues. 'Night after night the old March went out there in his winter coat, trying to hunt the ice stag. And some of the others went, too. November, January, even February. But the more they tried, the stronger it got, and the harder it became to even get close to Vale. By now, nobody even went there any more. Doors had stopped showing up. It was just a haven for cold nightmares. And worst of all, the cold was spreading. It was coming down from the mountains, and frost was appearing all over the valley. Even here, in Babel, you could see your own breath. Those were scary nights. And that's what a young nightmare king can do. It can haunt the dreams of thousands and make them wake up feeling dread night after night. People start to lose hope. Suicide rates go up. The world starts its slow slide into self-destruction.'

March's cigarette is no more than a glowing stump in the dark.

'Eight Sleepwalkers went out together in the end,' he says. 'And I've never seen anything else like it. I watched from the tower as they crossed the valley towards the mountains. Eight out of twelve proud and squabbling Sleepwalkers, putting aside their differences for the sake of killing a nightmare king. And by the point they reached the mountains, I couldn't see them any more. But I stayed up in the tower, I watched those frozen peaks, and I swear, time passed so slowly it could have been years.

'Then suddenly there was this great bright light, and for a

few moments there were two suns visible in the sky. I almost went blind trying to work out what was happening. It might have been a nuke, if it hadn't been so perfect and round and yellow. There was no blast either. Just waves of heat. And then the light faded, the mountains stayed black and the air stayed warm, and I knew that the nightmare king was dead.'

The helicopter leaves the shadow of the tower at last, and the light through the slats is sudden and warm. I am glad that it has returned. March stamps his cigarette out, a great frown across his face.

'August razed Vale. They're always the strongest, the August line. The others couldn't do much. From what I heard, they were each woken up one by one, while they tried to hunt the ice stag through the forests. And when he was the last one left, August did the only thing he could think of. He summoned the sun from his dream. The whole damn sun.' March shakes his head. 'He burned the forests, blackened the slopes and turned the lake to mist. All that's left there now is this great big black crater. But the nightmare king was banished. And that's what matters.'

I speak up, at last. 'And that's what's imprisoned at Solomon's Eye? A nightmare king?'

Slowly, March nods. 'Solomon built a black road to the eye of his great storm, where he'd made his prison. Then, he imprisoned whatever it was that he imprisoned, and he locked that prison up, and threw away the keys, and demolished the road, and made damn sure that everybody forgot what was locked up inside. So by my reckoning, June's heading there now – racing all the way to Solomon's Eye – to open it up and be chummy and friendly with whatever the hell is in there. And if I were a betting man, which I am, then I'd say that whatever it is that Solomon put in there must have been insanely powerful. A nightmare king so strong he couldn't kill it, so he locked it away.'

March pinches the bridge of his nose. His story seems to be finished.

'March,' I say. 'This might be a silly question, but what you do need me for?'

He looks up at me.

'Because you've got another copy of the map, right? So we can go stop her?'

A pause. 'Well—'

'Jesus, Will. Tell me you've got another copy of the map.'

'I do,' I tell him. 'But only while I'm awake.'

March rubs at his temple. 'Oh, hell. Hell hell hell.'

'What about the ruins of the black road? Couldn't you just find a way to follow them?'

The boy soldier chuckles humourlessly. Then, he moves across to the door in the side of the helicopter, and rolls it partially open. The cabin is immediately filled with rushing air, and he has to shout across at me, pointing at a section of the tower. 'Damn vultures will use anything!' And with my arms wrapped tightly around a railing, I peer out, and see a whole section of the tower which seems to be made of a kind of black stone. The rock of the black road, scavenged and used to heighten the tower.

With his hands clenched almost rigid, March fumbles to light another cigarette but accidentally drops it out of the side of the helicopter. The two of us watch it tumble away. 'What in hell's name are we gonna do?' yells March.

Before I can make any attempt at a reply, an incredible sight comes into view.

There are shapes hanging from the tower ahead of us: a tapestry of wooden walkways and scaffolding which make for a kind of peculiar set of docks. I can see the distant silhouettes of dock workers, high in the air, as if we are standing beneath crystal-clear depths of water and looking up at them. And moored at those docks is a singular ship, or mechanism, that defies easy understanding.

It looks as if someone has attempted to build a clock but did not know when to stop. It is a cataclysm of clockwork parts in synchronised motion arranged in the shape of a frigate. The ship has no sails, barely any hull beyond a few lengths of wood along its flanks, and between brass and copper lengths of girders, I can see endless cogs and cables, whirring and winding and ticking in gentle motion. The whole thing just hangs there, impossibly, in the sky.

I realise that I have forgotten to breathe.

Most remarkable of all is the bizarre clockwork ship's figurehead. Its sharp beak is at the very forefront, and behind that beak is a long wave of golden feathers. I recognise that bird; I would read tales of it to Samantha when she was still small enough to sit on my lap. It is the mighty phoenix.

I find some words, at last. 'What kind of ship is that?'

'That's a skyship!' calls March, over the winds. 'She's called the *Metronome*. And she just so happens to have a captain with a vested interest in Solomon's Eye. Normally, I wouldn't bother with the skydocks – it's quicker to get around through the doors. But if June's going to Solomon's Eye then that means she's going to places where there are no doors, and if we're going to catch up to her and stop her, then we're going to need to use a skyship. Will. Look at me.' I tear my eyes from the awesome sight of the clockwork skyship.

'Are you sure there's no other copies of your map? I mean, can't you even remember any of it? This is important.'

A desperation grips me. I hate the idea of being responsible for something as terrible as relentless dark dreams for thousands of people – and the consequences of those countless horrible nights – just because I was foolish enough to give away my notepad. I bow my head and try to think, but all that comes to mind is a memory of years ago.

The first month after Lily passed away, Sammy suffered a terrible nightmare. Every night she dreamed that there was somebody waiting in the upstairs laundry cupboard to hurt her. It got so bad that she could no longer walk past the cupboard, and because her room was at the far end of the hallway, she ended up just sleeping in my room. And though it was something of a great comfort to me in those dark days to not wake up alone – suffering through my own dark dreams – poor Sammy became withdrawn and quiet, and would use any excuse to be out of the house. I was not capable of helping her. I did not know how.

An idea strikes me.

'It's possible,' I call to March, 'that I could remember the songs. Using muscle memory. Using my violin. It would be tough, with my hands the way they are. And we'd need to find a new string, because I broke one. But it's possible that I could remember the songs of Solomon's Eye by just trying to play them again. If it's the songs that you need?'

March sighs a long sigh of relief. 'Yeah,' he calls, as our transport begins to approach the skydocks. Then, he grins at me. 'I knew you'd come through. You're a bright spark, Will.' Maybe it is something in his cheerful expression, but then I remember the second month after Lily passed away.

That one day, Sammy woke up and all seemed well with her again. She regained her flighty fearlessness, and there was no more need for her to sleep in my bed, because she was no longer frightened of the upstairs cupboard. I remember that I asked her, a few weeks afterwards, what had become of the horrible thing in the cupboard. And that she told me, cheerily, that a woman came with a silver gun and chased the monster away.

We land at the skydocks with a thump.

March yells a thanks up at Karl, and rushes across, towards the *Metronome*.

I stop for a moment, my view taken up by a second skyship further up the tower at a second set of docks. This one is far bigger than the *Metronome*, and it looks a lot closer to a traditional galleon, except that all of its sails are a brilliant gold and flow as if they are made of liquid. The name across the side of this ship reads *Sunshine*. I find my thoughts drifting away from the urgency of the situation and back to awe; it would be so easy to lose myself in the sights and sounds of Babel.

'Come on, Will,' calls March. I tear myself away and follow him onto the *Metronome*.

I am led through the low corridors of the clockwork skyship by her Bosun.

She has a steady tick, like a clock, or indeed a metronome, and her tick is all around us, but it is not unpleasant. It feels like a sign of life – as if, without it, the *Metronome* would be without her heart. The crew – a motley bunch of dreamers

– rush to and fro. We pass signs of industry – a shower of sparks where a cog is being welded into place, and a team of engineers attempting to free a knotted coil of cables.

'Captain Reid will want to see you soon,' says the Bosun. 'Once she's done with March.'

The Bosun is a large man, his belly almost protruding from his shirt, and I wonder if the pipe given a jaunty position at the corner of his mouth is a permanent fixture.

'She's a wonderful ship,' I tell him, and he grunts.

Near the stern of the ship, we emerge into a larger room, and it is there that the Bosun stops. 'This is yours,' he says, 'if you're telling the truth about your map.'

The room is in shadow, but I am still able to make out the great many shapes along the walls and shelves. In contrast to the rest of the ship, these walls are completely covered in thick wood, and upon entering, the *Metronome*'s tick is muffled. 'I am telling the truth,' I say.

He grunts at me, and his pipe wobbles. 'Just wait here,' he says, and he leaves.

I take the time to explore.

On one wall there is a rack of tuning forks, and inside a glass case there are rows of what look to be panpipes. Nearby, there is a set of mystifying and almost unrecognisable brass instruments. A large collection of wind chimes hang from the ceiling.

I step tentatively across to one of the many bookcases and squint through the low light at titles. They appear to be place names, or kinds of atlases. Collections of maps, I think.

Mystified, I head to the back of the room. There is something beside the window, not easily visible. It is a large frame, and contained within it is something like a scroll or a contract. I peer through the gloom, and see that it is a length of parchment titled *Babel*. And that beneath the title is a musical score.

It is a lengthy piece and takes up most of the back wall with its size, and between and upon the bars of its body dance the notes of a grand and regal song. It is a complicated composition, and it takes me some time to glance through and absorb it even partially.

It is in reading that I find something of an understanding.

This room is for the ship's navigator. And here, at the back of the room, framed and in pride of place, is the map that belongs to Babel. I do not understand how one would follow a map made of music, but I would imagine it has something to do with all of the strange instruments gathered around me.

'You're the map-maker?' A voice, from the doorway.

The Captain is tall and stern. She wears a long red coat with golden buttons, and she has a long braid of grey hair, tied behind her back, but it is her face that commands attention. It is an expanse of leathery and weather-worn skin, from within which a pair of wild eyes glare. And inscribed into the skin of that face is an unusual tattoo.

I am delighted to see that it is another musical score. There is the staff, with its five black bars running from ear to ear. Curled to the far left is a treble clef. And set upon this framework, taking the space across her eyes, touching her top lip and even drawn across her forehead, is a strange song.

'I am,' I tell her, and smile.

My smile is not returned. The Captain looks me up and down.

'While aboard my ship, you'll adhere to my rules. No weapons of any kind. No disobeying orders. And you'll pitch in as well. I'll not have a still body aboard my vessel. Understand?' She takes a step forward and into the room. 'The Sleepwalker March tells me you can make a map that leads to Solomon's Eye, and I have taken him at his word – his line has earned that much from me. But if I find you a liar, or a cheat, using my goodwill to secure yourself passage to some elsewhere place, then I'll have you both thrown overboard. Understand?' And before I can make a reply, she says, 'Show me your hands.'

I have never met a captain quite like this before.

Stepping towards her, I raise my aching hands, and as I do, I notice that they are not shaking as much as usual. Their tremor seems somewhat subdued, and even the tattoo visible at my wrist seems somewhat better defined. I frown.

Expecting Reid to comment on my arthritis, I am surprised when she says, 'You've sailed.'

'Aye,' I tell her. 'On and off my whole life.'

At this, she gives me a cold smile. 'Good.'

I lower my hands. 'I'll do my best,' I tell her.

'See that you do. Now: explain to me from where your map came.'

There is no easy answer. I settle for, 'A fever dream, a few years ago.'

'Mm,' says the Captain, thoughtfully. 'Prophetic, perhaps.'

Black boots clacking across the wood, she makes to leave. Only, at the door, she pauses, and turns back to me. 'I'm given to understand that you have a broken string?'

'Yes. And I'm not sure if I can give you the map without it.'

The Captain gives this a moment's thought. 'I'll have Callister informed – our chief engineer. And if we have nothing on board in service, then we'll make a stop.' Her stern face softens, and she says, 'For ages beyond reckoning, I have searched for a means to return to Solomon's Eye. There's an honesty in hands like yours, master map-maker, and I am led to believe that you and your Sleepwalker are truthful. Should you take us to where the black road once led, to the edge of Solomon's Storm, then I will take us through it. And not a thing on hell or earth can stop me.'

I believe her.

I head up on deck as we pull away from the docks.

The ticking of the *Metronome*'s engine is louder now, as it propels us in a slow arc. Captain Reid stands tall behind the ship's wheel, rolling it with one hand, the other behind her back – a regal pose. I notice that her wheel is a pointed star, like a sun, each spoke spiked.

Without orders, the crew dash from edge to edge, pulling on levers and adjusting valves. If the *Metronome* was slumbering before, then she is now awakening – the creaking of levers is her yawning, and the glinting of the sun across her bow is the opening of her eyes to see the day. The beak of the phoenix figurehead cuts clean through the air.

March has his rifle in pieces before him on a strip of canvas. He sits cross-legged at the ship's prow, and with a thin length of cloth, carefully cleans each part. As I approach, I notice the unusual quality of his ammunition.

Free from its housing, there is a bullet visible at the top of the rifle's magazine. It is a cloudy kind of silver, and as I watch it, I can see that the cloudiness is formed of condensation, as if the bullet is very cold.

'Hi, Will,' says March. 'I guess you met the Captain?'

'I did. She's pretty remarkable.'

'Definitely.' The boy soldier squints across at her. 'She's also mad.'

'Do you know what the song tattooed onto her face is?'

He shrugs as he puts his rifle back together. 'Not a clue.'

'She's letting you keep your guns?'

'An exception for a Sleepwalker, apparently.'

The city rolls out beneath us as we steadily glide around the edge of the tower. We appear to be adjusting our heading so that we can set out to sea, and I watch as the city streets, like the strands of an infinitely complex web, are netted out below us. I see the crowds of the city stop as we pass, casting their eyes up to watch us go.

March joins me at the railing, the warm wind causing his hair to flicker like fire. We both watch the streets and canals of Babel as they unfold beneath us, and a part of me wishes that I had spent more time here, simply exploring the place.

'Where are we heading?' I ask him.

'We need to go to another city first,' he tells me. 'Called Binary. So I can go to Parliament and warn the rest of the Sleepwalkers about what June's doing. Maybe get us some help.'

At last, the *Metronome*'s arc has brought us to the point where we are confronted by the sea instead of distant mountains. The sun is cut in half by the tower behind us. Ahead, at the edge of the city, there are beaches and docks and breakers, and a swarming of people like ants spread across them. I have spent so long without leaving a city that the sea seems infinite before us. I feel my heart beating faster in my chest.

'March?'

'Hm?' He also seems to be absorbed in the magnificent view.

'I get how the doors work. But how does Babel work? I mean, whose dream is it?'

A pause from the young soldier. Then he says, 'Everything dreams, Will. Worms dream of rich earth, and birds dream of open skies, and pebbles dream of being mountains. The difference is that, while people have doors, everything else doesn't. It's just one great big mass of dreaming, dreamed up by all the animals and plants and everything else. Wild dreams. And in some places, the doors come together, and people make cities in the wild.'

'Like Babel.'

'Like Babel. And a few other places.'

I watch the tower as it thins out behind us. 'It's beautiful,' I say.

'Sometimes,' says March, and he leaves it at that.

I hold my breath as the *Metronome* begins to find speed and heads for the divide between land and water. It feels as if I might tumble overboard into the blue, sky or sea. And then, all at once, we have crossed that border, the city of Babel is behind us and I feel as if I can release my breath. The air I breathe now is frigid and laced with salt, and the air coursing across deck seems colder. It whisks the edges of my coat around. I feel suddenly free, so free, and better still as the tower of Babel becomes a line, becomes a thin line, becomes the horizon turned vertical, dividing the sky behind us.

I laugh, and my laughter is caught on the wind and whisked away. The *Metronome* is as fast as promised, and the waves blur by beneath us. Her ticking is noisy and in a quick step now, as if time is passing faster, and the deck feels warm beneath my feet. We are a glinting golden jewel in the sky, retreating into the blue.

We fly out beyond the horizon, in pursuit of June.

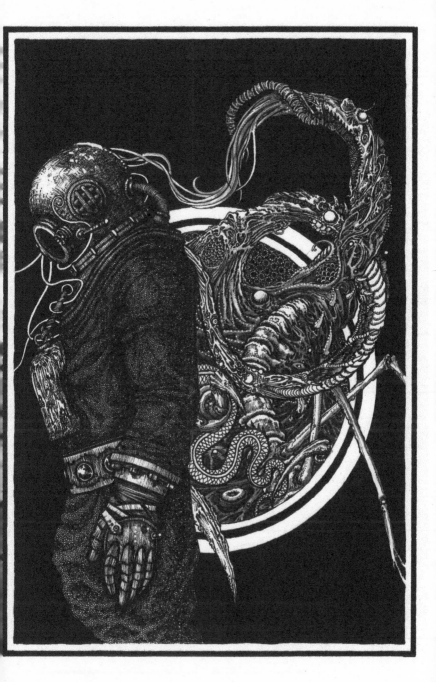

PART TWO

PART TWO

CALLISTER'S BIRDS

BINARY

Beyond the *Metronome* the sky turns from blue to faded blue, to white, to grey.

As we soar into a deep gloom, it reminds me of my first voyage.

It was an unusually overcast day in August, not long after my twenty-ninth birthday, when I drove up to Aberdeen in my little beaten car. With all my training complete, I probably should have felt some excitement. After all, this is what I had been yearning to do since I was young: to sail and see new places. The ship waiting for me was a hauler called the *Prince Regent*, and I had a place on board as a deck rating – perfect for me, because I was never officer material. Yet driving towards the docks, all I felt was a sort of slow dread. Samantha burbled in the back seat and Lily was silent the whole journey, refusing to look me in the eye.

I suppose that I had been expecting more cheer as we pulled away from shore. Like in wartime with the crew leaning over the side of the ship, waving to their loved ones. But there was only me, watching Aberdeen slowly recede. And there was only Lily at the docks, and she did not wave. She held on to Samantha, and I remember the way her white dress moved in the cold wind. It was my favourite white dress, stained slightly at the shoulder because Sammy had thrown up a little earlier in the day. Lily did not smile her sly slanted smile for me. Her dark hair swished across her shoulders, and I knew, more than anything else in the world, that I no longer wanted to leave.

The *Metronome* soars through clouds, and they let forth a hazy drizzle too fine to be rain, and too soaking to be a shower. With a sigh, I fasten my coat closed before the weather can drench me. Nearby, March does the same.

A city comes into view.

We fly above uniform towers arranged in blocks. The towers rise into the grey, and those panelled in glass reflect the dull sky and us: a black dot approaching. The streets beneath are arranged in an almost perfect grid pattern, where black and grey cars queue up, awaiting turns to cross intersections. Street lamps shine against the gloom of the drizzle, but they are unwelcoming white lights that do more to illuminate pavements than bring cheer to the place.

I realise that I am searching for any hint of colour in the streets. The roads are grey, the cars are grey and the buildings are grey.

'This is Binary, then?' I ask March.

He nods grimly. Even the colour in his uniform seems to be fading.

'The other side of the coin,' he says.

Looking at him now, a vision of green against the gloom, I realise why I feel so comfortable around March. He reminds me of Valentine.

When the *Prince Regent* finally took port in Cairo, halfway through my first voyage, I took to the bars there in order to try and drink some of my misery away. It was in one of those bars where I met a young soldier with an enormous bristling brown moustache and a ridiculous English accent, and the two of us continued the night together into oblivion, trading stories in the heat. He told me that he had been sent to Cairo with a diplomatic party in order to keep an eye on them, and he told me that his name was Sergeant Valentine. We laughed, that night. I remember the laughter.

I say to March, 'You ever hear of a guy called Major Valentine?'

Immediately, his face brightens up. 'You're kidding, right?'

'No. I'm curious. He never talks much about his army days.'

'He's still alive? Well I'll be damned.' March grins. 'He's a legend.'

'Seriously?'

'Seriously. I joined the army a couple of weeks before Valentine's day, so I was going through basic on the day, and they had us learn all about Major Valentine, and sing some stupid songs, and run about in the mud and the rain until we couldn't even feel our legs any more. Valentine was a cunning bastard. Won a lot of medals. Saved a lot of lives. There was one story where he sorted out a hostage situation at an embassy by rerouting the water supply. Flooded the place from the sewers. Lots of politicians with muddy feet, but lots of terrorists too. I think they kept that one out of the news. Can you imagine the headlines?'

I have to laugh. 'I'll have to ask him about that one.'

'Yeah,' says March. 'You should.'

The *Metronome* circles skyscrapers, and I am reminded of Manhattan, but without the spirit that brings Manhattan to life. The ticking of the *Metronome*'s engine rattles the windows of the skyscrapers we pass, causing droplets of drizzle to shiver.

Ahead, I can just about make out what looks to be a set of skydocks set into the side of a skyscraper. They seem as uniform and well maintained as the rest of the city, lacking in the haphazard rope and woodwork of Babel.

I shiver as the first of the drizzle manages to touch my shoulders through my coat, and hope that we are not staying in this place for very long. March slings his rifle over his shoulder as we set down, making for a gangplank being lowered by hissing pneumatics. He waves at the Captain – red coat turned crimson – who calls across to him. 'Make haste, Sleepwalker! I have little love for this place.'

March shrugs off the command and turns back to me.

'You should come with me,' he says. 'Everyone else is waiting here. Loading up supplies. Getting ready to run after June. But you'll be safer with me. Or rather, I'd feel better being able to keep a close eye on you. If you wake up, then we're all screwed.'

'What do you mean?'

'I mean, without you, we don't have a map, or any real way of catching up to June. And if I lose track for a minute and you accidentally get woken up, then the next time you fall asleep – tomorrow night, or whenever – you'll be back in your own dream and have to find Babel again. And by the time that's somehow happened, June's already gotten to Solomon's Eye, and—'

'She opens the prison.'

'A lot of people could die, Will. Nightmare kings are no joke.' March glances out at the grey city of Binary – dull and dull and dull. 'It's a hell of bureaucracy, here. Not very exciting. But I promise we're not gonna be here for long. I just need to warn the others, and see if we can get any help.'

I pull my coat closer and feel the kind of rush of blood I associate with pins and needles: a sudden flush of warmth through my fingers. The ache there feels different now, as if it is reparative instead of being indicative of damage. I wonder what is happening to me.

'You coming?' asks March.

'Doesn't feel like I have much of a choice,' I tell him, but my words come out more cynical than I mean. Perhaps it is just the gloom of Binary, making me bitter. I will be glad to leave this place.

I follow March through the streets of Binary.

We tread damp pavements, passing cars that all look identical; they are black, glistening with droplets and driven by hunchback shades with the corners of their mouths drawn down as if weighted. Drivers do not vie for space here: they are content to queue and wait their turn at the intersections, where the colourless traffic lights are shades of grey.

I shiver in the drizzle. 'This is what I imagine hell to be like,' I say, trudging along.

March is an unusual figure in this city. He is a soldier surrounded by men and women in dark suits and dark raincoats, carrying identical black umbrellas and briefcases. At crossings they wait in silence, their umbrellas forming an unbroken canopy overhead, but March pushes through. 'Hate it here,' he tells me. 'I keep imagining grabbing a bucket of red paint and just throwing it at walls, you know?'

As we carry on, I find myself yearning for the same. Worst of all are the doors. Because there are doors here – hundreds, if not thousands; easily as many as in Babel. Except here there is no telling where the dull individual dreams end and the dull city starts.

Off in the distance, there is a boom. The ground trembles slightly.

We both halt.

'What was that?'

March looks concerned, but shrugs. 'Not sure.'

Across an intersection, March takes us into a park. He has sped up a little.

I feel as if I am able to breathe a little better away from the claustrophobic streets, but I notice that the depths of the park's fountains are encrusted with coins like silver scales; there are so many wishes left unfulfilled here that the coins have become mountains. We pass people sat on wet benches. Everyone in this city looks tired, and I realise that it is possible, even in dreaming, to be dreadfully weary.

At a faceless, nameless statue, March has stopped. He is looking upwards.

There is a rumbling in the air, a thrumming, and around

us, the trees shudder. There are fires in the grey sky. Though it is not possible to make out any distinct shapes, it is possible to see the shadows of ships as they pass through the clouds above. The fires are the flaring engines propelling some of them along, but there are others lights too, piercing the gloom – winking red and green lamps, swinging torches and a scattering of portholes lining the edges of unseen hulls. It looks like a whole fleet of skyships are passing over the city.

'That's not right,' says March. 'I count thirty. Maybe forty. What do you reckon?'

I try and do a rough count of the silhouettes. 'Thirty or so.'

'Why would they…' says March, but he trails off.

Following the fleet is a behemoth. It fills the sky, looming over us as if it might eclipse the heavens, and it is surrounded by a black miasma of smoke, staining the clouds. The ground beneath my feet vibrates, and I realise that the ship up there is absurdly huge – maybe ten times bigger than the *Metronome*. It lumbers onwards, like a floating metal storm cloud, and it sounds a deafening horn, like a foghorn amplified tenfold. I have to clamp my hands over my ears to protect them, and when I feel safe enough to uncover them, dogs are barking and car alarms are going off in the near distance.

'What on earth was that?'

March's eyes are wide. 'Parliament's flagship. The *Smog*.'

'Where are they all going?'

'That's what I'm wondering.' He pulls the strap of his rifle onto his shoulder and nods towards the grey streets of Binary ahead. 'We should get a move on. I need to find out what's happening. Not much further now.'

'Something to do with June, do you think?'

'I hope not.'

March jogs across another identical intersection, passing the hissing grey hulk of a bus spraying water, and I follow behind as quickly as I am able. For once, there is a signpost, and it reads PARLIAMENT, directing us down the next street. Only... March begins to slow, a look of horror across his face, as it becomes apparent that something terrible has occurred ahead. There is fire, streaming out through the drizzle and smoke. I feel my heart sink.

><•<

Where Parliament should be is a vision of destruction.

It takes a while simply to take in. There is fire, smoke, and ruined and blackened masonry everywhere. It might be the remains of one enormous building, or maybe an entire block – it is difficult to tell. In the distance I can hear the wail of sirens approaching. Here the sky is grey, the surrounding buildings are grey, and the fire is flickering orange and yellow and red.

There is another great boom as something collapses in the wreckage, and I am startled from my stupor. March is wearing a grim expression. 'This isn't good,' he says.

Casting my eyes over the destruction, I am horrified to glimpse the body of a man trapped beneath a burning beam of wood. Without any hesitation, I rush across, keeping my coat over my mouth to protect my lungs from the smoke, skittering over hot rubble. I hear March call after me, but I miss the words he says. I can feel the heat of the flames as I approach. I lean down, grab a section of the beam that is not on fire and heave. The figure of the man, wearing a grey suit, wriggles beneath it.

I find that I am able to keep a grip. My fingers tingle.

There is a hand on my shoulder and I am pulled away. The beam settles back into place. March has a scarf wound around his face. 'Don't,' he tells me.

'What are you doing?' I am angry with him, turning back to try again.

'Don't!' he says again, keeping hold of my arm. 'Let him wake, Will. Look at him. Just let him wake up.' And I pause, and do look at him – the man beneath the beam. He could be anyone. Another dim face in the grey city. There is soot on his face, and I realise that he is not wriggling to be free of the beam trapping him. He is reaching out for his suitcase, on fire beside him. I stumble back, and as I do, the flames take hold of his jacket, and he crumbles into a fine dust, whirling away among the ruins. The man is awoken.

I turn on the spot. The grey city looms around me, and I can see hundreds of people doing nothing. They stand at crossings that no longer lead anywhere, and shuffle along the streets as if there is no great disaster here. I want to wave at them, to call them over, to tell them that we need help, but I know that it will make no difference. They are all too absorbed in their own little hells to notice the world burning down around them.

Keeping his hand on my arm, March leads me through the ruins.

'What happened?' I ask him. 'Terrorists?'

'Not terrorists,' he says. 'Just... breaking up communications. Now I can't get messages out to the others. Parliament's not... it's not a real government. How do you govern dreams? It's just a bunch of non-Sleepwalkers trying to help us out. And they do that by keeping the paperwork, passing messages along and keeping tabs on where everyone is. At least, they did...' He shrugs. 'Hard to terrorise a city that doesn't care if you blow it up.'

Ducking beneath a gout of smoke, we come to a rise in the rubble, and from there we are able to observe a bizarre phenomenon. At the heart of the ruins is a winter forest. It is bright, and the frost and snow covering it glistens as if it sits beneath a winter sun – only, above it, the grey sky continues raining its perpetual gloom. Pine trees litter the ruins thickly. Frost engulfs the flames.

'What *is* that?' I ask.

March lowers his scarf and grins at me. 'That's November's dream.' He almost skips down the rubble towards the edge of the forest. 'She's conjuring it to put out the fires. Come on, Will!'

I follow hesitantly, and as I do I notice that the forest is growing. Veins of frost are slowly clutching the rubble at its edge – rivers of ice filling the gaps and instantly sapping the heat out of the ruins. At the edge, I step through, and feel the bitter cold of the place. I immediately wish that I had brought a thicker coat.

Glancing at his compass, March scowls. 'Too many survivors. Okay, Will, you go that way, and I'll go this way, and if you spot November first, let her know I'm here.'

Crunching through the snow I have to tread carefully – the ruins still lie beneath. Here, a statue is half embedded in a tree, and there, an enormous collapsed pillar looks like a fallen tree-trunk, covered in frost and snow. There are people, as well. The worst is a man still sat at his half-burned desk, his frozen hands locked onto his ruined typewriter. I do as I am told and leave him be. At the entrance to a different section of the forest, I turn and see him collapse into dust and awakening.

I climb a hill surrounded on all sides by trees, and realise I am leaving the ruins behind. The dream of the forest remains disconcerting, however. The sky above should contain a gleaming white winter sun, but does not. And the sound is all wrong. I should be able to hear the flames, the sirens and the ambient noises of the city, but instead all I can hear is the bitter wind and the crunching of twigs and snow.

At the top of the hill the trees widen into a clearing. I see a woman.

She has a gush of silver hair, and she is wearing a white fur coat. Held between her gloved hands is a heavy-looking silver revolver. I watch as she aims the barrel of it at the head of a businessman half buried in a mound of snow and smartly executes him. No red sprays onto the white, though; he is awoken, turning to dust, and the blackbirds in the trees around the clearing all rise at once in a black rushing of wings.

The woman holds a compass. She studies it as I emerge from the forest path.

'Excuse me,' I say. Immediately, she fixes her revolver upon me, narrowing her eyes. I raise my hands and halt. 'I'm sorry,' I say, but she sighs and lowers her gun – holstering it at her side gunslinger style. She looks me up and down, and frowns.

'You don't belong here,' she says.

'I'm just passing through,' I tell her. 'You must be November?'

'That I am.' Her accent is soft, dulled around the edges. Swedish.

'March is here. We were looking for you.'

'Is he now?' She takes another glance at her compass. 'This way, then,' she says, and strides away among the roots of the forest. I struggle to keep up with her; by now my feet have turned numb from the cold. But before long we come to the foot of the hill, where March has dug a folder of frozen-looking papers out from the snow, and is thumbing through them. November halts at the edge of the clearing – a wasteland of icy office equipment – and hails him.

March looks nervous in November's presence.

'Hi, November,' he says, glancing at me and then back at her. 'It's been a while.'

'Long enough,' she says. Then, 'The fleet is compromised. An army of nightmares, I am told – came from the doors, woke the crews and stole their ships. I am concerned about the *Smog* in particular. She has enough guns to threaten the tower. But no Parliament. No means of leaving messages. I must send out messengers myself, just as we did in the old days.' She smiles, and I realise that she is older than she looks – skin so pale and winter-scarred that it lends her youth. 'You are here, though. Perhaps the two of us can rally the others quickly.'

'Was it June?' he asks. 'Was it her nightmares?'

November sighs. 'Of course it was June. It's always June.'

'In that case, I think I know where she's going with all those ships. And it's not Babel.'

'Where?'

'Solomon's Eye.'

November's face turns blank. I would imagine that if there

was any colour in her cheeks, then it would be draining from them. 'But... how? How did she get a map?' she asks, and her gloved hand instinctively goes to rest on the hilt of her silver revolver. I notice that the metal of that revolver steams, and I am reminded of the way that I saw March's bullets steaming. I find myself frowning.

'November, I'd like you to meet William Manderlay, the map.' He nods at me.

The icy Sleepwalker turns to look at me.

'I'm sorry,' I say, 'but I was wondering... why is your gun so cold?'

The two Sleepwalkers appraise me, and as they do, November idly answers my question. 'Ice-silver,' she says. 'A rare metal that nightmares hate. So we make guns from it, and bullets from it, and we hunt them with it. It hurts them; they are unable to even touch it. But it only can be found in one place. A rare luxury, for us.' Then, blinking, she turns back to March. 'A map. Fine. You have a skyship, then? You can follow her?'

'That's the plan. We're moored up at the East Dock because Reid wanted some cover, and I'm glad we did. By my reckoning we've got the only damn skyship left in the city.'

'Good. This is good. Stop her, at all costs, please. In fact...' November pauses, looking thoughtful. 'Yes, I will come with you. I will come with you both, and help you stop her. Go now. Return to your skyship. Reid means you have the *Metronome*, no? A fine choice. A flighty bird. I will put out the last of these fires, send messages to the others and then join you both.' She seems pleased with this decision, and nods to herself. 'Yes. We will stop June together. She cannot be allowed to reach Solomon's Eye.'

At this, March draws his feet together and snaps off a smart salute. He quickly lowers his hand when he sees the expression across November's face. It is odd seeing him so nervous; he does not seem to know how to conduct himself around the older Sleepwalker. 'All right,' he says, instead, and the two of us quickly rush away, in search of the edge of the forest and the way back to the *Metronome*.

>•<

The crew of the *Metronome* have opened up a partition wide enough to receive cargo in her side, and the two of us stand to one side of it, sheltering from the rain and keeping a close eye on the docks for any sign of November, while large cages filled with a very peculiar cargo are brought on board around us.

'Why birds?' I ask March.

The boy soldier has spent every moment since we arrived back at the ship cleaning his kit – trying to look impressive for November, perhaps. Currently he is polishing his boots while he wears them, dabbing a rag into a tiny portable tin of polish. He glances up when I speak to him. 'No idea,' he tells me.

From beyond the uneven opening in the side of the *Metronome* come the crew, carrying the birds. There must be hundreds of feathered bodies vying for space. The cages are not cramped, and have special little ledges upon which they can perch, but there is something close to a dozen birds per cage, of all different shapes and sizes. They are noisy, colourful and brilliant.

The hold behind us is slowly filling up with them.

The Bosun, who is overseeing the loading, has also chosen to remain in the dry interior of the ship. He taps his pipe and grunts at me. 'From what I hear,' he says, 'sometimes, birds get lost and end up in Binary. Bit jarring seeing a bloody great parrot larking about when everything else is grey. Disturbs the locals. So they have this special team they put out with nets, to catch 'em. Sounds like a bloody waste of time, if you ask me. Why not have a little colour?' The Bosun takes his time to remove his pipe and spit, making absolutely certain that his missile hits the grey concrete of the docks. 'Hell if I know what we're gonna do with 'em all,' he grumbles. 'Callister's orders.'

I do have to admit that I am enjoying the presence of the birds. It is a mad and chaotic colourful vision, making the *Metronome* feel even more alive.

Before too long the stream of noisy cargo stops, and the crew make to roll the doors shut.

March stops them. 'Hold on,' he says. 'We're waiting on an arrival. Leave it for now.'

The Bosun glares at him. 'How much longer?' he grumbles.

March can only shrug.

It is obvious that nobody wants to stay here any longer than absolutely necessary. There is no approach, however. I think that I was expecting the swift arrival of November, striding through the rains triumphantly, and I get the impression that March was expecting the same. Every now and then, he will glance up with a small frown upon his face. Eventually March runs out of things to clean, and stands tall instead, restlessly clutching at his rifle and peering into the rains.

'You take good care of your equipment,' I say, making conversation.

'Yeah,' he says. 'The last March always told me that if you look after your kit, it'll look after you. He hasn't been wrong yet.'

'What was he like? The old March, I mean.'

March looks thoughtful. 'The best guy I ever knew, honestly,' he says. 'He turned up one night in my dream, out of nowhere. Same dream every night, like you saw. Can't seem to shake it. And then this guy walks in, looking like something out of an old war film. You know, with the wooden rifle, and dented metal helmet. World War Two kinda thing. And he sits with me, and shows me his compass, and just talks for hours and hours. He tells me about dreams, and the doors between them, and that his name is March and that he's something called a Sleepwalker. And then he says to me, hey, you look like a bright young lad, want to learn how to do what I do?' March grips his compass tightly and watches the needles spin. 'I didn't realise he was training me to replace him. But I guess he must have known he was going to die soon. I miss him, a lot. It's hard,' he says.

'It's hard leaving my dream every night, chasing nightmares and using his name, like I'm pretending to be him. Like I'm pretending to be one of them. I'm not... I'm no November, you know? Most of the time I barely know what I'm doing.'

I squint out at the rains. I am not certain how to reply – whether attempting to be comforting would be patronising or not. Instead, I leave March to his thoughts, and hope that November shows up soon. I am firmly of the belief that we will all be better off once we have left the gloomy city of Binary far behind us.

An unusual quiet falls over the scene. The pattering of the drizzle seems to soften, as does the ticking of the ship's engine behind us, and the noisy calling of birds ceases altogether.

'What in hell's name...' March mutters. His voice sounds distant.

The far edge of the docks is wreathed in shadows, and from somewhere inside them comes the sound of heavy boots stomping. The birds behind us have flapped to the backs of their cages, as if to get as far away as possible from the approaching noise.

'Oh, shit.' March raises his rifle.

From the darkness lurches a heavy shape, and the shadows seem to linger upon it a little longer than they should, as if reluctant to let it go. It looks like some kind of bizarre ancient diving suit, heaving its heavy boots, one after the other, swinging its metal gauntlets and labouring under an enormous metal helmet with a porthole window.

March strides out and on to the docks to intercept it, his head angled across the sight of his rifle. I notice his thumb flick the safety catch above the trigger. 'Stop where you are!' he calls. 'Stop right there!'

The nightmare diver has no breathing apparatus. There are no pipes leading from its helmet, and there is no oxygen pack across his back. And yet, this is not the worst there is to see. Because it appears that the diver's helmet is filled with darkness.

The enormous diver's boots come to a clomping halt a few feet away from March, and it slowly raises one of his gauntlets, within which is a scroll of paper.

March's rifle is steady. With the utmost caution, March

steps as a dancer might, the end of his rifle trained on the diver's helmet, around to where he is able to snatch the scroll.

'Will!' calls March. 'Can you come and read this for me?'

I am afraid to approach the stand-off, but I cross the divide and take the scroll from the nightmare-hunter. I untie the fastening and read through.

'March,' I say. 'This says that November sent him. His name is Slint, and that he will help us recover the Smog.' I read it again to make certain. My throat feels heavy, and the drizzle from above makes streaks of some of the letters, but it is true. November has sent a nightmare to help us. 'I'm sorry, March,' I say. 'It says that she's not going to be able to join us. That nightmares are rioting back in Babel, and she needs to deal with it. But... she wishes us luck. And she says that this nightmare... this Slint, is a trusted ally. That he will obey orders without question.' My second sweep of the scroll done, I roll it up again in order to preserve it from the rain, and step back. It seems like a cruel joke and I am sorry to have been a part of it.

March takes a while to digest this news. He does not lower his rifle.

'Bosun!' he calls. 'Fetch the Captain!'

Grabbing the scroll from me, the heavyset Bosun seems more than happy to dash away. And in that moment, I realise that I too want to be away from this – that I have had enough of the grey city and its despair. I step back inside, and waver, watching the stand-off between the nightmare hunter and the nightmare inside the diving suit, wondering if I should stay and help. But then I see one last thing, and it is enough to cause me to retreat.

It was the slightest movement from the diver, the tiniest revolution of his helmet by the smallest degree, but it was enough – enough that the black porthole at the front of his helmet was staring at me, like a great black pupil composed of shadows. It was Slint noticing me – watching me with his unbearable abyssal gaze. I turn and leave the grey docks, in search of sanctuary.

Enough of this terrible place.

The map room is as I left it, a musty space where the sound of the *Metronome*'s ticking is muffled by its thick wooden walls. Except, this time, it has an occupant. He is sat at one of the room's long tables, and has a lantern lit to illuminate the intricate work he is hunched over. He is wearing a pinstripe waistcoat over a white shirt with the sleeves rolled back. And when he turns to see me enter, I notice that he has a great black moustache of the same colour as his well-oiled hair. His eyes are agleam, as if there is a great deal of work occurring behind them, cogs turning inside his head.

He twirls the delicate-looking tool he is holding between his fingers, and then flicks the lens over his right eye away, which is one of a collection hanging from a strip of leather about his forehead. 'Can I help?' he asks.

'I'm sorry,' I tell him, pausing in the doorway. 'I'm not disturbing you, am I?'

'You're not about to start welding or hammering something, are you?' The man's accent is distinctly London. He examines me for the tools that would produce any such offending noises, and seems to be pleased to find none of them.

'You don't look like a member of the crew,' he says.

'I'm not.'

'Good.'

He flicks the lens back down over his right eye, before turning back to his work. 'Bit of peace and quiet is all I ask. You're welcome to stick around, so long as you don't start making a racket.' The Londoner returns to his intricate operations.

I head inside, locating my violin where I left it, and turn back to him, my fingers paused on the rough twill of the case. With his complicated tools, the Londoner appears to be piecing together a device similar to the *Metronome* – fashioned out of clockwork. I notice that the man's hands are completely steady. He works with the precision of a surgeon.

'Are you making a clock?' I ask.

The Londoner replies, muttering beneath his breath to keep his hands steady. 'I tried a couple of times, back in Babel. And they were brilliant. Better than anything I could do awake. So accurate they'd never fall out of time. The problem, though,' he says, as he delicately screws a fixture into place, 'is that the time they were meant to be measuring was always wrong. Bloody nuisance, really. Drove me mad. You can make the world's most perfect clock, and it'll always be wrong because time is wrong in dreams. It always passes too fast, or too slow, depending on your mood.'

The man leans back from his work and looks up at me.

'I'm Callister,' he says. 'Of Callister's Clocks. You've probably heard of me, because I'm the best damn watchsmith in Britain.' He flicks the lens over his eye up again and folds his arms, observing me properly. 'And who the bloody hell are you, tramping around on my ship and leaving your soggy coat all over my chairs? Those things are made of Owlwood. Do you know how bloody difficult it is to find Owlwood in dreams? Near damn impossible. And it's the only wood we could find that could soak up the ticking.'

I remember that the Captain mentioned this man. She called him the ship's chief engineer, no less. Suddenly a lot of things about the *Metronome* make sense. 'I'm sorry,' I tell him, and reach for my damp coat.

Callister laughs at me, a great bellowing sound. 'Don't be sorry, you bloody great fool. I'm only joking. Leave your damn coat where it is. And to answer your question, no, I'm not making a clock. I gave up trying to make clocks a long while back. These days I have the pleasure of putting together great big flying boats in the sky so that mad captains can go chasing bits of sheet music across half of bloody dreaming. But this,' he nods at the stack of work in front of him, 'is more of a hobby. Something to pass the time.'

'Well, I'm sorry for disturbing you. I'm Manderlay. The man with the map.'

'Ah,' says Callister. 'The Captain told me about you.'

Setting his tools aside, Callister wipes his palms on a rag and stands, and when he advances his hand, I shake it, and the sensation is pleasant. I am momentarily astonished by the clarity of the tattoo on my wrist when I glimpse it – the heart for Lily. Indeed, it seems as if I am growing younger the longer I spend dreaming.

'Let's see the damage, then,' says Callister.

It takes me a moment to realise that he is asking about my violin.

I unlatch the clasps and draw her case open, to reveal her just as she was: lovely, worn from decades of use and currently so sad to see because she is still missing her fourth string. I run my fingers across the varnished wood of her body and idly trace her F-holes. It is as familiar as tracing the lines of my own skin.

The ship's engineer drops the lens back across his eye and peers closely.

'A thing of beauty,' he says. 'You much of a fiddler?'

I shrug. 'I played for the London Philharmonic, once.'

Callister chews on his bottom lip as he considers my violin. 'You know, I did see them play a long while back. And they were bloody brilliant. Never heard anything like it. Bit of a change from my old shop, too. Nothing but ticking all day is enough to drive a man to despair. But the London Philharmonic... well. That was something.'

I smile. 'I should never have left them,' I tell him.

After spending a good long while examining my instrument, he says, 'Nope. Don't reckon I can help you with this myself.'

'Surely you must have a length of steel wire on board somewhere?'

Callister straightens up and twists the end of his moustache thoughtfully. 'Absolutely. But nothing so slender. And truth be told, I'd struggle to shave enough off any of the cables we have. No, I don't think I can help here. What you need is an expert. Someone who knows his instruments. And lucky for you, I know just the guy.'

'Someone on board?'

Callister laughs. 'My lot wouldn't know good music if it slapped them in the face! It's all dub this, and house that.

Bloody great lot of useless lumps. But this map of yours is meant to lead to Solomon's Eye, right? Which means heading out into the deep wild dreams, way beyond the cities. And Reid likes to go by the Golden Gate, traditionalist that she is. Luckily for you, the guy I know just so happens to be set up there. So, way I see it, you head on up to the Captain and let her know we need to make a quick stop at the Golden Gate, and I'll take you to meet my man when we get there, and he'll fix your fiddle for you. How does that sound?'

'Sounds wonderful, Callister.'

'Mm,' he says, and returns to his work. 'Go tell Reid, then. I'll be up on deck myself, once we're clear of Binary. Can't stand the bloody place, myself.'

I close my violin case and head to the doorway with a spring in my step.

'Manderlay!' calls Callister before I can leave. I turn to see him sitting back in his chair. He is winding the back of the device he has been working on with a small key, and for the first time, I can see it for what it is. Made of copper, and brass, and maybe even gold, and glinting with the small jewels he has used to weight it, is the shape of a clockwork bird. Its head is currently against its breast, and its wings are folded in, but when Callister is done winding and removes the key, it begins to move.

The clockwork bird first raises its head, sharp beak flashing in the lamplight. Its eyes are rubies, and they glitter like fire. And then, ticking and juddering, the bird slowly raises its wings. One feather at a time, they part from its sides and splay themselves. With its magnificent head held high, and its wings spread broadly to either side, I recognise it for what it is. The bird is a miniature version of

Metronome's figurehead. Another phoenix, glaring fiercely in the lamplight, beneath the warm gaze of its creator.

'Say,' says Callister, thoughtfully. 'Got any gold on you?'

'I don't think so.'

'Mm,' he says. 'Don't worry about it. We'll find some somewhere.'

THE GOLDEN GATE

The air outside is warming as we leave the clouds above Binary far behind. It is night now, and the crew have lit a scattering of orange-glowing lamps about the ship.

I cast furtive glances around as I ascend onto deck, but there is no sign of Slint in his huge suit. The decks are mostly empty except for a scattering of crew making adjustments, the regal figure of the Captain behind her pointed wheel and the solitary silhouette of March stood on the shallow forecastle, above the ship's figurehead. The ship ticks steadily beneath my feet.

I ascend the aftercastle and address Captain Reid, whose eyes follow the stars.

'Callister says we need to make a stop at the Golden Gate.'

She nods, curtly. 'Then we shall.'

I attempt to make myself useful among the crew, and chat with them as they work. I speak to an investment banker adjusting a peculiar fluted valve, a yoga instructor elbow-deep in the deck and a man who tells me that he is homeless when he is awake, who listens intently at patches of the deck with a stethoscope, occasionally tapping at it with a hammer. I am put to work following a bearded zookeeper and handing him tools from a box as he works at the gyroscopes keeping the *Metronome* balanced. I feel like a caddy, keeping his golfer's clubs ready.

Beyond the railings is a wide vista of land, lit by the yellow moon hanging on the horizon like a counterfeit sun. The sky is awash with rolling pale clouds, and the lands are similar, rocky and mountainous and ridged in pale yellow where they reflect the moon.

I am reminded of the good years. The years I spent between home and distant lands, travelling to every continent, working hard. The thing about sailing is that by the time you reach your destination, you really feel as if you have earned it – as if that city out there, sparkling in the night, is the reward for all your work between the open waves. I saw places I never imagined could exist, those years, and I met such people – such wonderful, strange and endlessly fascinating people – that it is a wonder I ever came home. But I did come home. Year after year, I would return to my family, for lengthy holidays of months at a time.

After a while, Lily learned to smile again, and so did Sammy. And every time I returned to our cosy house in Edinburgh, Sammy would be a little bit taller and a little bit smarter. I would unlock the front door, and there she would be, standing instead of crawling, or calling me Pa instead of gurgling, and Lily would show me all the photographs she took while I was away – of Sammy's first steps, and of Sammy teething, and of Sammy trying out various foods for the first time. In return, I would show them both my own photographs: the streets of distant cities, the sailors I sailed with and the mighty ships we used to cross the longest stretches of sea.

I know that I upset Lily every time I left. But I still think back fondly of those times. I made enough money that Lily did not have to work, and so that she could buy everything that Sammy could possibly want. And though I know my wanderlust was selfish – that I sailed not for my girls, but for me – I do hope that Lily was proud of her husband, and that Sammy was proud of her father: the wild adventurer who returned from time to time, with brand-new tattoos and brand-new tales to tell.

Eventually, I head across to March. Below us, there are glinting points of light, like lighthouses in the dark. We are passing over a warm but mysterious land.

I notice that March has unclipped his side-arm. 'If I gave you a gun,' he says, 'would you be able to use it?'

I decide that I will not be offended by the question. After all, he is young, and he does not know very much about me. 'Please don't offer me a gun,' I tell him.

March regards me steadily. 'I won't lie. Slint worries me. The thing is... most nightmares look like people. Makes sense, right? Most people are afraid of other people. The evil dentist, the bad man who follows you at night, the clown that lives under the staircase. And all of that is fine by me, because it makes them easy to predict. I know how to deal with a nightmare that looks like a person. But... I don't think Slint's human, or even close to human. I don't know what's inside that suit, and it really worries me.'

I can see now why I am being offered a weapon, at least.

'I still don't want a gun.'

March carefully fastens his side-arm closed. 'All right, Will.'

'Where is he? Slint, I mean?'

'Somewhere below deck,' says March, quietly. 'Waiting.'

Time passes in a comfortable quiet. I lean against the railing and watch as the beak of the *Metronome*'s figurehead cuts through the air. A long way below, I catch sight of the coast, yellow-rimmed waves sloshing gently against curving beaches and rough cliffs.

'Someone back in Babel told me the sun never sets. I suppose he was lying.'

'No,' says March, 'he was telling you the truth. The sun's never set on the Capital.'

Wordlessly, I point at the moon.

'I can see why you're confused, but you're thinking about it wrong. Every place has its own sky here. The tower has its endless day, and the Golden Gate has its endless night, and every other place has a sky that suits its mood.'

We watch the sky together for a while. Eventually March leaves, off to patrol the ship.

Before long, a new city comes into view. This city is dark and obviously abandoned. It sits between the sea and a huge black lake, and from the horizon looks like a strange kind of mountain, formed of buildings that gradually get taller closer to its centre. By my reckoning, it does not look as if this city was subjected to any great calamity. Just that whoever was living here decided to leave. The very limits are being slowly washed into the sea, and instead of being disturbing, I find the scene somewhat serene.

Behind me, I hear Callister's voice.

'All right, you motley lot!' he calls. 'We're in need of gold.'

I turn to see that he's holding a small leather satchel open to the crew.

The crew approach him, and when they do, they each drop something into the satchel. First, the investment banker donates his gold watch. 'For the Captain,' he says.

The yoga instructor donates her earrings. 'For the Captain,' she says.

The homeless man reaches into his mouth and tugs out his golden tooth. 'For the Captain,' he says, with a wince.

And one by one, they all come, every last man and woman on deck, and even some from below. I wonder what is happening here, and what it has to do with fixing my violin. And more than that, I wonder at their devotion to Reid. I wonder what she has done to inspire such selfless giving in her crew.

Something big and dazzling comes into view below the ship, and I am startled from my thoughts.

We have come to a bridge. Except, where the city beneath us is abandoned, this bridge is still very much alive. It is a long tower bridge, and every square yard of it seems to be covered in small yellow lights – indeed, it is encrusted in lights like stars, as if they have fallen from the sky all in one place. The effect is that this long bridge, reflected brilliantly in the dark waters beneath it, looks as if it is made of glittering gold.

But this is not what makes me laugh. Nor is it the group of sailing ships I can see docked beneath the bridge. Nor is it the signs of industry I can see taking place all across the surface of the bridge, or the network of thin streets between the shanty towns, all as brilliantly lit as the rest.

What causes me such delight is the fact that I was

expecting some kind of literal golden gate. I was imagining something close to the gates of heaven as they are in stories. But what I have found here makes so much more wonderful sense. Because I know this bridge. I saw it once while awake, without all the lights and the folk occupying it. In waking life, the city beside it is bright and bustling, and in waking life, that bridge is inexplicably red.

Because those are the ruins of San Francisco, and that is the Golden Gate Bridge. We have come to the Golden Gate, and in dreaming, it really is the colour of gold.

I descend from one of the glittering golden towers of the bridge in a large basket, like that of a hot-air balloon. This close, it is possible to see that the lights woven everywhere around the bridge are something close to Christmas lights, thousands of small yellow bulbs joined together with endless ribbons of cable.

I lean over the edge and admire the shanty town below us, where there are the figures of sailors belonging to the dark ships docked beneath the bridge, mingling with locals. The entire bridge seems to be a great port town, where all manner of travellers bustle and trade.

'I don't get to come here too often,' says Callister. He is beside me, wearing a well-tailored pinstripe jacket and smoking a cigar. The satchel full of gold is tucked in beneath his arm. 'Take it in while you still can,' he tells me. 'This is it, really.'

'What do you mean?'

Callister blows a billow of smoke out through his nostrils.

'There are no more people after this. No more cities, or towns, or ports or anything like that. No more doors. We're heading into the unknown, Manderlay. The deep wild dreams. The places where nobody bloody comes back from intact.' He squints upwards, to the place where the *Metronome* hangs in the sky like a clock thrown into the air.

'Callister…'

'Hm?'

'This might be a strange question. But – back in Binary, March insisted that I come with him so that he could keep me safe. But… it's just the two of us, here. Is the Golden Gate safe enough that we don't need a Sleepwalker?'

At this, Callister chuckles. 'That's what he told you? No, no. March just didn't want Reid running off with you while he did his business in Binary. That's the only reason he took you with him.' The watch-smith glances over at me. 'You're his bargaining power,' he says. 'Reid's not especially fond of Sleepwalkers, from what I know – and especially not Sleepwalkers with guns. Hell, neither am I, truth be told. The only reason he's been allowed on board is because she needs your map.'

'But why?' I ask. 'Why does she want to get to Solomon's Eye? Isn't it just a prison?'

Callister frowns at me. 'You don't know?' He taps ash over the edge. 'Probably better if she tells you herself. She's got this way of telling her story… Better than I could, anyway. I think she can manage it, though. Getting us there, I mean. From what I hear, there's nothing but ruins, jungles and storms ahead. But I guess if anybody can take us through, it's Reid. She's mad, don't get me wrong, but sometimes you need a touch of madness if you want to get anything done.'

We disembark from the basket and make our way through the shanty town on the bridge. The routes between the shacks are relatively thin, but Callister navigates them with his native aggression, making himself twice his size through the sheer force of scowling.

We pass a building where car doors are used as swinging saloon doors, and we pass headlamps used as street lights, and ancient-looking engines rumbling away and powering all the tiny yellow lights everywhere.

There are doors to dreams here, as well: dreams of distant ports, bright islands and dark coves where furtive figures dart to and fro. From all of them stride more sailors and adventurers, bustling around or meandering drunkenly. Once again, I wish I had more time simply to stay and explore this place.

Callister arrives at the front door of a bungalow-sized shack with a tall chimney, from which a white stream of smoke is writhing, and he wastes no time in hauling open the reclaimed front door. A gust of warmth pours out. There is a great blazing furnace to one side of this wide room, flames licking the black walls of their housing. Callister stamps his feet and ushers me inside after him. 'Alder!' he calls.

The walls of the hot bungalow are covered in all manner of golden things. From golden weapons, such as swords and shields and guns, to golden tools, including hammers and tongs, and even more peculiar artefacts, like the golden horseshoes hung over the door. The glorious centrepiece of this display, however, sits beside the furnace, where there is a shining anvil made entirely of gold.

The very idea of this golden workshop is absurd, but delightful, because I know that there is no way that gold is strong enough to support things like anvils or hammers or swords. It is a soft metal, surely? It is as if some troublesome soul has played a prank on the place – wrapping every available artefact in gold leaf.

From between a pair of oily hanging curtains strides a great man with skin so dark that it causes the flecks of gold scattered across it to look like stars. From his thick arms hang golden bracelets. When he grins at seeing Callister, I can see that most of his teeth are gold as well. But most impressive about this man are his eyes, each of them housing an iris as golden as the rest of his ornaments.

The robed man opens his arms wide as if to embrace Callister. 'My friend!' he says, warmly. 'It is good to see you again! Come, come. Tea, is it? And tales of the cities. It has been far too long.'

I can see the beads of sweat forming on Callister's forehead already. 'I'm not here long, Alder. Captain's orders. We've gotta make haste. Hunting her white whale at last.' He chews at the end of his cigar and drops his satchel on the nearest workbench.

'Of course.' Alder nods politely and rubs his hands together. He empties the satchel and makes a little pile of gold trinkets. 'You do not have much of an eye for the yellow stuff, my friend,' he comments as he sorts through. His gold-rimmed eyes peer intently at each article. 'Fake,' he says, of a watch, and pushes it aside. 'Leaf only,' he says of a locket, before running the chain through his fingers. 'Ah, but this chain… yes. This I can work with.'

I exchange a glance with Callister, who shrugs.

Before long, Alder has made a large pile of fake or unusable gold items, and a very small pile which the goldsmith deems worthy. 'A disappointing haul,' he says. 'But I can work my magic, even for this. What do you need, my friend? More cogs for your engine, yes?'

Using his cigar, Callister points at me. 'Alder, I'd like you to meet an acquaintance of mine. This is Manderlay, the musician. Manderlay here needs a new string for his fiddle.'

Alder the goldsmith is an imposing figure. He stands with his arms folded and his golden eyes taking me in while I find some space and open the case to my violin. The thin steel of her three remaining strings feels out of place among all the gold. I wipe at my brow – the heat in here is stifling.

Alder makes his way around so that he is standing beside me. He seems unaffected by the fire of the forge. It makes a glittering shadow out of him.

'A fine thing,' he says, of my violin. Then, 'You need a new string, I see.' The goldsmith reaches out, and with the tip of one of his gold-flecked fingers feels the dark space where her fourth string should be.

'Steel is so unsubtle,' he says. 'Make music with steel and it will suffice, but it will be a strict thing. A predictable thing. But make music with gold... Ah. Now there is the art. There is the subtlety.' Alder raises his hand to his chin, thoughtfully. 'Yes. I can help you, Manderlay. I have forged strings before, and I would be happy to do so for you. Your offering is enough for this. But you should know that any string forged by my hand will change the songs you play. They will be sweeter, softer, brighter, just as gold is to steel.' He turns towards me. 'I could replace all four strings, should you wish it.'

It takes me a few moments of careful thought to come to a conclusion, and Alder is kind enough to give them to me while he goes in search of whatever tools it is he might need. But in the end, I feel as if I would be more comfortable with the hybrid version of my instrument. That she should have the three strings that mark where I have come from: that old, strict sound. And that she should have a fourth golden string, which will mark my journey so far and where I am going next.

'Please, only the one,' I tell the goldsmith.

'Very well,' says Alder, golden teeth glinting as he grins. He gets to work.

Callister's cigar slowly becomes a stub as he watches Alder work. The two of them exchange some good-natured banter, in the manner of old friends reunited, and I head across to the front of the bungalow, where there are two small open windows and a little relief from the heat of the forge. I unfasten my coat, and squint through the grime and soot to try and see what is happening outside.

I catch sight of sailors. Among them is a familiar figure.

The windows distort him, but there is something unmistakable in the manner of his solemn gait. I move across to the second window, where I see the same – a dusty old knight, striding across the bridge and carrying something in his arms.

Pulling open the door to the forge, I emerge into the street. 'Thyme?' I call, trying to find him. But I only glimpse the last white flash of his tabard as he vanishes from sight.

I make my way after him. Down the next street, between tall shacks, I catch sight of him again – trailing some sort of wires or cables as he turns another corner.

At a crossroads, beneath a latticework of tiny yellow lights, I pause, and this time catch a better glimpse – the

glint of his armour, and the bulky object held in his arms –
as he moves into an alleyway. The crowds here are too noisy,
so I do not call again. I stride straight across to the mouth of
the alley, where I stop.

Frowning, I watch as the frayed edges of Thyme's tabard
wave in the winds, and hear the clinking of his heavy metal
boots along the paved road. He is carrying what looks like
a television set, or perhaps two, with cables dangling and
plugs bouncing along the ground. I make to catch up to him
and ask what he is doing here, but before I carry on, there is
a hand on my shoulder.

'Manderlay?' says Callister, out of breath. 'What's got into
you?'

'I saw...' I turn back to the alleyway to try and point
Thyme out, but I can no longer seem to place him. There
are only sailors, meandering about beneath the thousand
yellow lights of the bridge.

'You saw what?' he asks, wheezing. 'Bloody hell, I haven't
jogged that much in years!' I notice that my violin case is
over his shoulder, along with his satchel.

'I don't know,' I tell him.

Callister rights himself. 'Well, don't do that again,' he
says.

I take one more glance about the crowds. No sign of the
dusty knight.

'Sure,' I say, mystified. 'I'm sorry.'

'Right,' says Callister. 'Come on, now. We should get back.
The Captain'll be wearing a hole through my deck with her
pacing.'

>•<

Back aboard the *Metronome*, I seek the cabin where the birds are kept. Dozens of beady eyes observe me as I enter. I am struck by the structures of the cages, as if this is a miniature city made of buildings filled with birds.

Of course, I could have used the map room for practice. But then, my first ever audience as a musician was composed entirely of birds. My parents never approved of the sounds that I made when I was eight, after being gifted my grandfather's old instrument. In fact, they took to sending me to the bottom of the garden whenever I wanted to practise. I struggled on despite them, and played with the birds in the trees as my audience. I liked to imagine that the songs I played were birdsong and that I was serenading the doves.

I open the case to my violin and see the golden string for the first time. It is a peculiar sight, as if a beam of sunlight has fallen over it. I draw my bow and tighten the horsehair, pulling off any errant strands. Then I run some rosin down the length. It is a wonderful comfort, to arrange my fingers at the end of a bow once again, and to see how strong they have become. I can only smile, remembering what March said to me back in Babel – words I dismissed as nonsense. 'Think young,' he said.

Replacing the bow in the case, I take my violin out and tune it. This time, I take care not to break another string.

Around me, the birds begin to quieten down, just as they did back in my old garden. As if they are listening.

And when I reach the golden string, high E, and begin to pluck and tighten it, the sound is somehow sweeter than I remember it being. At its perfect point of tuning, I pluck and hold the body of my violin close up to my ear, and the quiet in the cabin is wonderful, filled with the sweet humming of the string. Only the *Metronome* ticks on, like her namesake.

I close my eyes until the sound fades. When I open them again, Reid is there.

Her arms are folded and she is regarding me steadily. 'The first song, then, master map-maker,' she says. And I notice that March has arrived as well, and that he is lounging upon a cage nearby without his heavy pack or rifle.

'Before I play,' I say, 'I want to know why you want to go to Solomon's Eye. I made the mistake of giving the map to the wrong person before, and I don't want to do that again.'

'Will,' says March, 'we really don't have the time—'

Reid interrupts him. 'It's fine, Sleepwalker,' she says. 'It is a fair request, after all. For who would be mad enough to brave all the seas between here and there without good cause? I can respect a man who does not fly so blindly into peril.'

March grumbles to himself, and sits back on his cage.

'When I was a girl,' says Reid – all the birds in the room cease their twittering, as if they too are listening to her tale – 'I served aboard a galleon crewed by the finest figments belonging to the finest dreams in all of dreaming. The ship's name was *Sparrowhawk*, and her captain was the mighty Captain Murdock – the bravest figment I have ever known. I was the only dreamer on board, and naught but a mere cabin girl, but still they treated me with respect and friendship. And under the command of Murdock, we went out night after night into the deepest wild dreams, in search of treasures and wonders to bring home. We saw such sights, those countless nights, and we braved such adventures. For years, I sailed with the crew of the *Sparrowhawk*, until disaster struck.

'One night, lost beyond the farthest reaches of dreaming, we were greeted by a black boiling of clouds. A storm was ahead of us, and the winds were driving us inevitably forth. We had faced many a storm at sea before, understand, but none like this. I saw crewmen being swept into waves as high as the tips of our masts, our supplies tumbling beyond severed ropes and our sails almost torn clean from their rigging. And the only man beyond the chaos was Captain Murdock, tied with rope to his wheel and guiding us through, the force of his will against the storm.

'A great maw in the dark opened, deep in the storm, and a shattering of lightning raked the masts, turning them to bright splinters. And there, the sea itself parted, revealing a blackness like no other, the dark of the nether beneath us, and great waves like hands smashing together against her hull. No ship could survive such a calamity. The storm and sea conspired against her, and not even Murdock could hold them at bay. I watched as the *Sparrowhawk* was torn apart, and we all fell into the dark.

'In the dark, beneath the waves, surrounded by the splinters of my ship, I heard a song. It was low, beneath the storm, and though I was being tossed to and fro, and though the sea was pouring into me, and though I was alone and young and frightened, I heard that song, the song of Solomon's Storm, formed of its thunder and rushing waves and howling winds. I held on. I swam, and grabbed hold of a spar of wood, and floated through the worst, gasping for breath whenever it was given.

'And when later I regained my senses, my head full of pounding, I lay sand-encrusted upon a white beach with the sea lapping at my feet. I saw spars of wood sticking from the sand, and a long piece from my chest. Bodies were strewn from dune to distant dune. Somehow, I was still asleep. And though dozens of the crew were dead, more still were alive, and rising from their stupor much like me. The *Sparrowhawk* did not survive, but her crew did. Even Murdock, worn and harrowed, and commanding us to regroup and find survivors.

'There, upon that white beach, I recall clearly fixing my eyes on the horizon and seeing a sea like none I had seen before. Because out there, the storm that wrecked us still raged, filling the sky all around our bright island, and I knew that we had not escaped from the storm, but instead were contained within it – at the eye of it.

'Murdock knew we were lost and marooned. Murdock knew that rescue would not come. But Murdock was also a learned figment, and had heard of the island at the eye of the storm before. He knew that we had somehow stumbled across an ancient place, hidden for ages beyond ages. He knew that it was Solomon's Eye.

'Murdock came up with a plan. You see, there was only one way he could send for help.' Reid lowers her eyes, and I can see a glinting there. 'He could send a dreamer. He could send me.

'My dear captain told me to find a new ship and crew, brave enough to travel deep into the wild dreams, through Solomon's Storm to rescue all the survivors of the *Sparrowhawk* the next time I fell asleep. As he told me this, he woke me, as gently as he was able – by twisting the spar of wood through my chest.

'And as I was woken, I heard a song. I could hear a mad fluting, as the island faded. The notes of the song were delivered on the gentle wind from some distant place among the trees, and I remember those notes clearly, clearer than the song of the storm, and clearer still than the strange sea that surrounded us. For it was the song of the island, and the place where the crew of the *Sparrowhawk* were marooned. The song of Solomon's Eye itself.

'When next I slept, I returned to Babel. I did as I was told, talked to many captains and tried and tried again to get help. By the Gods, I tried. But who would listen to a little girl with no more than a pair of songs to guide her? So I waited, and I worked my way up through the ranks until I earned my own captaincy. I had the song of Solomon's Eye etched into the skin of my face, so every time I see myself, I am reminded of the urgency of my cause. And after a time, I found Callister, and helped him to build his finest dream: the mighty *Metronome*, swiftest ship in dreaming. And here I stand before you, the time having come at last. The time when I will return to Solomon's Eye, and rescue the crew of the *Sparrowhawk*.'

Both of Reid's fists are clenched. Lamplight dances in her eyes.

I am convinced of her cause. And instead of giving reply, I give her what she is longing for. I nestle my instrument beneath my chin, pushing my beard aside. Then I raise my bow, close my eyes and let my fingers remember the first song of Solomon's Eye. They arrange themselves across the strings, and I play for Captain Reid. I give her the first song – a pretty, fluttering introduction to the series, performed almost exclusively across high E.

The song comes back to me easily, and I find my foot tapping along to the rhythm.

Alder was right. Playing his golden string is different – so much sweeter than steel – and I play as I have not played in years, feeling the joy of the song fill me from the tips of my fingers to the tips of my toes. I give Reid the first part of her map, and I hear her coarse laughter – born of joy, or relief, or some other emotion – beneath the notes of the song. She can begin her journey at long last. She can rescue her lost crew.

SMOG

We pursue June's fleet through wild dreams.

Over black swamps, where clawed trees scratch at the *Metronome*'s underbelly and crocodiles snap in our wake. Over a steaming sea that covers her copper parts in condensation, and on to a colder climate, where icebergs float, and penguins halt in their march to watch us pass. We pause above a rocky island to get our bearings, before flying low over a sea so placid that for every tick of the *Metronome*'s engine, ripples cascade across the water, and for a time I am given to believe that we are skimming the sea instead of flying over it. Always, the sea is full of life; whales slap the waves with their tails, dolphins call out to us and flying fish cascade beneath us, defying gravity in a silvery reverse waterfall.

I am kept busy primarily by aiding the crew in any way they see fit – by carrying tools, adjusting valves, or simply mopping the deck. But from time to time Captain Reid will summon me, and I will be asked to supply the next song in the sequence that leads to Solomon's Eye. This I provide with pleasure, and I find that the songs get easier to remember as I go along.

'Don't you want to write them down?' I ask Reid, of the songs.

She shakes her head. 'I shall recall them,' she says, and I am fascinated by the way she uses them to guide our way. Reid stands tall behind her pointed-star wheel, steering with her eyes closed, and though it seems as if she is flying blind, I believe that she is listening for the route.

'How do you do it?' I ask. 'Could you teach me?'

'Perhaps.' She opens her eyes and glances at me. 'You are a fine musician, and you might make a fine navigator. But few ever hear the songs on the wind.'

I return to the crew, staying quiet – trying to hear anything beyond the ticking of the *Metronome* and the work of her crew, but I hear nothing.

Of the fleet, there is no sign until we come to a tremendous set of mountains.

The sea sweeps away ahead, but off to one side a jagged array of impossibly sharp peaks erupt from the waters, like a set of giant knives. Their tips are shrouded by clouds and snow. I am at the forecastle when the cry for contact with an enemy vessel is made, and at first I am unable to see what all the fuss is about.

I hear an argument erupt behind me, and I turn to see Reid and March involved in a heated exchange up on the *Metronome*'s aftercastle.

'We need to go after that ship!' March is gesturing at the distant mountains.

'Our route takes us around, Sleepwalker,' replies the Captain, sternly.

'Our purpose here,' says March, 'is to stop June. And she might be on board.'

'Our purpose,' growls the Captain, 'is to recover my lost crew.'

They glare at one another. Everyone on deck has ceased their exertions and is watching the argument unfold. There is a long, tense moment, before March glances about the lower decks and fixes his gaze upon me. Then, he says, 'You need the map, Reid. Go after that ship, or you won't get any more of it.' Reid's fearsome eyes lock on to me as well. I am pinned into place by both their gazes.

I quickly attempt to spot the enemy skyship again. At first, I am unable to discern anything out of place, until I turn my eyes to the deepest patch of dark among the clouds that smother the mountains' peaks. Some of those clouds are an inky black effluence, as if a hundred filthy chimneys are leaking all at once, and squatting at the centre of the swirling dark pollution is an enormous black shape, a hollowed-out circle of sky. I remember what March called it, that horrible bulbous skyship – the *Smog* – and even from here, it is a wretched sight.

Hoping that I am making the right choice, I turn back.

'I'm sorry, Captain, but March is right. We need to stop June before she can get to Solomon's Eye, and she might be on that ship.'

>•<

The crew are rushing about to ready themselves for action. We have a small while still until we catch up with the *Smog*, so I have borrowed a pair of scissors from March in order to ready myself – to get rid of my troublesome beard, which keeps getting caught on the buttons of my coat – and try to at least be of some help.

One of the crew has kindly filled a basin with water for me, and I am able to see a distorted version of myself in there. It is an unusual experience to see myself looking so young, not because I am so unfamiliar with youth, but because of how easy it is for me to fall back into the skin I left behind decades ago. I glance up, and the face in the mirror is me in my early fifties.

I cut away my beard. There are still lines of silver through it, but it is almost black.

Behind me, the crew are quickly pulling on tougher leathers, and rigging themselves up with harnesses so that they can tie themselves to the ship.

My beard falls away, and my face emerges at last. Then, water dripping from my roughly stubbled chin, I observe myself in the mirror. I can see the crew behind me, and Callister, who is leaning up against a wooden wall and watching me, idly tweaking the edge of his moustache as he does. I wonder how long he has been there for.

'Better?' he asks.

I turn to him, running a rough cloth across my face to dry it.

'Much better.'

He squints at me then, as if observing a piece of clockwork and looking for places in which to improve its efficiency. 'You need a new coat,' he tells me. I glance down at what I am wearing. It is a dreadfully cheap but warm thing, awkwardly put together and ill-fitting across my now stronger frame. I pull it off, and lay it down, and see all the tattoos across my arms – snake, heart, coil of rope – defined again.

Callister opens a locker further along, and draws a new coat from the interior. It is lengthy, and has an enormous stiff collar, and reminds me of the Russian military. 'Try this,' he tells me, and throws it across. 'Might take a bit of getting used to, but it's the kind of thing you're gonna need. Pull the collar up if you want to be able to breathe when we get up to speed.'

The coat is a snug fit. I am a slender man, but it falls well across my shoulders. I see myself in the mirror above the basin, and almost laugh. I now look as if I am a member of the *Metronome*'s crew. Callister is busy making his own preparations, pulling on a heavy-looking harness.

'Thank you, Callister.'

Callister shoulders the rest of his harness, and nods. 'Help keep my bird in the sky and you'll owe me nothing. I'll keep an eye on the Captain, and you keep an eye on your Sleepwalker, and together we might stand a chance of getting through this.'

An alarm bell begins to sound again from above. We both glance upwards.

Callister strides across to me and claps a hand upon my shoulder. 'Good luck out there, Manderlay. I'll see you on the other side. You can help me staple my bird back together when we're done.' Then he dashes away through one of the cabin's doors. I am left alone. I turn and see myself in the mirror once again – a younger man, ready for this adventure. I take a deep breath, and try to disguise my nerves, but there is no ridding myself of them. I turn my collar up instead.

'Good luck,' I say, to nobody but myself.

>•<

The *Metronome*'s tick is frantic.

Up on deck, flurries of snow whip at my skin. The crew rushing to and fro are already coated in a layer of frost. I can just about make out the jagged peaks of mountains as they emerge suddenly from the clouds, before vanishing again in the next instant as we weave a tight route around them, and it feels as if we are racing between deadly sharp icebergs in the sky.

The deck is slippery, and I have to haul myself across using handrails. The snow clears for a brief moment and I catch sight of Reid behind her wheel, her coat billowing, her fierce eyes in shadow as she steers us deeper into the mountains.

'There,' says March, pointing, when I reach him.

The Sleepwalker's fiery hair looks as if it has been extinguished. I follow the direction of his attentions, and see trails of black smoke through the white and grey. Almost at once, the *Metronome* meets the black, and a hideous stench hits me: burning tar, and petroleum, and all the worst pollution there is to sense. Where the black hits the deck, it leaves a greasy trail.

March hands me his harness. 'You're going to need this.'

'Don't you need it?' My voice is muffled behind my collar.

'I'll be fine. Remember: we're all screwed without you.'

The alarm bell sounds again, and I see that it is the Bosun, swinging an enormous hand-bell up on the aftercastle. Only, this time, he is answered by the almighty foghorn of the *Smog*. The deck seems to tremble beneath my feet as it bellows, sounding like the inversion of one of heaven's mighty trumpets – a hellish drone. They know we are coming.

I shoulder March's harness, and clip myself to the ship's railings as an eerie quiet descends upon the deck. All aboard pause to watch as the terrible nightmare diver ascends into view from below deck, his porthole swinging slowly about, as if the void itself is surveying the light. As soon as he has passed by, all industry resumes, but with furtive glances to the forecastle where Slint stands like a horrible glistening statue.

'What's the plan?' I ask March, as he checks his rifle.

He shrugs. 'I improvise.'

Somewhere in the smog-streaked clouds ahead of us, a black shape becomes apparent. Bristling with chimneys belching effluence, the *Smog* looms in the sky, utterly dwarfing the *Metronome*. Where we dart nimbly around the mountain peaks, the Smog simply smashes through them, leaving a trail of destruction in its wake.

'All hands!' the voice of the Captain cries. 'Brace!'

I see Reid haul upon a lever. There is a great thump beneath my feet, and the deck of the *Metronome* tilts, taking me by surprise. Before now, I have only seen her adjust our height while keeping us level. But now, the Captain's pointed wheel has a third axis; a means by which she might make her skyship dance intricately through the sky. I am quick enough to take a tight grip of my railing as she pulls back on it and we soar upwards, the *Metronome*'s tick becoming a quick-step rhythm. I am blinded by the snow.

Suddenly, there is blue sky, and the sun.

For a moment we hang there, free of the mountains and free of the clouds. The *Metronome*'s tick is so slow that it feels as if time is about to stop.

Tick.

I see March grit his teeth, and flick his rifle's safety off.

Tick.

I see Slint grab hold of the forecastle railing with both gauntlets.

Tick.

Below us is swirling darkness, and we fall towards it.

If I cry out, then my voice is lost on the wind. There is no more time for sound. Only a vertigo so powerful that it is like being on a roller-coaster plunging for miles instead of yards. I am gripped by the overwhelming fear that we will smash against the clouds, but instead we pass through. There is no time for me to see the *Smog*, only catch the blurred edge of it as we dive beneath – a hundred cannons belching brightly in the dark.

None of their payloads hit. We are too fast. The *Metronome* soars.

There is a wall of black effluence beneath the *Smog*. I am showered in choking pollution before we rise again on the other side, dodging more cannon fire and mountain-tops.

I see March, rifle raised as we come alongside their metallic glinting decks.

So many nightmares. Hundreds glare up at us.

I am thrown back as something collides with the side of the *Metronome*, and in one dazed moment I see not one soldier before me, but three. There is March, raining a silvery trail of bullets down upon the *Smog*, but there are also two more soldiers beside him, conjured from nowhere, with the dust of the desert whirling around them. Only, I know where they have come from. I have glimpsed them before, back in March's dream.

Hauling myself back to my feet, I see the crew rushing around me. Something else slams into the *Metronome*, and we dip momentarily before she is righted.

'Harpoons!' someone yells.

Glancing over the side I can see a set of three harpoons embedded into the side of our skyship, thick chains joining them to the *Smog*. Below, a group of nightmares are operating winches, attempting to bring us closer. We are pinned into place.

I see someone approaching through the snow, carrying a set of cutters.

Without a second thought, I vault the railing, and lower myself as far as I am able to see if I can get to them, but the harpoons are just out of reach. The crewman with the cutters yells something down at me, but I do not hear him. I hurriedly try to work out a way to reach those chains without unclasping my harness, but I can see no alternative. My only hope is that those three harpoons, grouped so closely together, are secure enough to support me.

I reach up and set myself free.

There is a gut-wrenching moment before I land on the harpoons. Thankfully, they are embedded so deeply that I am able to use them as a sort of ledge. Gripping hold of the slippery cold metal, I reach up. 'The cutters!' I cry. 'Hand me the cutters!'

The *Metronome* shudders as she is hit by another cannonball. I see pieces of her falling away, but I just about manage to keep a grip, and grasp the end of the cutters.

The first chain falls away easily, snipped in two, and the *Metronome* bucks.

I am thrown forward, but stop myself from falling by

wedging my boot against a barbed hook set into the side of a harpoon.

The second chain puts up more of a fight, and I have to duck as it breaks – the pattering of gunfire from below pinging from the harpoons, and from the copper parts of the skyship ticking behind me. Only one more chain remains. The *Metronome* pulls hard against it, longing to break free and soar away. I brace myself as best I can. I haul the cutters into place, and press hard.

The chain snaps.

The *Metronome* is jarred backwards with a greater force than I had been expecting, and I am thrown forward. The cutters slip from my hands, the harpoons slip from beneath my feet and I am falling. No more *Metronome*, no more *Smog* – only empty air and the jagged-knife peaks beneath me.

I reach out, panicking, trying to grab hold of anything.

My hands hit a chain – the chain I just cut – and I grasp hold with all my might as it swings down and around, still attached to the *Smog*. My hands are numb, and I am screaming as the chain swings past chimneys and cannons, clanging as it meets the side of the ghastly slick metal skyship.

Just about managing to keep my grip, the chain rises quickly – still being hauled in by its winch. Before I meet the uneven shell of the Smog, I swing myself out, so that my feet clang against a surface, and I run vertically up her flank.

With all the force of the winch, I almost fly onto the upper deck. Rolling to a halt, I gasp for breath, and catch a fleeting glimpse of the *Metronome* above, free of chains holding her down and weaving back and forth.

There are nightmares around me.

I see them advance, holding on to weapons or bracing claws – hideous demonic shapes shuddering in the cold. Trying to grab hold of the chain again, hoping that I might somehow use it as a weapon, I find that my arms are now completely numb. I have no strength left in me to fight.

Something lands on the deck beside me. The metal surface shakes.

Rising from its point of impact is a humanoid shape, but larger, bulbous. Slint has arrived. He seems twice the height of every other nightmare here. I see the uncertainty in the warped faces of the nightmares who had been advancing on me, and then an emotion I have never seen in a nightmare before: fear.

Slint slowly lumbers forward.

The nightmares around him trip over each other, dropping their weapons in their desire to be as far away from Slint as possible.

I catch my breath – feeling the bruises blossoming everywhere across myself already – and pull myself up to my feet again, just as Slint reaches a sort of small hatch in the deck. There are no other nightmares around him any more. They have all run away.

I am unable to draw my eyes from the bizarre sight that follows, as Slint tears the door off the small hatch – no bigger than a chute – and kneels before it. With his helmet turned away from me, I am unable to see precisely what he is doing, but I am given the impression that he has opened the small porthole window in it. Then, he presses that open window against the open hatch.

Like a fly wriggling free of its maggoty skin, Slint empties.

His metal helm rolls free and his rubbery suit flops. Whatever was inside that suit is gone, somewhere into the bowels of the ship. A wave of nausea hits me, and I hold on to my stomach, trying not to throw up.

Glancing around, I can see that the upper deck of the *Smog* has mostly emptied. Only a few nightmares remain, up in a cabin on its jutting metal aftercastle, where there is an array of alien-looking controls. I quickly grab hold of the nearest weapon I can find – an enormous wrench – and advance upon the cabin.

The rest of the *Smog* has fallen eerily quiet, punctuated only by the occasional scream, quickly cut off. There is no more cannon-fire, either. Whatever it is that Slint is doing below deck, free of his suit, is obviously having some great effect.

Keeping my head low, I am glad to see that the trio of nightmares still steering the ship do not notice my approach. Then, just as I reach the doorway, I spot the *Metronome* as she comes alongside the *Smog*. She looks wounded – ragged holes torn in her sides – but still noble and flighty. As soon as she is close enough, I see March jump across, joined by his two conjured soldiers.

It is strange how the dust of his desert dream gusts warmly around him.

Gripping hold of the handle to the cabin door, I bide my time, waiting for them to get near enough. The instant I see March nod at me, I swing it wide, revealing the cabin interior. All three soldiers open fire at once, and a hail of bullets shiver into the cabin. The fight is over in an instant, and March lowers his rifle. The two other soldiers from his dream vanish in a whirl of dust.

Rushing into the control cabin, March pulls the door closed behind himself, and the howling of the winds between the mountains is snuffed. He is grinning, but he looks tired – his eyes are bloodshot, and when he reaches for the controls he fumbles, taking a few attempts to slow the *Smog* down. 'Jesus, Will,' he says. 'Jesus holy Christ.'

'Is it over?' I ask him, leaning back and trying to slow my thundering heart.

'It's over. If June was here, we would know it by now.' The *Smog*'s rumbling engines begin to soften. We are in control.

It is then I notice that March is wounded, a dark stain against his ice-covered fatigues, damp and still spreading. 'March,' I say, because he does not seem to have noticed his bleeding arm. When he glances over at me he seems confused, mumbling something I do not hear. 'Your arm,' I say. 'Look at your arm.'

Frowning, March glances down at the blood soaking his sleeve.

'Oh,' he says.

Back on board the *Metronome*, I am sent to fetch March's pack.

I find it nestled in among heavy-looking equipment deep in the belly of the ship. A steady stream of crewmen pass me by as they retrieve spare parts. The usual buzz of industry on board has doubled, but the general feeling in the air appears to be one of relief. We have survived the *Metronome*'s first real trial, and have come through a little broken, a little bruised, but triumphant.

Given how easily I have seen March wear his pack, I am surprised to find that it is absurdly heavy. It is in the manner of a snail weighed down by a particularly heavy shell that I make my way back to him.

I come to a porthole at the end of a low corridor, and glance outside. We appear to be flying steadily alongside the titanic *Smog*, and I can see the sullen forms of nightmares lined up on that larger deck, strange silhouettes of a hundred different varieties – all monstrous things born of dark dreams. I wonder what it is that is keeping the nightmare crew of the *Smog* in check, before noticing the tall figure of Slint, who is stood nearby, back in his massive diving suit. The black porthole of his helmet glares impassively out over the rest of the vessel. Slint is now in command.

I turn from the frost-rimmed window and, one step at a time, make my way back to one of the upper decks, where a small infirmary has been set up. Despite our victory, there is a feeling of dread in my gut. March is hurt. And – though I am not superstitious – it was among mountains like these that I suffered the worst day of my life.

I was on a private yacht named *Prince Albert*, testing its seaworthiness just outside Reykjavik with its new owner, fifty years ago when it happened. Even though the snowy mountains in the distance were wonderful to behold, and though the cold city was a magnificent sight in the dusk, a slow dread gripped me that evening which I could not explain. And before the sun could fully set, a small motorboat rushed urgently out to meet us, in order to quickly get me ashore. I was told that the harbour-master had great sympathy for my situation, and that a flight home had already been booked.

'But why?' I asked, oblivious.

I do not recall who told me that Lily was dead. It might have been one of the sailors aboard the speeding boat bringing me in, or perhaps it was the harbour-master himself. But I remember nothing of Reykjavik, or of who took me to the airport, or of the conversation I apparently had over the phone with Lily's father. The only memory I have of the city of Reykjavik is those mountains as my flight home soared overhead, feeling as empty and cold and barren as they seemed. And just as quickly as my time in Iceland passed, my time across the Atlantic seemed to stretch on forever – for longer than any sailing trip I had ever taken – until, by the time we set down in Edinburgh, I felt as if I had aged by decades.

The worst was not the fact of Lily's death. The realisation that she was gone, so suddenly, had not hit me yet. All the way home I was entertaining the absurd notion that the two of us would deal with her death together. No, the worst was when I alighted in Edinburgh, stepped from the taxi and walked up to my own front door. Halfway down the little path that led to my front door, I saw Samantha – still so small, at five years old, and wearing an expression of childish bafflement – and I realised that my own daughter was a stranger to me.

The *Metronome*'s infirmary is filled with a scattering of crew being treated for minor wounds by other members of crew. March is sat upon a bench with his jacket removed. His arm is currently immersed in a basin of water, red clouds rising. He looks weary, drained of vitality; something of his proud and upright stature has been lost.

He still smiles as I approach. I lower his pack beside him, and am glad to be free of it.

'Can I help?' I ask him.

'You've done enough,' he tells me, as he rummages around with his free arm. There is still a thin layer of desert dust mingled with melting snow coating his trousers and face. For a brief moment I feel a fatherly urge to brush it from him.

March locates some white bandage, and removing his arm from the water, he begins to bind it. I am given a brief glimpse of the deep gash along his forearm.

'How did that happen?' I ask him.

'Just a side-effect,' he tells me.

I imagine that he must be talking about that feat of conjuring he performed outside: somehow summoning soldiers from his dream in order to fight. I remember my encounter with June, the way that she conjured life back into the wooden handle of my knife, and November, conjuring her whole dream to put out the fires in Binary. 'What was that?' I ask.

March binds his arm tightly, and then rests it. 'Just something the Sleepwalkers are taught to do,' he says. 'I don't think it has a name. Just... using your dream to fight. The last March taught me how, and I've seen some of the others do it. August and his sun, you know. I'm not very good at it yet, though. Controlling which bits of my dream I pull through, I mean. The figments from my dream are the easiest, but there's always side-effects. I seem to bring the desert with them. And this.' He nods at his arm. 'Every damn time. Stings like hell.'

He frowns a tired frown. 'I got hurt pretty bad. Out in the desert, I mean. That's... that's sort of what I dream about, every night – the pain. The old March showed me how to get rid of it, but whenever I try to summon anything, it comes back again. He told me I'd get better at it, the more I practise. But the others, the older Sleepwalkers, they can do it perfectly. I don't know if I'll ever be as good as them.'

I try to reassure him. 'You did well.'

March lets out a long sigh. The ship ticks warmly around us in the manner of an old comforting grandfather clock, a homely sound that I am beginning to realise I would sorely miss were it to stop.

March shakes his head as if to clear it. 'The truth is,' he says, low, 'I don't know how much longer I can hold on here. That fight drained me.' Then, he pulls his coat back on and stands, stretching in that way the defeated do, as if there is still energy in him despite the obvious lack.

'I think I'm going to wake up soon,' he says.

DELAWARE

The sun continues to confound me.

Whenever I look up from working at repairs on deck, it is in a different place. Sometimes it will be low and cast long shadows, and sometimes it will be directly above us and there will be no shadows at all; it will be very close for a while, and burn the back of my neck, and then it will be a distant cold coin. When I give Reid the next song that leads to Solomon's Eye, I appreciate why she uses music to navigate. The sky is unpredictable; it changes depending on the mood of each place we pass through, just like March said.

As we coast steadily between two islands – rich wildlife visible on both shores, dreaming the dreams of wild things – I am called to help with a gyroscope near the prow of the *Metronome*, where the crew have gathered. Unfortunately the piece of equipment in question seems to have been hit full-on by a cannonball, and as such looks more like a twisted piece of modern art than a gyroscope. I give my verdict: 'It's a lost cause.'

The crew grumble, but nod in agreement.

'Go fetch Callister,' says one, while they get to work removing the wreckage.

I head below deck. As I go, I glance behind us to see if the *Smog* is still following, but there is no sign of the massive warship. The *Metronome* is so much quicker that we have left her behind. Slint was made acting captain, with orders to follow in our wake.

I consider Slint as I go. He is terrifying, and powerful, and despite his impact on the *Smog*, I still do not trust him. Just how close is he to being classified as a nightmare king? And what is it that motivates him to help at all? Still, I hope that he continues to help us. He is certainly an imposing ally – the nightmare that other nightmares fear.

In my search for Callister, I stumble across a corridor that I have not seen before. I head along it, and pass endless small cogs and coils and gears, as if I am inside the very heart of the *Metronome*.

There are two very unusual doors at the end. The first is covered in steel plate and locked shut with an extraordinary number of chains and combination locks. And beside it is a perfectly ordinary red-painted wooden door, with a mail slot and the number 29 in silver attached, as if it is the front door to any building in Britain.

I open the red door. Immediately there is the sound of rain.

These are doors to dreams, then.

I emerge into what looks like a small workshop. Around me are shelves covered in all manner of clockwork parts, and were it not for the noise of the rain, I would have imagined that this was just another part of the *Metronome*.

But through a pair of curtains I come to a shopfront, and beyond its rain-smattered windows is a city. I see a man on a blue bicycle trying desperately to escape the sky's worst by holding a newspaper above his head. A red bus rumbles by, spraying the cyclist as it goes. The buildings all around are tall and white, and I know that this is a dream of London.

The shopfront itself is filled with clocks for sale. Their ticks are not synchronised, creating a melee of ticking, but I think that it is a rather wonderful noise. In my curiosity, I spend some time simply looking at all the marvellous designs, and most remarkable of all, the shelves beside the front desk, where there is a 'NOT FOR SALE' sign and rows upon rows of clockwork toy birds.

There is a pigeon with a lever in its back, and when I push the lever, it thrusts its metal head forward as if pecking for seed. And there is a penguin, which, when wound, waddles in little circles, flapping its mechanical wings as it goes.

'Having fun, are you?'

I turn to see Callister, with his arms crossed, looking angry.

'I'm sorry,' I tell him. 'I was looking for you, and I got lost...'

'I'm sure you did. Who gave you permission to go rooting around in my dream?'

'Nobody...' I place the penguin back on its shelf, feeling ashamed. 'I'm very sorry, Callister. I should have just left.'

He sighs, his anger fading. 'You'd be better off knocking first. I guess you've been hanging around March too much. There's a boy who goes stomping around dreams without permission. Well, tread softly, Manderlay. Tread softly. You've got no idea what you might disturb.' He frowns.

'What did you need me for, anyway?'

'There's a gyroscope on deck that needs replacing.'

'All right, then. Let's head up.'

As we go, I say, 'Your dream is very pretty, Callister. I like the birds.'

'Mm,' he says. 'I make them for my boy. Keeps him busy and out of my hair while I'm trying to work. Or rather, they did. Nowadays they're just sort of… reminders. Truth be told, I'd give anything to have him back and under my feet again.' The watch-smith pauses in his workshop to gather some equipment. 'He passed away a couple of years back. Leukaemia, it was. Don't know what he did to deserve it, but I'll tell you this much: if I ever meet God, I'm gonna punch the bastard right in his stupid face.'

'I'm so sorry,' I say.

'Not your fault, Manderlay. And anyway, my boy comes back to me sometimes, when I'm asleep. He'll be running around my workshop and driving me up the walls. My little ghost.' He shoulders a satchel and opens the door that leads back into the *Metronome*. 'It's funny, really. I don't know if he's a figment, or a nightmare, or whatever else. But it's nice. Sometimes it's nice to dream of the good old days, when everything was okay.'

Back in the corridor, we pass the other door, chained shut.

'Whose dream is that?' I ask, still curious despite myself.

'Reid's. No idea what's in there. But no snooping, okay?'

'Okay. I'll stick to the *Metronome* from now on.'

'See that you do.' Callister tweaks his moustache as we go. 'She tell you her story yet? About why she wants to go to Solomon's Eye?'

'She did. To rescue her old crew. It sounded like a fantastic reason for heading there. I'm not sure why people keep calling her mad. She doesn't seem mad to me.'

'You mean you haven't worked it out yet?'

'Worked what out?'

Callister fixes me with a gaze, trying to see how I tick. 'Her story. About going to rescue a crew made of figments. Whose figments do you think they are, Manderlay? I'll spell it out for you: they're Reid's. She's taking us all to Solomon's Eye so she can rescue her own damn figments. That's why we call her mad. And that's why nobody's been listening to her all these years. It was a childhood dream she had, I'd imagine – exploring the wild dreams, on a ship she dreamed up herself, among a crew of her own figments. She's been dreaming about rescuing them her whole life. Of course she's mad.'

I frown, troubled by this revelation – suddenly unsure of the *Metronome*'s captain.

'Why do you follow her, then? Why did you build this ship for her?'

The watch-smith laughs. 'Because she's a legend. There's nobody else like Isabelle Reid out there. You've got to understand – I only put the ship together. She's the one who inspires it. She's the one who gives it all purpose. Trust me, Manderlay. If you don't see it yet, then you will. Keep a close eye on Captain Reid.'

Making our way back onto deck, it becomes apparent that the *Metronome* is slowing. Her tick is changed from quick-time to a steadier rhythm, closer to a heartbeat.

'Why are we slowing down?' I ask Callister.

><

Out on deck, the air is muggy and filled with insects.

March bats them away, and calls me over when he sees me. He looks tired – there are dark rings around his eyes, and a limp cigarette hangs from the corner of his mouth – but he is also excited. The low sun makes his fiery hair seem hotter.

'Will! We've hit some real luck. You'll never believe it.'

The *Metronome* has slowed to a crawl. We are circling above an autumnal swamp. The waters are reflective and filled with shapes that might be logs or might be crocodiles, and the trees are an endless golden flourish. From horizon to horizon, the swamp is thick and hot.

Directly below us are ancient stone ruins, sunken at an angle into the waters. Once upon a time they might have been a set of pyramids. Tethered up to one corner of those ruins is a strange-looking contemporary boat, somewhere between a single-man yacht and a hovercraft. It has a folded-up sail, an enormous fan attached to the back and is curiously streamlined in a way that I have never seen before.

Standing beside that vessel, and waving up at us, is the silhouette of its owner.

'Who is that?' I ask. March hands me his binoculars.

Adjusting the lenses, I get a better look at the figure below. He looks heavily worn in every aspect, as if he has lived several hard lives simultaneously, from his ragged duster coat and shirt, to the strips of yellowed cloth wrapped around his hands, to his burnt skin. And more than that: there are tremendous scars warping his face, making him hideously ugly, as if he has had a long career as a competitive knife-fighter. Indeed, there are two large knives strapped to his belt, as if to illustrate my thought.

'Marcus damned Delaware,' says March, as the *Metronome* comes to a halt above the ruins. 'Of all the people I didn't expect to see out here, he rates as pretty high. He's an apprentice. May's apprentice. They're a funny line of Sleepwalkers – more like archaeologists and explorers than nightmare-hunters. But Marcus has been around for a long time. Knows a lot of things about a lot of things.' The Sleepwalker clutches his rifle tighter.

We head below deck, down to the hold filled with birds where the Bosun is pulling back the enormous rolling doors. Around us the cages tremble with the excitement of the birds as daylight is revealed. March squints at them unappreciatively. The two of us grab a gangplank and haul it into place, so that it bridges the gap between us and the sunken ruins where the apprentice Sleepwalker waits.

As soon as he is able, the scarred man boards the ship and shakes March's hand. 'Good to see you, boy,' he says with a warped smile. His voice is very deep, with an American drawl – he is Texan, perhaps.

'We can't stay long,' says March.

'Nor should you. Let's get going. I'm coming with you.'

I help the Bosun pull the gangplank back in. He tugs on a rope dangling from above. Somewhere within the clockwork hull a bell tolls, and without a second to spare the *Metronome* rises from the golden swamp and resumes her course, tick returning to quick-time.

When I turn back to March and the newcomer, they are deep in conversation.

'Nothing to worry about,' says Marcus Delaware, leaning up against a cage. 'The ruins are pretty much empty. Didn't find what I was looking for, anyway. Hell of a journey to waste, but there were some pretty interesting carvings. This far out, everything starts to talk about something called 'the first dream'. I'll be damned if I know what that means, but I'm damn well gonna find out. I mean to come back as soon as I get a chance. Right now, though, I have some news for you. Some things you need to hear.'

As I wander across, March nods at me.

'Delaware, this is Will. He's been helping us out. Will, this is Marcus Delaware.'

The Texan shakes my hand; his skin feels like sandpaper. 'Call me Delaware,' he says. 'Everyone else does. You must be the man with the map.'

I nod. 'Nice to meet you. What's this news?'

The scarred man crosses his arms. 'Not good, I'm afraid. I've been out here a while now. It's been a long dream. But you got lucky – I was out here before June passed by. And holy Jesus she's got a lot of skyships. You seen them? There were dozens, all shapes and sizes: battleships, escorts, and gods-damned pleasure cruisers – every single one of them filled up with nightmares. Hell of a force. I managed to get my boat under some trees before they could spot me. Thought I'd just sit out of sight while they passed on by.'

The Bosun closes the rolling doors and heads away to his duties, leaving us alone with the birds.

'She took Binary's fleet,' says March.

'I know that much,' says Delaware. 'And more. Y'see, I saw they were flyin' messages from ship to ship using winged type nightmares, so I fished one of them right outta the sky. Waited 'til he was overhead and roped him down. Tell you what, he put up a hell of a fight. We struggled for a while. But I persevered, and when that damn nightmare wasn't flyin' no more, I went through his pack and read all about June's plan to go to Solomon's Eye. Ran a chill down my spine, that did. What in hell's name does she think she's doing? Who does she think she is? There's places out here that're off limits. We all know that.' He glances at me. 'They were goin' on about the map-man too. How he'd managed to get to Babel and find March. How the two of you were flying out after June with the *Metronome*. I'll tell you this much – that made my heart lift. At least someone's trying to stop June from whatever it is she thinks she's doing.'

March looks troubled at this news. 'She knows we're coming, then.'

'Yup,' says Delaware, 'but there's more. She left the *Smog* behind to slow you down or maybe stop you. And she knows you managed to capture it instead. They must have had a radio on board, broadcasting everything that was happening. That whole fight pissed her right off, apparently. So she's decided to make a stand. She's decided to let you catch up, and then she's just gonna wreck you, straight up. She'll be just ahead, now. Somewhere between here and the edge of Solomon's Storm, I'd wager.'

The blood has drained from March's face. 'Ah, hell,' he says.

Glancing at both of us, the scarred man nods at the boy soldier. 'Why don't you go on up, tell your captain to expect a fight soon. I'll have Will here show me around. I'll help, if I can. Don't you worry about that. We can't let June get to Solomon's Eye.'

Running a hand through his hair, March nods, looking dazed. He rushes away, leaving me alone with Marcus Delaware. But instead of waiting to be led anywhere, the scarred man remains exactly where he is, leant up against a cage filled with birds, looking me up and down. It is difficult to meet his gaze; his eyes are set into rivers of skin so warped that his face might be no more than a horrible mask.

'Why do you have so many birds?' he asks.

'No idea.'

'Hm,' he says. 'All right.' Then, 'How is he? March, I mean. He looks tired.'

'The fight with the *Smog* drained him. He told me he's going to wake up soon.'

Delaware nods, and a quiet falls between us. I am not sure how to fill it. But then, 'You're getting younger?' he asks.

'Yes! I mean… yes, I am. But how did you know?'

'The nightmares were talking about it. They were talking all about you. Apparently they've been after you for a long time now. You've had June hunting the doors for a change – normally she just haunts Babel, makes a big noise about nightmares having rights too. But what I need to know is: did March teach you the ageing trick, or are you doing it by yourself?'

I frown. 'Well… March didn't teach me anything. But I'm not trying to be younger. It's just sort of… happening, I suppose.' I raise my hands and turn them over, admiring the ruddy flesh – the lack of blue veins – the heart for Lily, inscribed into my wrist.

'Good,' says the scarred man. 'Keep it that way. And keep your tattoos. Between you and me, if March is all we have against June, then we don't have much of a chance. He's so young – way too young – and the old March passed away long before this March was ready for the role. The problem is...' Delaware rolls up his sleeves, producing even more scars, valleys through his flesh. 'You and me, we wear our wounds. I wear my scars, you wear your tattoos, and we don't forget who we are. But this March... he doesn't get it, yet. He reckons that covering up his wounds makes him stronger, when the opposite is true. It's making him weaker.'

'I think I know what you mean.'

'Do you?'

'He made a joke about it, when I went to find him. And the way his arm won't stop bleeding... He lost it, didn't he? Amputation, infection, I don't know the details, but he lost his arm. That's why he's dreaming the same dream every night. He's remembering the last time he had it. And that's why it takes so much out of him to conjure bits of his dream. And that's why...' I do not finish my sentence, but I do not need to. Delaware nods.

'So it's up to you and me,' he says. 'If March is all the hope we have, then we've gotta keep him asleep. We've gotta help him out as best we can. We've gotta face that fleet of nightmares – and June – and maybe between the three of us, we can cobble together one competent Sleepwalker.' Then, he smiles a toothy smile, revealing crooked teeth. 'I reckon you and I are gonna be good friends, Will.'

And despite the terrible odds against us, I smile in return. Maybe there is some hope for us, after all.

ROOKS

The birdcages are being taken away.

From what I can gather, they are being relocated to a different hold at the stern of the ship, though for what reason I have not been able to discern. Fairly soon, there is only an empty dark space and me, sat with a pink finch with its own little cage, singing its lonely song as I listen. I have promised to take this bird through to the stern hold when I am done here.

The large rolling doors have been partly opened to air out the place. We seem to be finally leaving the heat of the swamp behind us. I sit with my legs dangling out over the drop, and I have opted to leave my harness unworn. A single errant gust of wind, or push from behind, or moment of imbalance, and I will fall. But I do not.

I am content to watch as the sky begins to blush, lines of red infusing the brilliant blue. But there are deep black bruises too, left in the wake of the other skyship flying alongside us, because the *Smog* has caught up. In our worry about what awaits us ahead, we have decided that we would be better with a second ship – a warship – to face June and her fleet.

The *Smog* is a big black and dull silver bulk, droning through the reddening sky and belching the choking effluence of its engines in its wake. We appear to be keeping mostly behind the larger vessel, as if we are using it as a shield against the darkening of the day.

We soar out over the last sparsely placed trees of the swamp, and are once more at the mercy of the open sea. Here the waters are gentle, and they reflect the red sky, turned to washing eddies of black and crimson that shudder. The first stars begin to wink into visibility overhead, and they too are mirrored in the waters, doubling their brilliance.

Despite the rumbling of the *Smog*, and despite the ticking of the *Metronome*, the scene seems tranquil and calm, like the quiet before a storm. Beside me, the finch twitters her songs. I have given Reid the last song she needs, and I feel useless.

When Samantha left home at last, I felt similarly. It was an early red dawn, like this, and the two of us loaded her cheap battered car with all the things she would need for university, and no matter how many times I offered to drive her through to Glasgow, she told me that she wanted to do it herself. To go off on her own adventure. Too much like her father, I suppose. I was proud, though. I was never any good in school, beyond music – too busy reading novels instead of textbooks, and too busy rushing off on my motorbike instead of doing homework – and I attribute the fact that Sammy managed to get onto a good course entirely to Lily's influence.

So, she left, and I became useless. The house was too empty, and so was I.

It took me less than a month to return to sea. I spent most of the next few years bouncing around the Mediterranean, shifting cargo from port to port.

In an upmarket bar in Rome, I ran into my soldier friend with his great bristling moustache for the second time. Only, he had one fewer eye than the last time we met. In truth I was surprised to find Valentine still about his business. He looked worn, much aged since I last saw him, but still beaming his ridiculous grin, as if he was in on a joke that nobody else knew about. Later that night, I asked him why he was still involved in the military. Did he need the money?

'No, no,' he told me. 'It's not about money. The money doesn't matter. There's always money. The only currency I give a damn about is time. The older I get, the more I do and see, and the more I realise I don't have much of the stuff left. It goes by so quickly, these days. And before you know it, you're an old man, your time is running by so fast that it's sprinting and you can't even do the things you love any more. So, this is me spending my time doing the things I love.' He grinned, then. 'Bossing people about and causing all manner of jolly trouble!'

There are islands out in the sea below me.

They are rocky outcroppings hardly large enough for a man to stand, but tall and twisted and pockmarked with black hollows. Shapes are moving among the islands in the half-dark: black, winged shapes, which flap and dive in tight arcs. By those that get close enough for me to see, I am able to ascertain that these birds are varieties of corvid. In the darkening of the day, the rooks fly and play, whisking themselves around as if to show their skill in flight.

I catch sight of something unexpected among the islands. There is a road between the rookeries, suspended among them, and using the rocky islands as supports. It is crumbling, and in places fallen through altogether, but the road seems to be made of some kind of ancient blackened stone, leading both back in the direction from which we have come and off into the direction in which we are headed. There are no particular decorations on it and its design is of no recognisable era; it is only very old.

We have come to the ruins of the black road at last. I do not find it reassuring.

There is the glint of something flashing ahead of us, like a star in the dark. I lean out as far as I dare in order to see, my face against the cool winds. And it is in that precarious position that I catch my first glimpse of Solomon's Storm.

The storm is still only a black line on the far horizon. But that black line is a tremendous shape – a dark so black that it feels as if we have come to the edge of the world – the edge of a chapter. That flash I caught before at the edge of my vision seems to have been the flashing of distant lightning.

I open the door to the finch's cage, and it darts quickly out, flying on rose coloured wings. In moments, we have left it behind. I watch as it flies away, in the opposite direction to the one we are travelling in. I drop its cage out over the edge and stand, to go and help keep a lookout for June.

>•<

Between the red sky and the red sea, June's fleet waits.

There is the guttering of flames from engines. Some of the

skyships hang in the sky beneath enormous balloons, while others hover beneath propellers or rotors, and more still seem to be suspended by arcane and less readily discerned methods. A twinkling of lights from portholes and decks and windows define their silhouettes.

March lowers his binoculars.

'What are they waiting for?'

The rest of us stand behind him at the forecastle – everything bleached red by the sky.

'They're waiting for you,' says Delaware, without looking up. He is checking and rechecking March's side-arm, taking it apart and putting it together again between his ragged fingers.

'What do you mean?'

'Why do you think she stole a fleet in the first place?' Delaware rolls an icy silver bullet around in his palm, before carefully loading it. 'She's scared of you, March.' Apparently satisfied by his work, the scarred man glances up at last, frowning at the Sleepwalker. 'You know they call you the "Lord of War", right? Nightmares, I mean. Where you go, cannons fire and people get shot. That's what they think of you. That's what June thinks of you. Hell, that's what I think of you.'

Reid's weathered face is a black web of shadows and song notes.

'Forty-two,' she says. 'We are two against forty-two, and my ship is not armed.'

With his back to the fleet in the distance, March observes us all.

'We have to stop June,' he says.

'What would you have us do?' growls the Captain.

'Throw ourselves upon their cannons? 'Twould be a quicker awakening. I promised you passage for the musician's map, and that much I have delivered. Your map is spent, Sleepwalker. You have no more to bargain with. I aim to make for the storm, and you are welcome to disembark. Use the *Smog* if you wish to fight, but I'll not risk the *Metronome*. The storm will be hard enough without flying through that fleet.'

A warm breeze curls the edges of my coat.

'He's right,' I say, but my voice sounds too quiet, so I try again. 'He's right, though. We need to wake June. If we don't, then she's just going to follow you through the storm and wreck your ship anyway.' I glance about at the deck behind us, where the crew are setting up a number of lengthy metal pylons. Perhaps something to help deal with the storm.

'Madness,' says the Captain. 'Madness, it is.'

'It's not...' March fumbles around with his good arm until he finds his compass. 'Look. All we need to do is wake June. And all I need to be able to do that is to work out where she is. So it's simple enough. We force her hand by making her have to deal with the *Smog* first, because if she doesn't, then it'll tear a hole right through her fleet. And while she's busy doing that, we use my compass to work out which ship she's on, fly across, and wake her up.

'Easy,' he says, trying his very best to look confident in his plan. 'It'll be easy.'

Scowling, Reid looks to Callister for his opinion.

The watch-smith shrugs. 'Could work,' he says.

The Captain abruptly stomps away, returning to her wheel and bellowing orders. I glimpse a pair of crewmen dragging chains up from below towards her, for some purpose. Then,

I return my gaze to March, who is watching all the needles turn on his compass with a small frown. 'It'll work,' he says, possibly for his own benefit. 'I'm sure it will.'

>•<

With the use of flag signals, we direct the *Smog*.

The atmosphere up on deck is tense. I have clipped myself onto a railing at the edge so I can see the deck of our pollution-spewing, nightmare-infested ally. Shifting shapes crowd the metal deck, and at their centre is the bulbous form of Slint in his diving suit, directing them. The *Smog* banks with orders received, and surges towards the waiting fleet.

Delaware joins me, pistol in hand. He has his own harness.

We both observe March on the forecastle. 'Do you think we'll get through this?' I ask. 'Do you think he can do it?' I am very nervous – a dreadful feeling in the pit of my stomach that this may be it; this may be when I am awoken from my incredible dream. The fact that March is still not wearing a harness does nothing to settle my nerves. I am unable to decide if it speaks for his confidence or foolishness.

'If anyone can win a war,' says Delaware, 'then it's him.'

There is a tremendous noise as the *Smog* sounds its great horn, like a foghorn amplified a hundred times. I feel it tremble through the wood of the deck. When it has finished resounding, this time, it is answered. The fleet ahead of us sound their own horns – whining sirens, and the clanging of what must be enormous bells. And with this clamour, they too surge forward.

I unclasp my harness and rush up to join March above the *Metronome*'s figurehead.

The ticking of the clockwork skyship quickens, and the crew stumble as we lurch into motion. We soar behind the *Smog* like a flighty finch behind a buzzard, and the fleet drawing swiftly closer to us is like a parliament of sinister black crows – a flock ready to devour us.

I hear the voice of Reid, audible over all the noise, and see that she has been chained down behind her wheel; there are great links pinning her in place.

'All hands, brace!'

The deck tilts just as I fasten myself to the forecastle. March grips hold of it with one white-knuckled hand, and he looks so weary – as if he has already been beaten. 'We can still turn back!' I tell him. 'We could turn away, go around the fleet, find a different way to stop June!' But when he glances over at me, his features ghastly white, I can see the resolution in his face. We are going forward with his plan, even if it costs us all our dreams.

There is a hellish grumbling and cracking as the *Smog* opens fire. The black effluence of a hundred cannons streaks out before it, utterly consuming the first skyship it hits and damaging the next two. Pieces of ships rain from the sky, along with the rag-doll figures of nightmares where they are flung from their broken vessels. The might of the *Smog* is terrifying to behold.

'Where is she?' March is staring wide-eyed at the face of his compass.

We bank hard to starboard as a slender battleship streaks through the sky beneath us, cannons roaring as it flanks the *Smog*. I just about catch sight of the enormous flagship returning fire, overwhelming everything with its absurd battery assault, and I cling on as the *Metronome* threads itself a clever route through a sky filled with hulls – black against the red – forcing them to either hold their fire or risk shooting each other.

Gasping to keep my breath as it is whisked from me, I turn and see that the *Smog* is actually winning. Nothing seems to be able to get close. Pieces of skyships fall everywhere, turned to splinters by its relentless firing solution.

'Come on, come on!' March taps at his compass.

The *Metronome* narrowly avoids being crushed between two jagged hulls by coming about, and suddenly the *Smog* comes into full view before us.

We all witness June making her move, and it seems to happen in horrible slow motion – as if she has stretched time so that we can fully behold her wrath. Even as the impact of a cannonball slamming into the side of the *Metronome* jars us, there is no taking our eyes from the terrible view.

The *Smog*... blooms.

Wooden supports grow branches and leaves, as if life is returning to them. Where there are the slightest stains, fungus sprouts. Where there was a gigantic metal skyship, there is suddenly a malicious living forest, with vines crushing its hull and trees tearing at its guns and crew. The *Smog* explodes outwards with greenery. There is a horrible groaning as its engines start to fail.

The fleet direct themselves away as the *Smog* drops from the sky.

When it hits the red waves, it smashes them apart, making them silver, and for a brief moment there is an island in the sea beneath us. Then it sinks. I lean out as far as I am able, and witness those few nightmares still on deck as they struggle with the vines and branches, and the last thing I see of the *Smog* is its acting captain, Slint, with his gauntlets grabbing at the sky as if he might find something there to hold on to, before he too is pulled beneath the waves.

Suddenly, we are very alone.

March is staring at his compass with horror.

'I can't find her,' he says. 'I don't know where she is.'

The remainder of the fleet turn their attentions on us.

'Hold fast!' calls Reid. The ticking of the *Metronome*'s engine reaches a panicked apex – *tickticktickticktick* – as we desperately avoid gunfire. Innumerable blurred hulls form about, trying to pen us in. I am panicking. I do not know what to do. The only thing keeping us from being wrecked is Reid's artful flying, and there is no telling for how long she will be able to keep it up. I duck as we narrowly avoid the base of a long metal hull.

Winged nightmares sweep down upon us, and the only thing keeping them at bay is Delaware. He fires off rounds from March's pistol, and when that is empty, he throws it aside and draws his knives – one steel, one flashing ice-silver. He throws his steel knife into the wing of one nightmare, runs up a flight of stone steps suddenly conjured from his dream, leaps high and plunges his silver knife into the head of another, before rolling back down onto deck. The stone steps vanish instantly.

'March!' I cry, as more winged nightmares approach.

There is a wild moment of horror as I see a group of vessels forming a solid blockade ahead of us. There is no way past. I know – I *know* – we will crash into them. Only Reid does not seem to share my sentiment.

The world turns. The hull of the *Metronome* splinters and grates. I see a mess of cogs sprinkle around me. My feet are lifted from the deck, and I am jarred backwards as we fly straight up. Then, before we slam into the enemy skyship above us, Reid spins her wheel, and corkscrews us around in an absurd manoeuvre. The *Metronome* soars upside down.

I see March drop beside me, and I reach out desperately, grabbing for him.

Snatching at the air, our hands meet. With all my strength, I keep hold of him. We both watch as the compass is jarred from his grip, spinning and falling like a wishing-well coin into the red sea far beneath us.

The *Metronome* spins around, and we both slam back into the deck.

Reid is calling out, crying out for Callister to do something – anything – to give her more power. I can hear Delaware conjuring more stone – anything to slow down the nightmares attacking the ship. Blood leaks from March's sleeve, dripping down his fingers as he hauls himself to his feet. With his good arm, he pulls me up.

'You have to…' he says to me, coughing and spluttering. 'You and Delaware. *You* have to stop her, if I fail.'

March turns to face the fleet now crowding around us. The *Metronome* rocks again and again as errant shells and cannonballs hit us. The dust of his desert dream whirls around him.

'What are you doing?' I cry out to him.

'I'll see you in another dream, Will!'

March raises his hands, as if he is about to conduct an orchestra. In one fluid motion he clenches his fists.

The first skyship blocking our path explodes – white-hot shards spinning. The one beside it is peppered with white lights as it too is torn apart. I have no time to grab hold of anything any more. The *Metronome* shudders horribly as we narrowly avoid the destruction raining down around us. I can hear March screaming, and his injured arm is crumbling as if it is made of sand.

There is another screaming. The screaming of jet engines.

Thin, flighty shapes surround us. I catch a glimpse of a glinting pilot's helmet. I see the smoke as rockets are discharged from beneath their wings. I witness the impossible reflection on their wings – the reflection of a desert sun.

The next skyship blocking our path blooms into white-hot fire.

The *Metronome* soars, faster and faster through all the destruction.

I feel the heat across my back from the haloes of fire we pass through.

Then, all at once, we are free. There are no more skyships blocking our path. There is only a great stormy wall ahead of us – lightning licking the sea at its edges. And though there is still a steady thundering of explosions from behind us as March's conjured jets continue their assault, there is a greater rumbling ahead – Solomon's mighty storm.

March falls to his knees, and the dust of his desert dream vanishes. His jets cease to be.

'March!' I grab him before he collapses onto his side, but his eyes are wide and unseeing. There is blood streaming from the young Sleepwalker's nose. His entire arm is gone. There is only the pouring of blood from his sleeve.

'All dead,' he says, coughing red. 'No survivors.'

He wakes. The weight of him becomes insubstantial as he turns to a whirling, fading nothingness that drifts from my arms. I am left alone on the forecastle of the *Metronome*, with nothing but the storm ahead.

><•<

The stern hold is all noise.

I rush from cage to cage and unfasten doors. Out pour the terrified forms of endless colourful birds. Most fly around the wide room, colliding with others and calling out, while some simply locate new perches and trill about their new-found freedom. There are birds sitting on both of my shoulders, another on my head, and every time I lift one of my arms a new bird settles down on the vacant space.

Beneath it all is the frantic tick of the *Metronome* as we race to meet Solomon's Storm.

Callister looks as if he has aged a decade. His sleeves are rolled back, and his hands and arms are so covered in oil and long cuts that it looks as if he is bleeding black. With an enormous metal wrench, he is hauling hard on one of the bolts keeping the stern doors closed.

The constant flow of colourful profanity from his end of the hold appears to be spurring him on to greater speeds. 'Bloody set of infernal bastard bolts!' he roars. 'Got all the cages open?'

I reach one of the last towers of cages, and by now the hold is so full of free birds that it is difficult to see the walls. 'Nearly! Open the doors! I think there's enough now!'

'What do you think I'm bloody well trying to do?'

I attempt to wade through hundreds of flapping bodies towards Callister. I catch a glimpse of the red sky behind us through a porthole, and in that sky I believe that I can see one of the skyships still in pursuit.

A handful are still following us. And maybe one of them has June on board.

Callister roars at me, just as I reach the doors, 'Find something to hold on to!' Then, with one last great heave, there is a metallic clunk from his bolt. I grab hold of a protruding pipe beside the doors just as they swing open. The sudden massive gust of air through the hold washes away the sound of all the birds, and even the ticking engine, and I see Callister as he too grabs hold of a pipe.

The birds fly out in one flowing mass of wings.

They are a massive rainbow blanket of feathers, streaming out behind us. I count three skyships in pursuit, but none of them is quick enough to avoid the birds. I hear Callister laughing over the winds.

The birds fly at brilliant speeds, so glad to be free, and where they collide with the skyships chasing us, there are small explosions of feathers and colour – they are awoken. I see flames burst in the turbine engines of one, where feathers and the whirling dust of awakening have impacted its machinery, and I see a second thrown wildly off course by the sudden barrage of birds, swinging about and crashing into the third, nearby. I find myself laughing as well, caught in the same joy as Callister as the last skyships from the once-huge fleet falter.

The birds have done their job.

Those three remaining ships begin to fail and turn about. They limp away, appearing to have had enough, fire leaking from their engines. Behind them, the sky still burns with the last wrecks from the damage done by March. Further back still is the red sky itself, with its thousand glittering stars.

'That must be it!' I cry, my words unheard. 'There's no ships left! We must have woken June! We've done it!'

We speed beyond the battle, so quick above the sea that there are no waves, just an endless silvery red sheen.

Only, the red is now being stifled by black. The dark is getting darker. We are passing beyond the rookeries, beyond the fleet and beyond the wild dreams. We are entering Solomon's Storm at last. We abruptly hit the edge of the great black clouds and continue beyond.

Reid is not reducing our speed. If anything we seem to be accelerating.

We hurtle into Solomon's Storm as if we have been shot from a cannon into it, and all light, all sight, is lost. We are swallowed up by the dark, speeding into darker chasms of chaos beyond, where wait deeper dangers than a mere fleet of skyships: the wrath of the sky itself.

PART THREE

THE FIRST DREAM

SOLOMON'S STORM

Lightning licks the hull.

When it touches the rods bristling out on deck, the charge courses below, directed by long rivers of copper wire. Electrical lamps have been strung up along the *Metronome*'s corridors, and they glow white hot every time the ship is struck.

There is another flash from outside, gifting me a glimpse of the boiling clouds and lashing rains, and then the inside of the ship is lit up, bulbs burning like stars captured in glass. Slowly, they fade. Between flashes is a darkness so complete it feels overwhelming, a promise that the light is never coming back.

Hunched silhouettes dart from doorway to doorway, and I am among them. Every time the ship is struck, we cower as the hull shudders. Yet, the lightning is not the worst. The worst part of the storm is the terrible winds. From what little I know of storms, they are composed of streams of wind like waves, rushing upwards and downwards, and from what I know of hurricanes, they are one tremendous wheel of wind, predictable in its speed and strength. Solomon's Storm – the stuff of nightmares – is neither. At one moment, winds push us forward so quickly that the rains become long streaks across portholes, and at the next an almighty gust slams into our side, rocking us.

I find Delaware sharpening his knives between stacks of broken cogs and coils. He is watching the porthole at the edge of the cabin with wide eyes, unblinking as the sky unburdens itself of lightning again and again. 'How's the ship?' calls the scarred man, over the roar of the storm.

'We're down to half hands. A skeleton crew. And the lower decks are off limits. Too many holes in the hull. But we're flying! Reid's still out there, chained to her wheel. And if anybody can get us through, then it's her. What she did to get us through that fleet...'

Delaware attempts a smile, but it comes out looking grim. 'I saw. You should help them, if you can. They need you now. You're the brightest dreamer left on board, by my reckoning. You're like a candle against the dark. They'll believe in you, and it'll give you strength, if you let them.' Another flash of lightning makes the ship shudder, and we both wince. 'Go on,' he says.

I quickly head away, following the string of electrical lights slowly dulling down to darkness. Beyond the corridor, beyond the hull and beyond the tips of those spires out on deck, the storm attempts to digest us within its tremendous black belly.

I stop and listen as we hurtle through a lull, and it is then that I hear the song of the storm for the first time: the last song from my album, Solomon's Eye. It is an amalgamation of the roaring and whistling winds, the rumbling of thunder where clouds collide, the electrical crackling of lightning and the waterfall hissing of the rains, and even the groaning hull of the *Metronome* herself. For a few moments I do not notice the rocking of the ship; I am rooted to the spot, and in awe of what I am hearing. The song of Solomon's Storm is more than the sum of its parts. It is a majestic and terrible symphony, sung by the sky itself in all its rage.

Another brilliant flash of the white lights, and I glimpse someone unexpected, the edge of his white tabard at the end of a corridor. Another sighting of Thyme. I rush after him in the dark that follows.

Through a door which should be closed – slamming in the winds – I see him descend into the gloom of the lower decks, where there are no white lights and all crew have been forbidden to go. I pause at the edge, unsure how the beams of wood barring this door have been broken. They look torn as if by great force. The storm, perhaps.

I see Thyme vanish into the deep black, and try to call after him. 'It's too dangerous down there! Come back!' But my voice is drowned out by thunder.

I cautiously make my way down the steps. A flash of lightning reveals the jagged holes in the hull all around – entire cabins ripped clear of the ship – and I take care navigating the corridor, eyes wide to welcome in any light.

The winds howling through the ship whirl my coat around me. Debris skitters along the ground, and I am unsteady as the ship is buffeted about. The storm rages on.

I come to the place I saw the old knight go. I no longer need to wait for the next flash of lightning; at the base of a rudimentary set of steps, descending between all manner of cogs and coils in motion, is a pool of flickering white light, as if the heart of the *Metronome* is aglow.

As I draw closer, I hear a loud hissing like the release of steam. And when I navigate my way across a set of unmoving pistons and get close enough, I am able to see the silhouette of someone sat beyond, haloed by the flickering white lights. I duck beneath a pipe.

There are screens everywhere in here, and arranged around them are speakers. Every single one of them is playing empty static. The screens flash and fade just like the white lights above, and there are screens on every wall, and even attached to the ceiling.

Sitting cross-legged at the centre of his chaotic grotto is the last liar with a multitude of shifting shadows cast across his lap. His head is bowed, as if in prayer. Thyme has removed his chain mail, which sits in a heap up against the corner of the room, and wears only a set of heavily scarred leathers beneath his stained white tabard. The rest of him is exactly as I remember it, as if he is a knight made to wait centuries for his calling to come about, as if he is overgrown and old beyond his own age.

He is a stowaway.

I glance around, and locate his sword at the very back of his grotto, where it hangs on the wall between the screens. Still wrapped up in its scabbard, his sword seems to be taking pride of place in the room, as if I have entered a bizarre cathedral.

When Thyme looks up, I see the static reflecting in his eyes. 'Manderlay the Bard,' he says, and I cannot read the expression upon his wizened face.

Now that I know what he was doing with all the equipment I saw him carrying back at the Golden Gate, it raises even more questions than it answers. I begin with, 'Thyme? What are you doing here? What is all this?'

'Sit thyself down,' he commands, and I do not know if it is something in the manner of his speech or the shadows across his face, but I find myself obeying. The ship shudders around us, yet in this place, I have come to a moment of calm among the chaos, as if Thyme has constructed a temple of peace.

'Tell me,' says Thyme, 'art thou a man of Christ?'

I find myself considering his bizarre question, even now, even here.

I have never been religious. Even as a young boy, the various churches I was taken to did not feel significant. The problem was that my father could never settle on a denomination. While he was certain of God's identity, he was never quite sure about His exact message, and as such, during my childhood I was baptised by three different churches, and tasted the flesh and blood of Jesus in two different forms.

None of it felt special. 'From time to time,' I say.

'As all men are,' says Thyme. He draws one of his hands up so that it points at me, or perhaps even through me, pinning me to the spot. 'I'll tell thee a lie, then, in the fashion of thy occasional faith. I'll burden thee with a new thought or three, as I must, for what is to come next. Listen well, Manderlay, for this is a lie that is not often told, and rarer in this way; it is a lie favoured by the oldest liars, and remembered only by the mad and departed. It is a lie older than thee, older than me and older still than the ancient storm we cross. It is a version of the first lie ever told.'

Thyme draws both of his hands together, as if he might capture the light of the static screens between them. 'On the seventh day,' he says, 'God rested. He saw before Him His garden, and all the light and life He had made, and saw that it was good. He saw the setting of His new sun, and the rise of His new moon, and saw that they were good. He saw the stars come alive, lighting up like candles might, and saw that they were good. And when He saw all of this, He became lulled by His creation, as if Eden and all the constellations in His new sky were a child's mobile, spinning around in His thoughts. And it was thus that, on the seventh day, God rested, and on the seventh day, God fell asleep, and at the end of the seventh day, God dreamed the first dream.

'There is little known of the first dream. From time to time, a glimmer of it can be gleaned from the glitter of the oldest forgotten rocks. Dig down to the depths below the oldest mountains in dreaming and thou mightest glimpse a colour never before seen, or hear a sound not meant for mortal ears. There are wonders yet hidden from mortal dreamers that might reveal more of that first dream, when God Himself slept, and let His wildest thoughts come alive and shape the very foundations of dreaming. But while there is little known of that first dream, even in the brightest and wildest lies I know, there is one tale told of God's most terrible creation, born of that dream. For it was written that

God did not only dream of colours beyond imagination. It was written that God dreamed... of darker things.

'As a matter of induction, the oldest of my order – the once great and prosperous Order of Liars – told me the tale of an ancient tome they knew to once exist. Within that tome, now lost to the ravages of time, was written the story of Creation's last secret. The pages of that book said that, when God slept at the end of the seventh day, there was the tiniest sliver of doubt at the back of His thoughts, buried like a worm in an apple.

'This was the first lie. The lie which all liars must learn and remember.

'The book said that while God slept, dreaming the first dream, His doubts... awoke. It said that God's doubt was made up of seven questions: seven shards of doubt, which, among all the impossible colours and sounds of God's dream, became seven voices – seven voices that echoed God's doubts back at him in seven different ways. The book did not say what those seven questions were, but it did attach a name to the voices. In that most ancient, hallowed and secret of tomes, those voices were called the Seven Satans, and it was written that they were the first nightmares. God's own nightmares.

'And there the Book of Lies finished, half burned as it was when our citadel was sacked by Solomon's knights – the eldest among us killed, and our most hallowed of lies almost forgotten. It was only half a tale, half a lie, and the last of its secrets were lost. Nobody knows what happened to the Seven, or where they went. But those in my order whispered the first half of the story to one another, and it reached all the way through generations to me. For I am the last liar, and none but thou and I have heard the story of the Seven Satans. None but thou and I know they even might have existed, once.'

Thyme's voice is low, now, and he drops his hands and his head, as if he has no more energy to hold them up. I can see long lines across his brow. 'This was my first lie,' he says, 'and it will be my last. Remember it well, Manderlay the Bard, and have faith.'

Around us, the storm growls louder and the static of his many screens pours into my ears like waterfalls. I stand and brace myself against a wall. There is a new sound beneath the rest now, ticking in time with the skyship's engine. It sounds as if the *Metronome* is developing a kind of cough.

I can only frown at Thyme, apparently returned to his deep contemplations and meditation. I do not know what to make of his wild story and why he has stowed away on board. Most of all, I do not know why my ghost keeps leading me to him.

I am given little time to consider, as the engine's cough becomes steadily more apparent. Something bad is happening to the *Metronome*. I rush to the entrance to Thyme's grotto, ducking beneath a coil of cables. I should climb back above, and help if I am able. And then, tell them that there is a stowaway on board. Let Reid deal with the old knight.

Thyme's voice calls out to me as I go, and I turn. His arm is raised, and with one gnarled finger he is pointing at his sword, where it hangs like an icon on the far wall. I can see the static of his screens as they cascade white light across his pale skin. He is grinning his wolfish grin, teeth bared, as if I am prey.

'Remember, Manderlay!' His voice finds me above everything. 'My sword is the sword that once guarded the gates of Eden! Should it be pulled from its scabbard, then it will burst into bright flames! Remember this, and have faith!' He raises his face up to the light and I can see the glint of madness in his eyes. For a moment, I am afraid. 'Above all else, have faith!' he cries.

The *Metronome*'s ticking is slowing, like a clock winding down, and the crew are milling about in a panic. Nobody seems to know what to do.

I run into Callister rushing along a corridor, and am almost bowled over. He helps me up before continuing. 'Come with me!' he orders. Every flash of the white lamps lends him years, and I realise that he is getting so much older while I find my youth.

I make to tell him about our stowaway – about Thyme, but he interrupts me. 'One of my main gears has gone and bucked a bloody tooth,' he tells me, 'and by my count we have just under two hundred ticks until the whole damned engine skips a beat and throws us out of the sky. No time to chat, Manderlay!'

Behind the watch-smith is the Bosun, the sleeves of his coat rolled up. The heavy man's shirt is torn, and by the monochrome light of the lamps I am unsure whether there is more oil there, or blood. I lag behind. 'There is a spare!' Callister yells back at me, over the noise of the storm, 'but the only way to replace the broken part is by either stopping the engine, or doing something very foolish. So we're gonna do something very foolish indeed and jump the entire central gear-shaft!'

When the three of us reach the door leading out onto deck, the Bosun retrieves a claw-hammer from his belt and begins to hack at the boards nailing it shut. The ship ticks around us, but slower, so that it feels like a pendulum losing its momentum.

Callister pulls a new cigar out from somewhere within his waistcoat, bites the tip off, spits it out and places the rest in his mouth. He does not bother to light it. 'I've forced us to reduce speed as much as I can, which'll have the Captain in a fine mood. But if I hadn't, we'd all be halfway to the bottom of the sea by now.' He glances up at the ceiling, unseeing, but I can hear him counting down beneath his breath. 'A hundred ticks left, maybe,' he says.

The Bosun rips at the last plank across the rattling door.

Callister pulls his jacket closed and fastens it. 'The only way we're staying in the sky is if we pull three levers at the same bloody time, freeing up the new gear-shaft and letting it brute-force the old one out. I've got lads waiting to catch it below. There's one lever up front, which I'll get to, and two on the aftercastle, which are for the both of you. Bloody great copper things, set into the wood in a way that makes them bloody difficult to pull because I didn't reckon we'd ever need to do anything like this mid-flight. Can't miss 'em.'

The door finally comes free, and the Bosun leans against it. It shakes beneath his broad shoulder. Callister looks from him to me. 'At the count of fifty ticks from my mark. Got it? Fifty exactly. On fifty, you pull your lever. And I don't care how much the wind wails, and the rain splashes, and the whole damn ship sounds like she might be tearing in two, you get to those bloody levers and pull them on fifty, or I swear to the almighty I will find you both in awakening and make sure you never sleep again. Got it?'

I do not think that I am prepared to face the storm. I swallow hard and pull my own coat closed. 'You take port,' yells Callister to the Bosun. 'And you take starboard,' he yells at me. I still have my harness around my shoulders, but I do not know if I will have enough time to use it. I brace myself against the wood of the deck. 'On my mark!' shouts Callister, biting down on his cigar so hard that it bends upwards. I take a last few deep breaths, as if I am about to dive into a deep lake.

'Go!' calls Callister.

The Bosun does not need to pull the door back, because when he lets go of it, the winds slam it against the wall. The corridor is instantly filled with a tremendous and freezing cold gale, along with the first lashings of rain. I begin counting down from fifty in my head.

The first up is Callister, who vanishes instantly into the dark. Next is the Bosun, a little less steady despite his superior size, who rushes to port. Last is me. Battling up the final few steps, I finally experience the full force of the storm, and it is a wonder that I am able to stay on my feet.

The winds are so strong that the rains are horizontal and sharp, endless lashings, a wall of water so icy that it feels as if I have frozen instantly. The only thing allowing me movement is the fact that we are currently facing into the wind, and that I can use it for a little momentum, to push me across to the starboard railing.

I was correct in assuming that I would not have time

to attach my harness to anything. I have already lost fifteen ticks. The howling of the storm around me almost completely muffles the *Metronome*'s failing engine, so that its ticking is an absence of noise rather than a presence.

I count on as I pull myself towards the upper deck. There is an almighty flash of lightning and the ship is lit up. I catch a glimpse of the slick deck, railings bent and dented. By the time I reach the steps leading up to the aftercastle, I believe that I have only twenty-five ticks left. I have used half my time.

I haul myself up two steps at a time, feeling the rains pound against my back. It does not feel as if I have time to breathe. When I reach the top there is another great flash of lightning, and I am granted a startling glimpse of the state of the Captain.

Behind Reid the boiling clouds of the storm are whirling. The golden buttons of her coat have torn free, so that a stream of red whirls out behind her. One of the chains keeping her attached to the deck has snapped and is trailing along with the rest. But still she stands tall behind her wheel, wild eyes reflecting the lightning.

I notice that her wheel has been so badly damaged by the storm that it is now a crescent moon, and though I have only the slightest moment in which to see her, I believe that the expression across her face is one of fierce anger, as if it is her wrath against the storm.

There is no sign of the Bosun. I have twenty ticks left. With my feet slipping, I skate across to the back of the upper deck, where there are indeed two levers, one to either side. I crouch down, with fifteen ticks remaining, one hand on the railing nearby, my other on the lever. I say another little prayer to whoever might be listening. Then I look up and try to locate the Bosun in the dark. In the next flash of lightning, I see him.

The Bosun has been caught up in an errant gust of wind. I can see him clutching hold of the port railing, but he is on the wrong side of it, having been blown overboard. The bulk of his body is trailing out behind him. I can see the wild panic in his eyes. I have ten ticks remaining. There is another flash of lightning and I have no time left to consider how to respond.

I make a decision.

Clutching hold of the lever beneath me, I tear at my harness until it comes clear.

Six ticks remaining.

The rain stings my eyes.

Four ticks remaining.

With all the strength I can muster, I whip my harness around through the air, throwing the far end of it as hard as I can.

Three ticks.

In the next flash of lightning, I see the Bosun as he is swept into the storm, tumbling wildly. But my harness catches the lever he was meant to pull.

Two ticks.

I haul as hard I can on my own lever, and with the harness, the other. And though I cannot feel my own hands for the rains, and though I am sliding to find purchase against the deck, I am sure that something moves. I let go of them and wrap my arms around the nearest section of railing.

Something is happening beneath my feet. The ticking of the *Metronome*'s engine has been replaced with a kind of grinding thump.

For a few moments, I worry that I was too late, that my timing was off, but then the grinding stops, and is replaced by a new tick. It is a quick ticking again, healthier than before, and as it erupts into life, the ship bucks. We are speeding up, and the rains whip harder across me. I try to shield my face against the torrent and wonder how, if at all, I am going to make it back below deck.

The darkness seems to go on forever, along with the cold and the trembling of the ship. But I believe that I glimpse a flash of colour ahead of us. I stare out, hooding myself against the wind and rain. And there, I am sure that I see it again. A flash of colour, a window of blue in the black, swallowed up as quickly as it was revealed. The ship shudders beneath me as the Captain hauls against the wheel, finding us a new current to sail across.

And then, all at once, we are free.

With the storm trailing behind us, we soar into clear air. There is a sudden blue sky above, and a sudden blue sea below, and the last smatterings of rain as the clouds behind us spit their contempt.

I am so dazzled that I remain in position. I can breathe again, and for a long while I simply crouch there on the upper deck, unable to move.

The ship begins to slow down, by the Captain's hand. Eventually I am able to stand on shaking legs and see where we are. Solomon's Storm whirls about us in an enormous loop – surrounding our little sea of calm. But above is a blue sky, empty and fresh, with a happy yellow sun. The open waters below us sparkle pleasantly. The air is warm and soothes my poor rain-whipped skin.

We have come to Solomon's Eye.

The *Metronome* looks as if it has been to hell and back. A lot of railings, pieces of machinery and even whole sections of hull are battered, bent and broken. Those pylons meant for the lightning that still remain are black stumps. The only intact part of the ship appears to be her tick, which is healthy and slowing to a leisurely pace.

Upon wobbly legs I venture forward. At the prow of the ship I can see the shape of Callister as he too begins to move, one hand against the base of his back, and though I am very sorry for the Bosun, I am so glad to see that my friend the watch-smith has survived.

The Captain, who is still clutching hold of her wrecked half-moon wheel, has her head bowed. As I move up to her side, she stumbles and falls to one knee. But even in that position, she does not let go of her wheel.

Instead, she cries out, her voice so hoarse that she wheezes her triumph, and I hear her call beneath the blue sky. 'Solomon's Eye!'

The Captain's clothes are torn, and her skin looks bruised and beaten, but still she raises one hand to the sky as if she could anchor herself to it. 'Murdock,' she says. 'I came back for you. I kept my promise. I'm here, now. I'm here.'

The crew blink bleary eyes as they shudder onto deck.

Despite the state of the ship, there is a great deal of cheer. Hammers and welding torches are brought to bear with enthusiasm, and those chunks of hull deemed unredeemable are broken off and left to drop to the gentle sea below.

There are wispy white clouds above us, like the storm's

afterthoughts, and as we move at a leisurely pace through the blue sky – through this great patch of calm – our clockwork home begins to look something close to herself again.

I have been set to work hauling some of the black stumpy pylons from their places and throwing them overboard. The crew chatter and laugh around me as I work. Most seem anxious to see what comes next. To see what we came all this way for.

Nobody has been able to pry the Captain away from her broken wheel. She sits, cross-legged beneath it, with one hand still guiding us onwards. She looks as worn as her ship, almost a skeleton of herself, but there is still that determination in her eyes. Reid has delivered us through conflict after conflict, across great wild dreams to be here. She is not letting go yet.

The Captain still has her eyes fixed on the horizon, and is keeping silent. I would guess that she is listening for something on the wind.

Before long there is a cry.

'Land ho!'

We gather at the prow.

Ahead of us is a great tropical island. The sun reflects on countless palms, across which the flitting forms of tropic birds can be seen. The hills could be compared to mountains for their gushing green waterfall slopes, arranged almost theatrically around rocky tips, all the way down to deep patches of thick jungle below. All is surrounded by a long and golden belt of beaches, pockmarked with rocky caves and long hooks of sand, reaching out into sea as if the island is an octopus and they are its tentacles.

There are no signs of human dreaming anywhere, except

for the object at the very centre of the island.

It is this that brings the crew to a temporary silence. The ticking of the *Metronome* seems loud beneath our feet. There is a building at the tip of the tallest hill, upon a plateau surrounded by the rim of a dormant volcano, as if it is walled in. The structure is difficult to see, except for in those places where it directly reflects the bright sun, because it appears to be made entirely of silver. The crew murmur among themselves, unsure of what to make of it.

Could this be Solomon's prison?

'Prepare to make landfall!' cries Reid. She hauls herself back up to her feet, and pulls back on a lever. The ticking of the skyship's engine slows, and we turn gradually to port.

The crew begin to rush around, making final preparations, but I wait at the prow, standing above the blackened beak of her phoenix figurehead, and watch the mysterious island we head towards, thinking about nightmare kings and ancient Sleepwalkers.

Callister joins me as we slowly soar about.

'You did good back there,' he tells me. His clothes are torn in places and his moustache is now completely grey. He claps a hand on my shoulder. 'We made it, after all,' he says.

I sigh and lean against the railing. 'The Bosun...'

The watch-smith shakes his leg idly, to free it of something. 'Don't worry about it,' he says. 'We'll find him sooner or later. The crew always come back to us, when they dream again. Like... they're magnetically attached to the ship or something. I don't bloody know.' He shakes his foot harder. 'Bloody great lot of useless lumps, leaving bits of cable all over my damn deck. Can't train them to save their lives...' He trails off as he looks down.

A green vine is winding its way around Callister's leg and tightening.

He looks up, meeting my eyes. 'Oh bloody hell,' he says.

The ship rocks as a long trunk of wood erupts from the deck behind us. I turn, too late to shield myself, thrown onto my back. The *Metronome* is shaking beneath me, and there is a screeching as if she is screaming. The air is pushed from my lungs and I have to take a moment to try and catch my breath. In that moment, all hell breaks loose.

Planks of wood shudder and branches sprout from their edges in fast-forward. The crew are thrown about as those branches curl and cover themselves in leaves. I can hear the crew shouting, and the ticking of the engine faltering, and above it all a long howl from the Captain, hauling hard on levers, trying to save us.

I try to reach, to grab Callister, but the vines are up to his waist. I can only watch as they crush tightly around him and he is awoken, eyes filled with surprise.

The *Metronome* is tilting to starboard. More trees are spawning from the wood of her hull. I can hear gears groaning, and her ticking becoming an unpredictable thing. I skitter around sudden trunks, trying to find some balance between them, and run towards the Captain. She is snarling at the forest tearing her ship apart.

'Will!' calls someone, over the sound of the *Metronome*'s slow death.

I see Delaware vaulting across sudden branches, until he meets me at the centre of the new forest. The deck tilts further beneath my feet as the scarred man thrusts something into my arms. I see that he has given me my violin case.

'Delaware?'

As the ticking of the *Metronome* begins to fail, I feel the scarred man pull something across my shoulders. 'June's still asleep! We didn't wake her!' he snarls, as he pulls me across to an empty patch of hull, where the railing has been pried free. 'We've got to carry on, Will. We've got to stop her!' Only at the edge of the ship do I realise what Delaware is doing. I have no time to put up a fight. There is no ticking now, only the ripping of the hull, the howling of the Captain and Delaware shouting unheard commands at me as he pulls something onto his own back.

Then I am pushed.

As I fall, I see the *Metronome* as it is wrecked. Trees have sprouted at every angle across her, and there is barely anything recognisable left of the clockwork skyship. It is green from bow to stern. The last trees pull apart the skyship's guts, raining cogs and coils, gears and levers, but I can hear nothing more of its distress. I only hear the rushing winds as I plummet, and see the silhouette of Delaware as he makes to follow, ready to leap after me.

He is stopped. The branch of a tree whips out and skewers him through the chest. The scarred man is awoken.

Through my horror, something of Delaware's commands comes back to me.

The speed of my velocity shakes at my arms, and though I am terrified, I reach across to the place at my shoulder, where there is a cord, and I pull hard. I catch a glimpse of white cords and canvas, and I am hauled hard suddenly upwards.

Then, I am floating, as the parachute billows above me. Breathing heavily, I watch the waters below as they are sprinkled with glinting copper parts from the wreck of the *Metronome*.

The *Metronome* is being destroyed in the same way that the *Smog* was, but I do not know how it is possible. I do not know how the Sleepwalker June is wrecking us. I do not know where she is. There are no other ships in the sky.

The remains of the clockwork skyship hurtle past me. Somehow, Reid has steered her wild descent towards the shore of the island. And though the ship is nothing but green ruins, and though it ticks no more, the *Metronome* still meets the sand, drawing a long line through it, crashing to an ugly halt.

The world is suddenly very quiet.

It is then that I hit the water, the cords of the parachute winding themselves around me. I barely have time to take a breath as I am pulled under. The sea is warm, and I struggle to find air. There is only the confusion of the deep blue, and the canvas and cords of the parachute.

No amount of kicking is getting me free. I realise that I am drowning, and if I do not save myself, I will wake up.

DRIFTWOOD

A moment of clarity.

With my feet skimming the white tile floor of the swimming pool, I take stock of my surroundings. Teenagers dive and cannonball, wearing too little, and older folk swim lengths, dressed modestly. The sun glows across all their backs, tanned and pale, slender and overweight, athletic and flirtatious.

Among them all, at the centre, as if she has been positioned there by divine hands, is Lily, caught in a pillar of sunlight.

She pirouettes as if she is dancing in slow motion. Behind her the pool is a chaos of limbs and bubbles, but she is a picture of calm, as if she is the eye of a storm. Her suit is white with a small bow at the breast, and she is fascinated by the tiny bubbles rising from between her lips as she turns.

She is completely absorbed in her moment, and I am completely absorbed in watching her, with the chlorine stinging my eyes, and my lungs complaining for oxygen.

Her nails are painted white, and her arms are raised,

fingers moving as if she might weave the sunlight. Then she rushes upwards all at once, dark hair streaming behind her. The girl in white is gone, and the moment is broken. I kick up from my dark corner of the pool.

Gasping for breath, I break the surface.

The ruins of the *Metronome* litter the waves of the bright sea around me, bobbing and colliding. The strings of the parachute are cutting into me in places, and I am bounced between waves, but I kick hard, keeping my head high. I breathe.

Blinking enough to clear my vision, I spot the case of my violin as it too bobs to the surface nearby. I pull myself across to grab it. Then I kick and struggle, and haul myself through the sea towards a floating shard of the broken skyship's hull.

Grabbing on with one slippery hand, I take the time simply to catch my breath and get my bearings. The salty sea slaps my back, birds wheel overhead, the sun is warm and I am not certain about what just happened. I was drowning, tangled up in my parachute, but then... I was at the swimming pool where Lily loved to go in summer.

I saved myself, somehow – with a fragment of a distant dream.

I can see the island in the near distance, but I am given no time to judge how long it would take me to swim there. There is an enormous dark shape in the sea below me, rising fast.

The creature narrowly avoids me as it comes to the surface. The surface of the sea domes, before bursting. It could be a whale, spewing its breath into the air, except that it is covered in irregular protrusions, and has hatches along its back all in a row.

A submarine.

I watch the froth of water as it slides from the submersible's streamlined back, and see the silhouettes of crew as they haul hatches open and clamber to their feet. I bob as the sea ripples, struggling to keep hold of my raft. When the waters have stilled, a rope ladder is rolled into the sea, and I am called to climb it.

I lope across, struggling against the weight of the parachute. Still tangled, I wearily clamber up the curved hull of the submarine. The hull is made of a kind of wood, flecked with salt stains and barnacles. Rough hands help me up the last rungs, hauling me to my feet and reaching around me with knives to cut the worst of the parachute away.

I take deeper breaths, and were it not for the hands beneath my arms, I would collapse to my knees. I do not even have a voice to thank the folk that have offered me salvation from the sea.

The figures around me are an unfamiliar gathering of rough-looking dreamers with dark rings beneath their eyes, and they seem jolly in the light of the sun, stretching their arms as if they have awoken from a lengthy sleep. They wear practical wools and carry the equipment submariners might – knives, and wrenches – but just like the crew of the *Metronome*, they are a motley lot, with no distinctive uniform.

From somewhere behind them an unusual figure emerges. I try to step away, but I am the only one out on the narrow deck who seems surprised by its approach. It has to be a nightmare.

It looks as if it is made of stone. It is the shape of a man, and the size of a man, but constructed out of rocks, as if a statue has come to life. It hauls itself completely free of the interior, and none of the crew runs screaming, or seems even slightly perturbed. The rocky nightmare stretches itself in the light of day, a minor mountain come to life.

When it laughs, it sounds like a rock-slide. 'We caught ourselves a fish, mates!' I find it difficult to determine the direction of the nightmare's gaze, because its eyes are no more than two shallow reliefs, like empty sockets in a skull. 'Welcome on board, little fish,' it rumbles at me. The rocky nightmare thumps the wooden deck of the submarine with one of its oversized fists. 'I'm told we're to keep you for now. Our Captain wants a word with you before you wake. We'll have no nonsense from you while you're on our little boat, mind, or you'll be answering to me.'

I finally find my voice, and every word tastes of salt. 'Who are you?'

'My name is Dust, first mate aboard the *Driftwood*.' The nightmare flexes its pebble fists, and they clatter like marbles in a bag. 'Take him below,' it says to the crew. 'Put him with the other fish. The Captain will call for him when she's ready.'

Beneath low ceilings I am led.

The submarine's corridors are made of trees. Their trunks are pressed together so tightly that there is no space between. The floor is a tangle of roots matted into a flat surface, and judging by the occasional green leaf dangling from an errant twig, these trees are still very much alive.

It feels as if I am being led through some kind of peculiar secret garden.

Eventually, I am brought to a room where there is a pair of barred wooden cells. My captors have allowed me to keep my sodden violin case, and I clutch at it as I am directed between the bamboo bars of the nearest cell. Within, there is a comfortable-looking bunk, and even a wooden bowl with a metal tap. I am told that should I feel hungry at all, I am only to call out and food will be brought. The tired-looking crewmen mutter happily to one another about the sunshine as they leave, locking the gate to my cell as they go.

This room is much like the rest of the interior of the *Driftwood*: an airtight alcove. There are some wild red roses in my cell, lit up by a dull orange lamp, and beneath them is a thicket of thorny stems. It is a pretty sight.

I sit down upon my bunk with a sigh. Placing my violin down beside me, I tug at the last strands of parachute cord still wound around my leg. While I pull ineffectively at it, I remember the look on Callister's face when he saw what it was winding its way up his ankle, back on the *Metronome*. I recall his terror as he was awoken, and I feel a sharp pang of regret – that I could not help him, help any of them, or perhaps that I did not try hard enough.

Glancing about, I find I am not alone. There is movement in the shadows of the far corner. Whoever is inside the other cell appears to have either broken or dimmed their lamp, obscuring them from sight. I squint, letting my eyes adjust, and when I realise who it is that I am seeing, I feel my eyes widen in surprise. Standing at the very back of that other cell is Slint.

The dull metal of his helmet is covered in dings and dents.

There is still that pool of utter blackness in the porthole of his helmet, but Slint looks wounded. With one heavy gauntlet, he is holding the fabric of his suit closed. There is a great long tear across his belly.

I spend some time considering what to do.

Eventually I manage to get the coil of white parachute cord free from around my leg. There is still a good length of it, and winding that length up around my wrist, I make a new coil. Then, I lean over the thicket at the edge of my cell and take the time to find the perfect thorn. The one I choose is wickedly sharp – a red hook – and there is enough roughness in its edge that I am able to tie the end of the parachute cord around it.

With my labours complete, I hold my peace offering between my palms and wonder if it will have any effect at all.

'Slint!' I call, nervous about getting the dark nightmare's attention. I throw the coil of cord across to his cell. For a small while there is no sign that he has seen what I have done. But then, as slowly as if he is moving through water, I watch the nightmare diver approach the coil and bow down so that he can pick it up.

With that, he vanishes back to the far gloom of his wooden prison.

In my own cell, I watch, and wait to be called up by the *Driftwood*'s Captain, considering if I am correct about her identity. I think about my friends as well: those members of the *Metronome*'s crew that must be awake now. I hope that their awakening was gentle. And as I continue musing upon my predicament, I find a small amount of relieved amusement in the idea that I have just presented a proverbial lion – thorn in its paw – with a literal thorn.

›•‹

I am escorted through to what I am told is the submarine's bridge.

The room we emerge into is stunning. Not for the crew behind various instruments, or Dust the stone nightmare, who is steering, but for the display that encompasses the entire nose of the ship. It looks like a window. Or maybe a hundred windows, in a vast crystalline concave arrangement, as if we are standing inside the eye of an insect.

The light in here is strange because the windows are uneven and flawed, and each gives a slightly distorted view. I approach in awe. As I get closer I see that each window is a large scarred block of glass, embedded together in a tight network of branches. The submarine bobs between the waves, and while the upper half of the windows show the blue sky and island, the lower half reveals the sandy depths below, where fish dart to and fro.

Pieces of the *Metronome* clatter gently against the glass.

'If you follow the coast shadow-wards from Babel, then you'll eventually get to a city called Impetrus.' I blink and turn to see June, who leans against a small desk beside me. Somehow I missed her. She is just as bright and wonderful to behold as the last time I saw her, wrapped up in luxurious yellow cloth and gold sequins, as if a shaft of sunlight has tumbled through one of the windows and come to life.

She continues speaking. 'It's an old, old city. Mostly ruins. But some doors still show up there, because people are interested in it. It's great for looking at what people used to dream about, a long time ago. It's full of statues, just sitting or standing around, as if the whole city was turned to stone one night.

'The stories say that it was ruled over by a benevolent nightmare king during the Nightmare Monarchies. A sort of gorgon, apparently, which makes sense. But according to that same story, the people of Impetrus loved their ruler. She was wise, powerful and peaceful, and the city prospered. That is, until Solomon came along, woke everybody up and killed their nightmare king.'

June shakes her head sadly. Her gold-star earring swings and glitters. 'One of the strange things about Impetrus is its beaches. Instead of sand, they're made of marbles. Hundreds of thousands of marbles, clattering with every wave. And the way the marbles work, they vanish every time the waves cover them. It's beautiful.

'I got curious. I wanted to know where all the marbles came from. So I put together a team of nightmares and dreamers, and I built a submarine – the first version of the *Driftwood*, in fact – and we all went down together to see.

'It was even better than I'd imagined. There's another city out there, sunken beneath the waves. A city even older than Impetrus, and made completely out of glass. It's in ruins, now. In fact, it's been down there for so long that it's mostly just marbles rounded by the tides. But here and there are some chunks of buildings. Maybe towers or maybe temples – it's difficult to tell.'

June stands before the *Driftwood*'s windows and presses her palm against one. 'We took some samples with us. There aren't any carvings or symbols on them, and they're so worn and scratched by the sea that if there ever were any, they're long gone. But we polished what pieces we had, until they were as clear as they once were, and I incorporated them into the nose of the *Driftwood*.

'The point isn't so that we can see outside, though. We've got periscopes for things like that. The point is that we're looking through glass reclaimed from dreams maybe thousands of years old. Older than us. Older than anything any person can remember.' She turns back to me, folding her arms and appraising me. 'Remembered only by the sea.'

I am unsure how to respond. Indeed, I believe that I should be very angry with June – for taking my notebook, waking my friends and wrecking the *Metronome*, and for trying to do whatever it is she is trying to do here. But now that I am before her, I cannot find any rage inside myself. Perhaps it is the brilliant windows affecting me.

'Hi, June,' I say at last.

'Hello, William,' she replies. 'I really didn't expect to see you again. I certainly didn't expect you to find your way to Babel. You've caused me a lot of trouble, you know that? I'm telling you the truth when I say that I didn't want to wake anybody tonight. But I had to. March is… tenacious. His whole line is. If they get an idea in their head, then they follow it to the edge of dreaming and a lot of people get hurt on the way.' She sighs. 'I am so sorry for every dreamer that I had to wake tonight. Worse, I'm sorry for all the nightmares that sacrificed themselves for me. I know you thought that getting March involved was good, William. But it wasn't.'

She returns to her desk, leaning against it and opening a drawer. She takes a familiar object and holds it out to me. Of course it is my notebook. I take it, but as I do, I notice the desk behind her, where there is another familiar object. Beside her own compass, which is a finely carved wooden affair, is March's compass – salt-stained.

It takes me longer than it should to realise how she has it. I remember it falling from March's outstretched hand, tumbling away beneath us and in to the red sea below June's fleet. And suddenly everything about that fight makes sense. I can imagine June here, stood before her incredible windows, conjuring life back into the wooden supports of the *Smog*.

Our plan to find her was doomed from the start. We had assumed that she was on one of her stolen skyships, but she never was. She was below us the whole time.

'Was it worth it?' June asks.

My notebook feels unimportant now.

I know I should do something. Find some way to stop her. But here, before her, I have no answers. I am no Sleepwalker – I do not know how to deliberately conjure my dream. I cannot fight or wake June. I cannot fulfil March's last order.

The bright young dreamer before me shakes her head. 'I still owe you, after everything,' she says. 'I'm going to go ashore, but I'm not going to wake you again. That was cruel of me. So I'm going to have you put back into your cell, and you can spend the rest of your dream in peace.' She steps forward, and with one finger pressed against my chin, gently lifts my head. For a moment I believe that she is going to kiss me again, but she does not. 'You were handsome,' she says, 'when you were young.'

I find my voice at last. 'Why?' I ask.

'Why what?'

'Why do you want to release a nightmare king?'

This causes laughter in the young Sleepwalker. 'A nightmare king? Is that what March told you? It's not a nightmare king, William. That's not why I'm here.'

Another realisation dawns on me. It is a tentative realisation, I am sure, but... it would mean that my last bizarre encounter with Thyme would make a lot more sense. Maybe his story was not just a story. Maybe it was his way of warning me about what really lies at the heart of Solomon's Storm, imprisoned here. I was afraid, before, afraid of the idea that I might be responsible for something as terrible as the release of an ancient nightmare. But this might be so much worse.

'Is it...' I try, '... the Seven Satans?'

June's eyes widen in surprise. 'You've spoken to the prophet?' she asks. 'Oh, William. You are so wonderful. You keep surprising me. You're close, but you're not quite right. They're not called "Satans". You must have misheard, or maybe he was telling you a different version of the story. They're the "Seven Sorrows". And all seven of them aren't imprisoned here. Just one. What else did he tell you?'

'The prophet? You mean Thyme?'

June plays with the golden rings around her fingers as she remembers. 'It took me a long time to find him. There used to be hundreds of liars. You can find stories about them in some of the old books. They were great, once – they shaped dreams with their stories, turning tales into beliefs. But one by one they were killed off. All except Thyme. The last liar. And it's very difficult indeed to find a liar who doesn't want to be found. But I persevered, for the sake of curiosity – the same curiosity that drove me to see what caused the marble beaches of Petra. I'm no nightmare-hunter, William. I'm more of a... historian.

'The thing about liars is that they understand how to

craft the perfect lie. They understand that silly things like admitting to a lie doesn't matter. People will still believe, all the same. But liars also understand that in order for a lie to work, it's best to plant the seeds of truth in it. Enough that the lie will feel real. And it's because of this odd paradox – that a good lie must contain some truth – that made the liars brilliant archivists. Nobody hoarded knowledge and rumours like they did. Which, I hope you understand, is why I sought Thyme out. Not for his lies, but for the ancient truths buried in the lies he tells.'

June smiles at her memory. 'I found him, and he told me such a brilliant lie. Such an amazing, incredible lie. The truth of it was obvious.

'He told me that when our world was yet to be born, when there was nothing but the endless dark sea, where lord Vishnu slept, curled up in the coils of the great serpent Ananta-Shesha, that Vishnu dreamed the first of our dreams. And before lord Vishnu was awoken – when the lotus was still only a green shoot, rising from His belly – He heard the sound that would be our cycle, the great Ohm, and lord Vishnu turned in His sleep. He was moved greatly by the Ohm. And as lord Vishnu dreamed, He wept seven tears for the beauty of that sound, and those seven tears dropped from His cheeks, and rolled over the coils of Ananta-Shesha, and dripped into the endless dark ocean, which was a sea of dreams. Seven tears – seven sorrows – which joined the first dream, and took on shapes. Seven sorrows that still endure, now. Sorrows from the dawn of our world.'

For a few moments our eyes meet, and it feels almost conspiratorial between us. Two dreamers having shared versions of the same tale. The differences between them are vast, but the similarities are obvious. The grain of truth in Thyme's lies is apparent.

'He said something similar to me,' I tell her.

She looks out over the island. The yellow beach is close.

'One of them is imprisoned here,' she tells me. 'All the clues are there for anyone to find, if they know what they're looking for.

'Solomon said that it was a nightmare he couldn't defeat, so he built a cage for it out of fear. But you and I know the truth, William. Maybe it is a nightmare, or maybe it isn't. But the fact is that whatever is imprisoned here is a piece of God. An actual piece of God from the creation of our world, for anyone to meet.' When she turns back to me, her eyes are agleam. 'I'm going to see God,' she says, and then she rushes across to me and embraces me tightly.

I do not return the gesture.

When she releases me, June smiles. 'When I come back, I'll tell you what it looks like. Try to stay asleep.' With a gentle thump, the *Driftwood* meets the sand of the beach and comes to a stop. I glance out at the trees before us and feel a great lump in my throat. I know that I cannot let June open the prison on this island. I know that the version of the tale Thyme told me was not brilliant, but terrifying. 'God's own nightmares', he said.

I know that I have to stop her. But I am powerless.

June calls for someone to take me back to my cell. Then she addresses her crew. 'I'm going out,' she says. 'Dust has command while I'm gone. I shouldn't be long.' She waves to me as I am led away, and I am unable to bring myself to return the gesture. I am frightened of her – frightened of what she might do. Worse, I can do nothing to stop her. I am a useless old man. I feel the strength of my youth slowly ebbing away, and as I am led through the low tree corridors of the *Driftwood*, I feel my hands tingling with affliction.

>•<

Back in my overgrown cell, I watch my hands twitch.

The thing about getting old is that it is very difficult to notice. There is no one day when you wake up and think to yourself, 'I am an elderly man now. I should stop doing all the things I was doing when I was young.' Instead, the things you take for granted begin to slowly get harder, until they become impossible.

I watch the rivers and valleys that are the map of my hands until movement from the other cell rouses me from my self-pity. I see Slint, half in shadow. He appears to be watching me. There is a set of white stitches across his belly where he has repaired himself. I frown, finding that I am no longer afraid of the nightmare diver.

I feel powerless.

After Lily died, I became obsessed with the place where she passed away. I drove the A9 until I knew every yard of it, and I parked up beside the dented barrier where it happened, sifting through the remaining broken glass like an oracle trying to interpret the fall of the bones. As days passed, rain washed the worst away, and men came to repair the barrier and sweep up the last bits of glass, until all traces of her death were gone. It always bothered me how easy it was for the site to return to its former state – just another layby between Perth and Pitlochry – as if it had no significance at all.

I dreamed about coming to rescue her.

I sailed over Scotland in my old patchwork boat. The whole country was flooded with water deep enough to settle above the highest buildings, but everything beneath the waterline was perfectly preserved – there were no fish, and no seaweed to distort the view. From my vantage in my little home-made sailboat, I could see the grass moving with the currents, and the A9 itself, populated with cars missing their drivers.

I followed the road, holding my patchwork boat together with will alone, and I sailed all the way from Perth to the point I had memorised while awake. There, I could see below me the thick traffic, and the collision – the result of an attempted overtake gone wrong. The broken glass from the cars reflected the sunshine, and so did Lily's white dress – a beacon showing me where she lay across the bonnet of her broken vehicle.

Removing my shoes, I dived into the water. Like a pearl-diver, I held my breath until my lungs burned, and I kicked until I reached her, and took her in my arms, and launched myself from the wreckage of her car, with bubbles trailing. I dragged her into my boat, gasping for air and praying that there was still life left in her. But she was already gone. It was the crash that killed her. I held her in my arms, pawing at her face as if I might put the life back into her, and waited there until my dream faded, and I woke, helpless and alone.

My dreams continued, night after night, and I was always too late to save her.

Inscribed into my wrist is the heart for Lily; it looks as fresh as the day it was first done. I remember those itchy, stinging nights afterwards, when she would soothe my skin with kisses, as if she was sealing her love into the scar as it healed.

I never could save Lily in my dream. But this is different.

I clench my fist and watch the heart stretch.

Perhaps I was wrong. Perhaps I do have some strength, in dreaming. Not the power of a Sleepwalker, but the power of my youth. All the wanderlust and heady carelessness, that apparent immortality. I am not sure if I can face June, but sitting here ruminating is not going to do anything. What good is it if I do not even try?

'Slint,' I say, standing, keeping my voice quiet so that the crew outside do not hear me.

There is no response.

I try again. 'Slint. We need to do something about June. Do you think you could break us out of here somehow?' I try to think, to consider what possible advantages we might have. 'Maybe… maybe we could get to the prison before she does. I think I saw it from the air. There's a silver building at the top of the island. And maybe June doesn't know what she's looking for. Maybe it won't show up on her compass. And maybe if we get there first, we could set a trap, or…'

Slint is impassive, a dark statue.

'What are you waiting for?' I ask him, remembering that moment back on the *Smog* when he subdued an entire ship full of nightmares. What does Slint have to fear, here? Not other nightmares, and certainly not any dreamers. What is stopping him? The Sleepwalker? 'June's gone,' I tell him. 'She's not on board any more. She said she was going ashore alone, and that was a while ago now. There are no Sleepwalkers here to—'

And like I have flipped a switch in him, Slint moves.

With terrible ease, he thumps up to the bamboo bars of his cell and crushes them between his gauntlets. Splinters rain down around him, and the ship groans as if wounded. I stumble back as he lumbers across and tears the bars of my own cell apart, snapping them as easily as if they were twigs.

I grab the case of my violin.

Two bearded crewmen rush through, carrying heavy-looking wooden batons. They both stop short when the Slint turns towards them. 'Oh, shit!' says one, and, 'Get back into your cell!' says the other, but the fright etched into each of their faces is clear.

Slint's helmet slowly rotates from one crewman to the other, taking them in with that pit of a porthole; a black pupil set into a gigantic metal eye. He reaches up to his helmet.

The first crewman runs at him brandishing his baton, and with one casual but almighty shove Slint throws that man bodily against a wall, where he bursts apart in the dust of awakening. The other crewman simply stands, frozen in terror, as Slint unclasps the porthole in his helmet. I hear the hideous creaking as its rusty hinges swing back.

From within Slint's porthole comes something... dark.

Black tentacles, or black spider legs, or some kind of black effluence, leaks into the air, and as it exits, his suit begins to deflate. And where glistening wet tentacles might reflect the light, this blackness does nothing of the sort. It is difficult to look at because there is nothing for my eyes to see. It is a virulent darkness – an abyssal blackness – and as Slint's suit diminishes and lolls onto the floor in a useless heap, the nightmare's true form unfolds itself and fills the room, expanding like ink through water.

It devours the light.

A low moan escapes the mouth of the remaining crewman. Like a rushing of sentient water, tentacles of darkness lash out and wrap themselves around him, choking and crushing. I do not see his ultimate fate, because that same dark fills the room, and then the corridor outside, removing all vision, until there is only me – stumbling in the stifling quiet – up against my cell's orange lamp.

I grasp for the lamp, and notice for the first time that there is a bulbous insect trapped inside, with its tail casting a glow. Tentatively I step back out and into the room.

There lies Slint's empty suit, like the discarded skin of a snake. I make my way nervously around it and into the *Driftwood*'s low corridor, glancing to and fro. My lamp barely casts enough light to see by, as if Slint's darkness is a thick thing filling the ship like liquid.

I need to find a way out, an escape. But first I need to return to the ship's bridge. There might be something important there that June chose to leave behind.

The walls around me are groaning mournfully, and the corridors I navigate are dark and empty. I catch flickers of recoiling darkness at the corner of my eye everywhere, retreating from my little lamp. There are no crew, only the remains of their dreaming – repair-work left unfinished, a table thrown aside, lamps without insects.

I can hear screams cut short, but they sound distant. The *Driftwood* is shuddering around me, as if it has swallowed a dark pill that it is unable to spit out.

After far too long in the dark, I finally find the bridge. By now bits of wood are falling, and I can see gaps in the canopy. The bridge is as empty as the rest of the ship – its occupants having awakened – and the dazzling set of windows at its nose are black, as if they have been painted with oil. I head across to June's desk, where I fumble through drawers until I find what I came here for. March's compass. I brandish it, with relief. She was confident enough to just leave it here.

'You!'

A grating voice from behind me. Quickly, I pocket the compass and back away.

Holding my lamp aloft, I can just about make out the shape of Dust. Eerie tentacles of dark lick at him, but he shrugs them off as he advances. The canopy above us is cracking apart, and shards of light fall across his rocky shoulders. 'You broke my ship!' he roars. 'This is your fault!'

I glance around in panic, looking for a way to escape, and there, so slender, is a slit of light between two of the hull's trees. I run across, dropping my lamp and noticing in horror how the glow of it is snuffed instantly. The gap between the trees is shuddering and leaking water. Without another glance back, I try and squeeze through.

I can hear the thumping of Dust as he vaults across the bridge, but with one great heave I slip beyond and splash into the sea.

The light outside is almost blinding. I am in the shallows here; my feet touch sand. I make loping steps, running as quickly as I can until I am free of the water.

The *Driftwood* looks as if it is imploding. From the outside it is like a dying beached whale, its nose buried in the sand. I catch glimpses of tentacle-like flickers of darkness between gaps in the hull, and shudder, even in the bright warmth of the tropical sun. The Sleepwalker's submarine slowly sinks as I run.

From among the ruins lumbers a flailing rocky shape. Dust has freed itself.

Throwing branches and ruined roots aside, Dust pulls itself to its feet and clatters onto the beach. For a moment, I am afraid that it is going to rush me, but then, something else emerges from the ruins of the submarine behind it, stopping it short.

Emerging from the sea, salty waves splashing against his helmet, is Slint, back in his suit. Bits of trees collide uselessly against him as he strides from the waters, advancing towards the stone nightmare with his same casual stride.

I can feel my heart beating in my chest. I am not sure if I should help, or if I can.

One enormous stone fist is launched towards Slint. It meets the nightmare diver in his stomach. But instead of slamming against something solid, it slaps against the rubber, and the suit seems to mould itself around the blow. The nightmare inside that diving suit is not a thing of flesh and blood and bone, and there is nothing to break. Slint barely stumbles. And then Slint raises his gauntlets and retaliates.

He pulls off one of the rocky nightmare's pebble arms. He kicks out with a boot and the stone nightmare's leg is smashed into bits of rock. Limb after limb, Dust is disassembled. As Slint casually pulls the rocky nightmare's lower jaw from its chiselled face, the whole mess of it crumbles away around his heavy boots. Dust is banished.

The fight is over, and Slint shakes his gauntlets twice to clear them of dust before raising one to his closed black porthole protectively, to shade it against the sunlight.

'Slint...' I say, finding my voice.

His helmet swivels around towards me. Behind him, the ruins of the *Driftwood* are bobbing around and gathering on the shore.

It worries me that somewhere out there is someone capable of dreaming Slint.

'We should go,' I tell him. 'While we still have time.'

And at this, he finally gives me a response. His free gauntlet rises, slowly as if he were swimming under water. The tip of his forefinger meets the tip of his thumb to form a loop, fingers splayed behind.

Okay, he is telling me. Okay.

SOLOMON'S EYE

The edge of the jungle is thick and impenetrable. With my feet sinking into sand, I search the island's beaches for a way through. In this manner, I eventually mount a rocky outcrop, and behold the landing site of the crippled *Metronome*.

There are cogs and gears and spars of wood like giant splinters being washed up everywhere. And at the end of a massive furrow ploughed through the sands is the bulk of the wreck: the shredded, glittering edges of what was once a clockwork skyship. Though it is no more than a shape now, like a crushed and beaten clock, I can still see the edge of a golden wing at its buried nose, bent upwards and heralding the rest of the *Metronome*'s figurehead: the fallen phoenix.

It is far too quiet here. I miss the *Metronome*'s tick.

I spot something familiar nearby. Sticking out of a pile of broken television sets and heavy cables is Thyme's sword. It is still wrapped in its leathers, and its silver hilt glints in the light, and for all the world it looks like a symbol of something – a crucifix, perhaps.

I scramble across and pull Thyme's sword free. It is heavier than I thought it would be, but I suppose that I have spent too long watching films where heroes heft their weapons as if they are made of cardboard. Turning the leather of its scabbard over, I wonder about Thyme – awake now, in all probability – and I wonder about the lies he told me. I wonder whether this blade really would burn were I to draw it.

'Have faith,' he said, time after time.

Slint catches up at last and stops behind me. Waiting for my next move. He seems uncomfortable in direct sunlight – smaller, diminished somehow, as if he is just a man in a suit after all – and he observes me with his black porthole shaded beneath a gauntlet.

'I found a sword,' I tell him, as if he might actually offer me an answer. I glance across at the wreck of the *Metronome* again, which is still and quiet, and feel a sharp pang of regret. Then I pull my coat aside and loop the sword's leather scabbard through my belt. There, the sword does not feel as if it is going to cause me to keel over.

'Come on then,' I say to Slint, and continue towards the jungle.

>•<

To the rear of the *Metronome*'s wreck, I come to a long tongue of earth, inviting me into the throat of the jungle. Only, there is a worrying set of heavy drag marks along it. Three parallel furrows begin at the edge of the sand, leading from the skyship's wreck into the dark of the jungle ahead.

Slint looms behind me, and I glance up at him. 'What do you think?' I ask, but of course he gives no answer.

I draw March's compass. There are four needles – one for me, and one for Slint, and two pointing ahead of us. Two more dreamers, somewhere else on the island. One must be for June, but the other is anonymous. 'It could be a survivor,' I say, still unsure. But I suppose that we should check it out, just in case.

It is noisy and busy between the trees, with the croaking of reptiles, the buzzing of insects and the calling of more mysterious creatures from further away. But I am glad to find that we are left alone by the island's wildlife. I put this down to the presence of Slint, who stomps nearly silently from shadow to shadow behind me. Back in shade he is regaining some of his dark majesty.

Before too long a figure emerges ahead of us, walking with a limp.

Heavy-looking chains are bound around the crescent-moon remains of the *Metronome*'s wheel, with its star-pointed spokes causing the strange furrows in the earth. The chains are the means by which it is being dragged, over the shoulder of a wild and almost unrecognisable figure. This figure is so muddied and bloodied that it could be a corpse come to life, and its limp is being caused by its left leg, which is bound tightly around the shin using two copper levers and the shredded remains of a red coat. The figure steps into a pillar of sunshine beaming down through the canopy, and is revealed all at once.

'Captain?' My voice feels too loud.

She turns, her grey hair become a crazed thatch-work around her worn features.

'Manderlay?' she says, and she drops her chains. The wheel falls flat with a thud.

I am too startled to respond when she throws an arm around my shoulder and embraces me. 'You look well,' she says. Then, taking a limping step back, she turns serious. 'You're armed? I'll not have swords and guns and all manner of foolishness aboard my ship. Have you no respect? Throw it overboard, so that we might be free of it!'

My hand hovers over Thyme's sword.

'Captain...' I say, uncertain. 'We're not on board the *Metronome* any more.'

At this point, Slint arrives. I watch him slide from the shadows. In the sun, it looks as if he is stood beneath a shower of light, with the cascading brightness bouncing from his dented helmet.

Far from being daunted by Slint, the Captain glares at him as well. 'Neither of you are in any state to serve,' she says. 'I'll have the Bosun find you some fresh clothes, and Callister bring up something to polish that helm. I may not have the respect of my peers, but I'll have the respect of my damn crew!'

'Captain...' I try again. 'The *Metronome* is gone. I'm sorry.'

This time, Reid seems to pause before reprimanding me. She glares into my face as if I am Solomon's Storm, needing to be conquered. But then, she looks around at the jungle, at the trees and the canopy, at the wheel of the ship fallen behind her. With one bloodied hand, she reaches up to her leathery face and traces the lines of the black tattoo there.

'This is my island?' she asks, tentatively.

'We made it,' I tell her, with a cautious smile. 'You brought us all the way here.'

The Captain nods. 'Then we must go and find my crew.'

'They're awake… They all awoke when the *Metronome* crashed.'

'No. Not them. My crew of old. The crew of the *Sparrowhawk*. I told my captain that I would return here, and so I have. They will be waiting for me somewhere. Murdock, and the rest. They will be waiting.' Captain Reid leans down and makes to grab at the chains, her eyes glassy. 'They have waited long enough.' Before I can respond, she begins to drag her broken wheel through the jungle again.

'Captain!' I cry.

She stops. 'What is it?'

'Your wheel…'

I consider telling Reid the truth. That she is mad. That her old crew are almost certainly gone from this island, because they were just figments from her childhood. That she is dragging the broken wheel of her broken clockwork skyship behind her, and that she should help me instead; she should help me deal with the very real and terrifying problem of June.

Only I do not think that my words would have any effect. Reid's madness is what brought us here: facing the storms and the skyships in between, for the sake of her lost crew. I do not think that I could stop her if I tried. But… there might be another way.

'Why not give your wheel to Slint so that he can carry it?'

The Captain stares. Then she nods. 'Yes,' she says, as if I have spoken perfect sense. 'Why not let the nightmare haul our cargo?'

Between the three of us, we manage to wrap the wheel's chains around the shoulders of Slint's diving suit, so that it is strapped to his back. Its spokes strike up around his shoulders, as if he is a grey cloud and the wheel is the sun beaming behind him.

'And if I can make another suggestion,' I say, feeling as if I am gaining momentum as I search around for a lengthy branch she can use as a crutch. 'Perhaps it might be worth us heading upwards, to higher ground, so that we can see more of the island. That way we have a better chance of spotting your crew.' I find a thick branch that seems to be about the right length, and work the wood to snap it. 'What do you think?'

When I glance across at the Captain, I see that her stern features are arranged into something that might actually resemble a smile. 'I say that you are a man of sound mind, Manderlay. Higher ground, it is. Lead away!' She thumps me hard across my shoulder. 'And perhaps we shall have you play a tune for Murdock when we find him. For he is a man known to appreciate a good song!'

Through the jungle we three tread, through tough thickets and murky, swampy patches of mud where claw-marks grate the ground. The air is thick around us but the native wildlife continues to avoid our advance. Slint is our vanguard, the dark diver pushing the undergrowth away with his heavy gauntlets. He barely seems to feel the wheel strapped to his back.

I watch June's needle twitch on March's compass. We are slowly gaining on her.

Almost all at once, we come to a wall: a sheer rocky face blocking our path up to the slopes of the island's central peak. Nearby, the slivering shimmer of a waterfall is visible.

We head towards it, hoping for some means of ascent.

From different heights gush pearlescent streams, turned into faceted droplets and sprays by the depths they fall, brilliant rainbows above each one. Trees perilously grip gaps in the rock face, glinting in their eternal dampness. And at their base is a row of ragged openings that give way to complete darkness.

The first cave yawns before us. Potentially a way up.

'Slint…' I say. 'Maybe you could scout? See if there's a way through?'

The nightmare diver unchains the *Metronome*'s wheel and sets it down beside Reid, perched upon a rock to rest. Then, without hesitation, he plunges into the darkness beneath the falls. It is an eerie sight to behold – how the shadows welcome him – and realisation grips me. Slint's suit is not meant to protect him from water, or from the darkness he inhabits. Slint's suit protects him from the light.

I shiver beneath the warm sun.

Reid rests with her hand upon her wheel, eyes unfocused. Her damp hair clings to her shoulders, but I am glad to see that some of the blood and grime smearing her is being washed away by the falls. There is a dry, flat rock beside her, and I place my violin case upon it. I take another look at March's compass.

The bright Sleepwalker, June, is ahead of us again, but I would wager that we are close to catching up. I feel nervous at that thought, because I have no idea what we are going to do when we meet her. Try to wake her if she cannot be reasoned with, I suppose. Whatever it takes. I glance down at the sword at my side and sigh. I have never tried to use a sword before, but it is the only weapon we have.

'Captain,' I say, and she frowns at me as if I am a stranger. 'This might be a funny question… but what do you have against weapons?'

For a moment, I am not certain that she has heard me. But then she speaks, measuring her words. 'Before the *Metronome*, I spent an age captaining for the *Wordhoard*. She was a fine vessel – as sleek and quick as a barracuda across the waves. We set our station between Castra and the Golden Gate, and there we darted from ship to ship and fought and plundered, night after night, until our holds were full.

'Grand times, they were. I was glorious, then. But understand: I was no pirate of doors. We took only books, and maps, and scrolls. Words were our plunder and we had our fill. We became traders of information, so bloated with books we were as sharp as knives. But for all that…

'I learned little of what I actually sought. Scraps of information about Solomon's Eye, and nothing more. No maps or charts or accounts. And beyond that, I learned that there was little in awakening for me either. That asleep and dreaming, I was mighty and brilliant – a legend, perhaps – and awake, I was nothing and nobody.

'But beyond all else, I realised how easy it is to wake, to be forced back to banality. A single strike is enough to fright a sleeping mind to awakening.

'There is no greater target than an armed dreamer. Point a gun, and it is almost inevitable that a gun will be pointed back at you. It is far more prudent to run – to dream on and see greater sights. And it was in this manner that my crew and I gave up our piracy, and dreamed longer for it. We forged the faster *Metronome*, speeding through the skies too quick to wake.'

I think that I understand Reid a bit better, now. While I am unfamiliar with the sword at my side, it is guns that make me truly uncomfortable.

In the years I spent travelling, I had many guns pointed at me, but the worst instance was in Philadelphia. I had a scattering of days off in Philadelphia a few decades ago, and I decided to wander the city a while, to take in the atmosphere of it. What I found was a bright but troubled metropolis, equal shades shining lamps and deep pools of dark. It was in one of those pools of dark that a man came towards me with a pistol.

I looked down the barrel of his gun, and I was terrified.

I gave him my wallet, and it was enough to send him on his way. But the encounter made me introspective, made me respect the weapon. I did not feel worthy of it, and that unworthiness stemmed from just how easy it would have been for me to die then and there. My life snatched away in an instant, as easily as waking from a dream. I never wanted the responsibility of possessing something so easily devastating.

Running my hands across the case of my violin brings me comfort. I unlatch it and open it wide, hoping that my instrument has been spared the worst. Thankfully, it has. By some miracle, my violin is whole and dry. I give silent thanks to whoever it was who designed the case.

'What happened to the *Wordhoard*?' I ask Reid.

She blinks, remembering. 'When I found Callister, we took the *Wordhoard* apart. She became the basis for a far greater vessel. You'll still see parts of her in the *Metronome*, if you look close enough. I never imagined I'd fly. None of us did. But we soar. Oh, how we soar...'

Removing my instrument from its alcove, I tune it. The

tuning does not take long, and it helps to calm my nerves. It helps me to forget about June for a moment.

'And what about the books you stole?'

Reid's leathery features crinkle into a proud smile.

'I have them all, still. Hidden away. The greatest library in all of dreaming, or so they say.'

I idly pluck at my violin, glancing at the dark caves and wondering how much longer it will take for Slint to return. Reid is staring glassy-eyed at the falls once more. I read the notes etched into her weathered features – that strange little song – and I mouth them, and as I do, I pluck them. I play the song tattooed into Captain Reid's face, and smile to hear it, because it is a pretty little dancing tune. A simple, pretty melody.

The island answers.

A great, all-encompassing sound fills the air, and the trees around us swish to its rhythm. The noise is tremendous and woodwind, as if someone is playing an awesome wooden flute from somewhere above. The silver prison, perhaps. The song hums through the rocks beneath my feet, and vibrates the droplets of the waterfall, causing it to dance. It is the same song, the song I just played. Reid's song.

The song lasts for as long as it lasts. Then silence, a fresh pause in the air, like a question mark, until I hear the waterfall as it finally comes back into the world, rushing and gushing and retaining its overpowering grip on local sound. I turn on the spot, violin at my side, laughing at what has just occurred. I know that it was wonderful, remarkable, brilliant, and that I do not understand it.

When I look at Reid, she is weeping, and I do not know if it is in joy or sorrow.

><•<

We emerge from the caves and into the light.

Ahead of us is the bare face of all that remains of the mountain, and never have I seen such an enormous sun. The top of the mountain is cut off in one great line where the basin of the volcano begins, and it is upon that line the sun sits, as if it is resting within its crater.

Before that overwhelming light, Slint is humbled. The only reminder of his true nature is his shadow, vast behind him. It is warm enough up here that I do not need my coat, so I offer it across to him, and he accepts it wordlessly, pulling it across his helmet and forming a sort of tent around his porthole window.

Reid is glaring back at the view behind us. From here, the island looks like it flounders heavily in the sea, as if it is a sunken wreck. In the far distance the horizon is a ring of deep black, where the storm writhes eternally around its hidden eye. 'I can see no ships from here,' she remarks, leaning heavily against her crutch.

'A little further,' I tell her, and she frowns at me, perhaps sensing my deception.

We toil on, and not far ahead we come to the ragged edge of a broken road. It is wide, dusty and ancient, made completely out of black stone. It is the end of the black road, leading to the top of the mountain. The antithesis of the yellow-brick road.

I glance at March's compass. June's needle is steady – it looks as if she is waiting for us ahead. She will have certainly seen us on her own compass. I conceal March's compass as best I can in a pocket, just like the first time I met June. It would not do to lose the young Sleepwalker's device again.

We come to a set of ruins, built into a rocky plateau near the walled rim. They look bleached and flattened by the power of the burning celestial giant in the sky. We walk the plateau, the black line of the road leading us beyond those time-worn ruins and up to the wall that surrounds the volcano's rim.

Finally, we find ourselves before a tremendous open archway. While gargantuan in size, perhaps five times the height of a man, it is half sunken into the ground and rests at an angle, so that its peak is off-kilter. It is a compass needle pointing in the wrong direction.

Waiting for us beneath the arch is June.

'You shouldn't have come, William,' she says. She has something at hand which might be a pebble, manipulating it as she watches us. Her whole form shimmers as she stands, her back to the awesome sun.

'I had to,' I tell her. 'I have to stop you.'

June scowls at me, and then turns to Reid. 'I'm glad you're here,' she says. 'Really. I have a lot of respect for you, Captain. I've heard all the stories.' June smiles. 'I'm glad I have the opportunity to apologise to you, in fact. I don't like having to wreck ships. I had to wake March, though – he left me no choice. I had to destroy the *Metronome* – and wake everybody on board – just to make sure he couldn't follow me any more. I am sorry for your loss, truly, and I hope to make it up to you. When this is over, I'll take you back to Babel.'

Reid's face is a complex network of shadows. She leans against her crutch and regards June steadily, but gives no reply.

'Slint,' says June, turning her attentions to the nightmare diver. 'I spared you because I really don't like having to banish nightmares. I still don't. Which is why, even in the light of the fact that you being here means you've done something terrible to my crew, I'm going to give you one last chance. So listen carefully. I want you to wake William. I'm done with him.' She gestures at me with the object in her hand. 'Then, once I'm done here, I'll take you back to Babel as well.'

I take a step back from Slint.

His helm swivels around so that he faces me. The rest of him follows. At once, I manoeuvre the case of my violin over my shoulder and place my hand on the hilt of the sword at my hip. 'Please don't,' I tell him. 'Please.' And yet he advances, slowly lumbering across the cracked ground.

Slint reaches up and frees the chains from his shoulders, letting my coat drift free and flutter away. He grips hold of the *Metronome*'s half-moon wheel and brings it before him, bearing it like a makeshift club.

I reach out with my free hand, taking another step back. 'Slint!'

He raises his weapon. At the last moment, he turns and throws it with all of his might at June. The wheel hurtles through the air towards her.

Crying out in surprise, she snaps her idle hand around to bear on the spinning projectile. The wheel bursts, devoured in an instant by what looks like fungus. A shower of mushrooms patter across her yellow dress.

Still, the Sleepwalker is startled. Even as Slint sprints towards her, thundering with his heavy boots, it takes her a moment longer to recover.

Her face changes, curling into anger.

June throws the object she was holding. I catch a glimpse of it as it rolls towards Slint. It is not a pebble, or a marble, after all. It is an acorn. The instant it touches the ground beneath his feet, it erupts.

The tree grows in fast-forward, exploding from its acorn in an instant. Branches as sharp as knives puncture the suit of the nightmare diver, one in each arm, one in each leg, and another through the stomach. The new tree winds around until he is brought to face the sun. Slint is crucified.

'No!' I cry, and rush towards him. Too late, I realise that it is foolish for me to try and help. Too late, I see the Sleepwalker's attentions turn on me instead, and her hands raise towards me. There is no need for her to throw another acorn. I am already carrying a length of wood that she can use to hurt me.

I feel the pressure against my back, and the force of the conjuring as it sends me flying through the air, landing hard on the black road. The air is knocked from my lungs as I impact, but it is nowhere near as bad as the sudden pain of loss. The realisation of what she has done to me.

My violin. She has used my violin.

I roll over to see the tree as it blooms from the case. I watch the strings as they snap, clinging on to the new bark. I watch the bow as it is warped in twain before becoming its own small sapling.

Feeling the thudding of my heart in my head, still gasping for breath, my distress turns to anger. It turns to a white-hot rage that burns through me, burns through my veins. And it is with no thoughts, only anger, that I draw Thyme's sword.

The searing white flames that gush from the red-hot blade blind me, but still I stand. I turn about, until I can see the shape of the Sleepwalker as she reaches into her satchel, drawing out more acorns. There is a look across her face now that might be uncertainty, but still she stands her ground. And with a flick of her wrist, she sends acorns flying towards me.

I begin to run towards her. To close the gap.

I am no swordsman; I have nothing but rage for what she has done to my instrument. But as the first tree erupts from the ground at my feet, I slash wildly with the burning blade, and see blackened branches as they fall away.

It is the second tree that catches me. I am quick to slash it out of the way, but not quite quick enough. Though I am not impaled, the sudden trunk of the tree slams into me and sends me sprawling. The sword is loosed from my grip as I hit the ground harder than before, my senses jarred by the sudden impact. The heat in my veins remains, but I have no breath left to breathe. I am a fish floundering for air.

The sword spins, a burning arc, and hisses into the cracked earth blade-first nearby, scorching it instantly. Still its bright flames crackle. I try to crawl across, to reach for it, but my chest feels like it might burst. I am struggling to stay asleep.

A different hand clutches at the hilt of the blade.

'For many an age,' says the Captain, 'I have not allowed arms aboard my ship. Night after night my crew and I have slept long and deep, kept dreaming by my words alone.' She throws her crutch away, and I watch it clatter down the slope. Then, Captain Reid pulls the burning blade from the ground. She tests its weight in her hand, and arcs it around with the skill of an experienced fencer. And with her bad foot behind her, she lowers herself into a stance, the blade pointed towards June.

'For you,' she says, flames reflecting in her eyes, 'I make an exception.'

The Sleepwalker throws another acorn, wildly. Reid turns the burning blade in a close arc, and where a tree erupts from its acorn, she cuts it cleanly. The edges of the cut catch fire, and the tree falls away. With her leg bound, the Captain advances slowly but inevitably towards June.

June still stands her ground, but she looks frightened now, fumbling around for more acorns. 'You have no idea!' she cries. 'You don't know what you're doing!'

The expression across the Captain's face is fierce, mirroring the burning blade in her hand. The next two acorns clatter to the ground at the Captain's feet.

'You wrecked my ship!' snarls Reid, and cuts the first tree in two.

'You woke my crew!' she snarls again, and slices the second tree away.

The Captain lunges, a brilliant leap, delivering a bright arc all the way across from her shoulder, until it clatters against the stone of the slanted arch.

June stares wordlessly down at the cut through her torso, burned black from the bright blade, then back up at Captain Reid, a moment of absolute terror crossing through her, just like the sword did. Then, she wakes.

The Sleepwalker bursts into dust, and the trees she conjured do the same, leaving only the splintered remains of my violin and the shapeless suit of Slint as it hits the ground, pierced rubber wobbling.

I finally catch a gasp of breath as the Captain falls to her knees, the bright blade of the sword planted into the hard ground beside her. She holds on to the hilt so that it can take her weight. And there, kneeling as if she is praying, she clenches her free fist.

Standing unsteadily and clutching hold of my chest, I limp across.

'Captain?'

'My crew,' she says, between gritted teeth. 'Now, we must find my crew.'

MURDOCK

I repair Slint.

Tugging at my shoelaces, I use them to tie up two of the tears running through his suit. Otherwise, the only materials I can find are the scattered pieces of my violin. Using lengths of horsehair from my bow to puncture the rubber and pull it together, I then use the four strings that once stretched the length of my instrument as well. The tear through the suit's chest, right above where Slint's heart should be, glints gold instead of steel.

With the last few rips sewn up, my fingers bleeding from handling thin wires, Slint fills out the rest of his suit again, that flabby, flopping rubber expanding out from his helmet as if there is a liquid pouring down. Slint rises as if from the dead.

Reid is watching the distant waves that coil around the island. She is frowning.

'They must be here, somewhere,' she says, but she no longer sounds certain.

Thyme's sword is sheathed at my side, and with the loss of its bright hot fire, so too my rage has dissipated. I am now a musician without an instrument, but I do not mind. I am still asleep, and June is awake.

Slint limps up to join us. One of his legs is now slightly shorter than the other – the rubber having to be rolled up to fill in the gaps – and the entirety of his left arm is gone, gauntlet tied to a knot at his shoulder.

I am beginning to feel weary. There is a tiredness in my legs, in the soles of my feet, and my chest still hurts with every breath I make. Yet, it is not a wholly unpleasant weariness. I feel as if I have earned my bruises, every one.

We watch the island below us for a while.

'Maybe,' I say, eventually, 'we should go and see what all the fuss was about.'

Limping and dragging our feet, we venture up to the slanted arch – that broken compass needle pointing at the sky – and cross into the dormant volcano's basin, where the black road eels into the dark earth beyond. The temperature drops immediately.

The silver prison looms ahead of us, casting a mighty shadow.

It is a huge and bizarre crystalline structure, so faceted with walls and peculiar angles of architecture that it shines diamond-like. Cyclopean in its height and proportions, it dwarfs us – reflecting us a thousand distorted times. It even dwarfs the sun, which seems small and distant behind its tallest twisted towers. Dust cakes the lower walls, and while there are glimpses of the intricate carvings once etched into it, most have been worn away by time.

In all regards, the prison looks like it might just be one

enormous chunk of ice. It has no windows, and from its highest edges it looks lumpy and melted; there is no telling if it was ever built out of silver bricks, or if it was simply carved out of one gargantuan nugget of silver. Every surface glitters with condensation and the hard earth at its base crackles with frost. A little condensation rises from its jagged heights, wisping against the blue sky.

The black road curls away around it to some hidden entrance, no doubt.

'It must be ice-silver...' I say, remembering what November said: the metal that nightmares loathe even to touch.

It takes me a small while to realise that there is movement below, on the grounds between the black road and the prison. It looks like there is an entire graveyard filling the base of the volcano. I can see rows of earthen mounds, coated in the same frost as the rest of the crater, and above each one a small wooden cross.

Among the rudimentary graves is a small dark figure, stumbling as if its legs are too stiff. It moves among the graves as if it has risen from one of them. Quickly, I fumble around for March's compass, but there is no needle pointing below. There are only three needles here: one for me, one for Slint, and one for Reid. That corpse-like creature must be a figment.

'Murdock?' says Captain Reid beside me, almost too softly to hear. Then, she is stumbling down the slope towards him. I glance up at Slint, who remains his usual impassive self, and then the two of us follow after her, navigating the scarred and icy slope towards the graveyard.

Up close, the shambling figure looks almost dead. It is ghostly pale, and little more than skin and bones beyond the black greatcoat draped across its wiry shoulders. Its cheeks are sunken and its white hair is thin where it clings to its skull. In one hand it drags a shovel, and when it catches sight of the Captain with its hollow eyes, it stops in its tracks. Its gormless mouth remains open, as if it is struggling to breathe.

'Isabelle?' it wheezes.

The Captain stops before him. 'Murdock...' she says. 'I came back. My captain – I came all the way back for you and the crew.' I can hear the wavering emotion in her voice, like nothing I have heard from her before. She sounds... childish. Keening. 'All the way from Babel,' she says, 'we crossed the seas. I gathered my own crew, Murdock. I had my own ship built. All for you. And I'm sorry it took so long, but I'm here. I'm here now.'

The corpse man's shoulders drop, as does his head.

'Isabelle...' he moans, a graveyard groan. 'Let me die. Please, let me die.'

Reid glances around, at the prison and all the graves, her brows knotted. 'Where are the crew?' she asks. 'Where is everyone, Murdock?'

With more strength than I could imagine in the shambling figure, he raises his shovel in both hands, and plants it firmly in the nearest grave. 'Nought but dust, but I marked them still. We waited, Isabelle.' The icy ground cracks around the blade. 'We all waited for you,' he wheezes. Then, he lurches forward, reaching out with one of his skeletal hands. He places his skull-like head against her shoulder and holds her in an embrace.

'Let me die,' he whispers with his parched voice. 'Please. It has been so long.'

There is a long quiet in the graveyard before Reid responds. 'I am... too late?'

The shambling man crumbles to dust. The grey stuff pours down Reid's arm, and I am sure that I hear a hiss of relief as it goes. The corpse-like creature called Murdock turns to nothing at all.

Only his coat is left behind: a great black coat with tarnished silver buttons. I watch as Reid kneels and picks it up from the ground, shaking it free of grey dust before pulling it over her shoulders. By some miracle it fits. She turns back to us, and there is that same familiar stern expression across her features. The only remnant left of her encounter with Murdock is a single tear, still trailing down her leathery face, all the way to the edge of her chin.

'I have found my crew,' she says, and she grips hold of the shovel's hilt where it stands, still buried in the ground. There are maybe a hundred graves here. I wonder what I should say, but I have no words.

'Time to find our way home,' says Reid, quieter, and she releases the shovel.

We follow the black road back up to the slanted arch.

Where it meets the lip of the volcano, something catches my eye. There is a crimson glistening across the dusty black surface of the road that I must have missed before. I crouch down to see. The substance is oily – still wet – and spattered in a trail that leads back down and into the volcano, following the road.

'Blood?' says Reid.

I follow the road with my eyes, watching it curl around to a hidden corner of the prison. 'It can't be June,' I say. We all saw her wake, chopped in two. I draw March's compass, but its face is empty except for the needles pointing to us three, and this blood certainly does not belong to any of us. It is a mysterious trail, freshly laid. I am hesitant to follow it.

'Come now,' says the Captain. 'Someone may be in need of aid.'

Warily, I tow behind Reid, who stands taller within her new black coat. Behind us, Slint shuffles to keep up. If Reid is the Dorothy of the black road, and Slint is the tin man, then what does that make me? The brainless scarecrow or the cowardly lion? Worse, does that make me Toto? Perhaps it is my weariness, but I find myself chuckling at the absurdity of it.

At last we reach the end of the black road.

It comes to a halt before an almighty set of double doors. They are huge, maybe three times my height, and set deep into the icy silver prison. The divide between them – a line through the silver – is only ornamental: they are well and truly sealed, and all around their edges, a frosting of deep ice keeps them airtight. Whatever hinges they may have are inside, and whatever carvings and inscriptions once covered them have been worn to a mirror flatness.

Sat with his back against them is Thyme.

It takes me a moment to realise that he is not dead. The old knight is so bloodied and torn that he is almost a parody of life; it is bizarre that his chest should still rise and fall. What little there is left of his white tabard is torn to bloody shreds, and there are great splintered chunks of wood sticking out of him everywhere.

'Thyme?' I rush across.

The last liar opens his blood-encrusted eyelids to reveal reddened eyes. This close to the ice-silver prison, I can feel the terrible chill of it. Where Thyme has his back against the metal a seal of frost coats him. It is no wonder that he shivers and shudders.

'Ah,' he says, throatily. 'Manderlay the Bard.'

'Do you know this man?' asks Reid. She stands behind me.

I do not think that this is the right time to reveal that Thyme was stowing away aboard the *Metronome*. The countless pieces of wood splintered into him must be bits of her broken hull. He must have dragged himself all the way up here after she fell from the sky.

'This is Thyme,' I tell the Captain, hoping that she will not enquire. 'He's a friend of mine.'

I lean forward, attempting to free Thyme from the icy surface of the prison, but he shakes his head. 'Nay,' he protests. 'I am done. Leave me, my friend. I only wished to behold this – the edge of the road that leads all the way from Babel to here. I only wished to sate my curiosity, and so I have. Leave me here, and return hence to thy tower and doors. I am done.' He coughs weakly.

Glancing back at Reid, I see that she is no longer concerned by Thyme. She is preoccupied with her own ailment. Sat upon a chunk of stone, she is unwinding the bindings from her splinted leg, and where flesh is revealed, it looks clean. 'Come then,' she says. 'I should like to reach the Golden Gate before I wake, and we have much work to do building ourselves a new ship.' She tests her leg, and it seems strong again.

I turn back to Thyme. 'Are you sure?' I ask him, but I remember what March said of injured people in dreaming. That it is better just to let them wake than keep them asleep and in agony.

'I am certain,' he says. 'Only...'

'What is it?'

'My sword. I see ye have my sword. Leave it here, I beg thee. Thou canst not leave a knight without his weapon, surely!' He coughs again, spraying blood with his spittle. 'Repay thy debt to me,' he says.

I unbuckle the leather-bound sword from my side, and hand it over. In truth, I am glad that I am able to leave it behind. Then I stand. I am not sure what else there is for us to do here. Reid is ready and waiting, freed of her bindings, and she looks impatient to be gone. And Slint is nearby, with his helm swivelling back and forth, looking uncomfortable beside the ice-silver prison. I am not sure what else I can say to Thyme before we leave, so I settle for, 'Goodbye, then.'

Thyme simply nods, clutching weakly at his sword.

Hesitantly, we make to leave, and it takes me far longer than it should to realise exactly why I am so hesitant. Again, I draw March's bulky metal compass, and again I see that there are only three needles upon its surface. Thyme does not have a needle. I pause, wondering what it means. If Thyme is not dreaming, or a nightmare, then he must be a figment. But what kind of figment? And if Thyme is a figment, then just who is dreaming him?

I turn back, just in time to see the old knight stand, ice tumbling from his back.

Across his bloody face is his wolfish grin. He clutches at the hilt of his sword.

'I saw thee!' he cries. 'I saw thee on the rise, whenst thou drewest my dull blade and gave it light! Thou art the spark, Manderlay the Bard, that ignites the blade! Thy faith is fire, and thy faith shall be rewarded! I promise thee, thy faith shall be rewarded a thousand-fold!'

When Thyme draws his sword the white fires gush again around it, and too late I realise what it is for, the purpose of all his lies about it. His sword is not just a weapon.

I try to run across, to throw myself at him and stop him from doing what he is about to do, but there is no time. I can only stumble short and watch in horror as he raises the red-hot blade, flames licking at the sky, and brings it down in a clean arc.

The divide between the doors melts like butter. With a clink, the burning blade meets the ground, and the severance is done. Thyme's sword was never just a weapon. It was a key.

There is a pause, like the world is taking a great breath, before the enormous silver doors slam inwards, sending shards of ice spinning. With the sudden rushing of air, Thyme falls to his knees. Beyond the doors is a terrible blackness. I am awed and terrified by the open prison. On his knees, Thyme raises his free hand and his bloody face, still grinning that wretched grin, as if in tribute to the thick dark before him.

There comes a terrible shape from the black.

Titanic fingers emerge, followed by the rest of a giant human hand, all of which barely squeezes through the gaping opening. Where that horrifying appendage taps the ground, searching, it causes the earth to tremble and jump. And beyond, in the dark, I can just about make out the wrist joining the monstrous hand to something impossibly huge.

The hand sweeps ponderously around until it finds Thyme, and it snatches him up like a rag doll in the hand of a child. The last liar is pulled into the open prison, leaving nothing behind but his manic, echoing laughter, and the burning sword, which clatters to the ground, still bright.

Then nothing. Nothing but the darkness and my horror.

The ancient prison has been opened.

We stand in silence for a long time. The opening of the prison remains dark and no more horrifying creatures emerge. I suppose I had been expecting the advance of an obviously evil figure, something with horns and hooves, wearing a cloak of shadows and a crown of bone. When March talked about nightmare kings, I imagined terribly warped visions of monarchs with cruelty in their eyes, and when Thyme talked about God's own nightmares I imagined fallen angels and demonic chthonians. But there is nothing. Nothing but the horror of the empty darkness and the memory of the titanic hand.

'I need to go after him,' I say.

Reid watches the dark beyond the open prison doorway and shakes her head. 'You would be a fool to do so, Manderlay. I have read hints of what lies within: an unnamed beast from beyond time, an invention of madness, an aspect of something that should have remained forgotten. Whatever you owe your friend, it's not worth confronting whatever occupies that darkness.'

I glance at Slint, as if he will offer an answer.

'I can't just leave him.'

'Return to Babel with me,' says the Captain. She is standing tall again. Her stature is regal within her new black coat, and when she regards me, she does so soberly, as if some internal storm of madness has lifted within her. 'Dream the rest of your dream sailing the skies. We'll gather the crew and find new horizons to venture, free of Sleepwalkers and their quarrels.'

The offer is very tempting.

'If I'm quick, I can find Thyme and we can all leave together.'

'You and I both know if you enter that prison, you won't be leaving it.' The fallen burning sword casts weird shadows and reflections across the ice and silver encrusting the gaping mouth of the open cage. I watch those flames flicker.

I retrieve my old notebook from its pocket, and flick through its ear-marked pages. The songs that led us here are still all intact. 'Here,' I say, and I offer it out to Captain Reid. 'All the songs you'll need to find your way back. Just follow them in reverse order.'

She takes the book with a nod of thanks. 'I'll return to the beach, then, see how much I can salvage of the *Metronome*. Mayhap a raft with enough of a tick to weather the storm and seas from here to the Golden Gate. But I'll walk slow, Manderlay. I'll take my time. Find your friend. Run quick enough and you might catch me before I'm gone.'

'Thanks, Captain.'

We shake hands. I turn to Slint. He is observing me through his pitch-black porthole. 'It's up to you,' I tell him. 'I'd be grateful for your help, but if you'd rather go with the Captain, then I won't blame you.'

The dark diver gives me no response, but he follows when I approach the prison entrance. I am glad that he has decided to come along.

I stoop before the almighty dark of the prison and grab the burning sword by its hilt. Its heat is a comfort against the chill, and by its light I intend to try and navigate the interior. With a deep breath, I advance, taking one last glance back at Reid before she leaves, black coat billowing around her, head up high.

The burning sword illuminates silver walls, casting my reflection back at me a hundred times. I can feel the cold of the ice-silver floor through my shoes.

A few steps inside and I realise that Slint is not following. I turn to see that he is having trouble at the entrance. When he attempts to tread the silver ground of the prison a terrible wreathing of frost grips his boot. He snaps his foot back as if he has trodden on something sharp. The ice-silver is hurting him.

'Go with Reid!' I call to him. 'And... thanks. Thanks for everything, Slint.'

He is still for a moment. I can see the glint of the gold across the chest of his suit, where the string from my violin holds him together. He is slanted, with one leg shorter than the other.

When he raises his single remaining arm, he folds his hand into that same universally recognisable symbol from before. Forefinger to thumb, other fingers splayed. Okay, Slint is saying, one more time. Okay.

THE MAGICIAN

This is a strange place.

Where I tread the crystalline passage my feet cause musical echoes, as if the walls are chimes. The cold is bitter and relentless, and my teeth are chattering despite my proximity to the burning sword. I have left the prison's entrance long behind, and now the sword's flames are the only light source, reflected from a thousand uneven silver surfaces back at me.

'Thyme?' I call. My voice echoes weirdly.

The passage is gradually sloping downwards. I keep both hands around the hilt of Thyme's sword, pointed at the dark as if I might divide it in two. I descend into the depths of the ancient prison this way, dearly wishing that I could have just left with Reid. But I need to find out what has happened to Thyme. I owe him that much.

The passage starts to open up. The ceiling slowly lifts away, along with the walls, until they are a distant glinting, and then nothing at all. I am surrounded by the dark, with only the cold silver floor beneath me. At first the echoes of my footfalls sound scattered and strange, as if I am navigating through a dark church, and then a cathedral, but then the echoes stop altogether. When I call out, my voice sounds so small.

'Thyme? Where are you?'

I draw March's compass and examine its face, but there are no answers there. Dozens of needles turn and spin aimlessly, some in colours I have not seen before. As I watch them dance, a hairline fracture cracks the glass. Quickly I find a handkerchief and wrap the compass up, hoping to save it from further damage.

I carry on, shivering in the cold.

Hunched against the dark, I notice that the path is beginning to thin. On both sides, I can see a ragged, crystalline edge with a drop beyond, and as I continue it slowly draws in. Eventually, the path becomes barely wide enough to contain me, and I find myself sweeping the sword over the perilous emptiness to either side as if I might banish the dark. But there is nothing. Nothing but me and the thin ice-silver road, thinning into nothingness.

Then, the road stops altogether.

I am confronted by a profound darkness. The path stops at a knife-sharp edge, as if it is pointing into the abyss. I am humbled by that emptiness. It gnaws at my extremities, numbing me, and I realise that I am blinking frost away from my eyes. Even the burning sword's flames crackle low across its blade.

'Thyme?' I try, but the silence swallows my call.

As I go to turn back, defeated by the empty prison with its impossible geography, I catch sight of something below.

Kneeling at the edge of the road, I hold the sword aloft and illuminate a surface down there. It looks like wrinkled cloth, spread across the ground a few feet below. A way forward, after all. I lower myself as far as I am able over the edge, and let myself drop.

An eternity in the dark before I land. Hauling myself back up to my feet, I examine this new place by the wavering flames of Thyme's sword, which are now blue.

While the air is still bitterly cold, this surface is warm and uneven, and the burgundy cloth spread across it rolls off to either side of me. There is a slope, and I imagine that this is a new path through the prison. I descend along it.

There is a faint booming that at first I mistake for my own heart beating. I stop a moment, turning to and fro to try and locate the source of the slow beat, before crouching, and feeling the ground tremble. The rhythmic thudding is coming from beneath the cloth – from the path itself. Warily, I stand.

A deep voice rumbles from somewhere beyond.

'*I see you,*' it says.

Suddenly there is a great, warm wind gushing at me. I struggle to remain standing as it gets stronger and stronger, pushing me forward. The flames of the burning sword gutter, and in one horrifying moment are extinguished, leaving nothing but a slightly glowing blade. Then complete blackness, and I am tumbling through it, driven on by that powerful warm wind, rolling down the path and crying out in confusion and fright. Somehow I manage to keep hold of Thyme's sword, but I am unable to get a grip on the path.

I come to a halt. The ground is warm and leathery, but no longer sloped. I spend a few moments simply catching my breath on my back and letting my eyes adjust. There is light here. It is only a small beacon, a distant orb above like a burning yellow light bulb, but it illuminates me and the strange pillars that surround me.

Wavering, I stand, and turning on the spot, I realise with horror what those pillars are. There are five of them – fingers. The surface I am standing on is a gigantic palm, and the faint booming I can hear even clearer now is the beating of a titanic heart, forcing blood through veins like pipes. Desperately I look for a means of escape, but I am trapped here, caged in by the fingers around me. Thyme's sword is no use; it no longer burns.

'Where is Thyme?' I cry.

The tremendous voice rumbles again, vibrating through me. '*Thyme never existed. He was an idea, an idle thought, a piece of me. If it's any comfort, he's a part of me again now. I know him inside and out. And he's very grateful for your help. We both are.*'

There is movement beneath me, and I fall back to the ground. The giant hand is moving: ascending. Its fingers widen, allowing me a better view. I am drawn close to the burning orb, and for a moment I find myself hypnotised by it. It looks so familiar, but I only realise why when I catch sight of the dark orbs spinning around it.

'*I wanted to show you,*' says the voice. '*I wanted you to see.*'

'Is that… Is that a solar system?'

There is a deep rumbling that might be assent. '*I made them a long time ago. They live on the third planet. All they do is quarrel and pray and die. There isn't a single original thought among them. It's like a mirror. It's like I've been watching me kill myself for eternities. Endlessly dull.*' The voice pauses. I try and locate the third planet from the sun, but it is difficult to tell.

'*Recently,*' says the voice, '*I've been plucking the stars from their sky, one by one. But all it did was make them kill each other faster.*' There is a sound that might be an avalanche, or might be laughter. '*They've been blaming each other for it. Not enough prayers, not enough offerings, not enough faith. But it's all pointless. A dull game. A predictable, boring game. This is what I've been reduced to. This is what you've saved me from.*'

I feel a terrified awe gripping me.

Another giant hand comes into view. It encompasses the solar system hanging in the dark, and with no more than a squeeze, snuffs the whole lot out like a candle. '*Enough of that,*' rumbles the voice. '*I'm free now, thanks to you. No more of that nonsense.*'

My breath catches in my throat. 'But…' I manage.

'*Don't worry about them. They were nothing but idle thoughts – idle dreams, like your friend Thyme. We can always make more if we need to.*' The hand beneath me shifts again, and I realise that even though that small sun is gone, there is still something casting light in the dark. Inevitably, I am drawn to the other source of light, which is white and flickering.

It is an eye. A gargantuan eye, full of static light, as if it is an enormous oval television screen. I try and shuffle away from that horrifying sight, but the palm draws me closer until it is all I can see. Like a hellish snowstorm, the eye watches me scramble. 'Please!' I say, and there is that avalanche sound again, but so much louder. The eye squints as the giant laughs, causing the static storm to dance.

'*Let's go,*' says the voice. '*Enough of this place.*' And the whole world shifts around me.

>•<

There is a lurching sensation, then vertigo. It feels as if I am pulled apart and put back together in a single instant, or perhaps the opposite: that it is everything except me that has been torn up and repaired. Suddenly I am somewhere warm and bright.

The sky is a blinding blue.

Sand. I am standing in sand. I crouch and raise a handful, sifting it through my fingers, and see that there are tiny cogs mingled with the grains. Around me more parts stick up from the sands, and the bulk of the ruined *Metronome* flounders nearby like a beached clockwork whale. I am back on the beach. There is no sign of the giant. Instead, a familiar figure is stood nearby. I frown, standing tall again. 'Thyme?'

He stretches in the sunlight and his chain mail and armour reflect it brilliantly, brought to a mirror shine. His stained tabard is now a fresh creamy white and he even wears a white cloak, gushing majestically across his shoulders. Somehow, he seems taller than before, and his silvery beard and hair have been combed back, revealing a face not pointed and grinning, but encompassed by a benevolent smile so genuine that it is almost enough to make me forget my existential terror for my gladness.

'I thought you'd appreciate a familiar face,' says Thyme. Except this is not Thyme after all. This version of him has the giant's eyes; they are each a static storm. I hold my ground, unsure how to react. Somehow, the giant has made himself small. And maybe it was my conversation with June, but I am reminded of the stories of Hanuman – the trickster monkey god who could change his size at will, and used that power for all manner of clever mischiefs.

'Thyme was your figment, then?' I ask.

The creature who looks like Thyme stands before the brilliant blue sea and seems to be admiring it, or looking around for something. Instead of answering my question he says, 'Ah, there it is,' and raises one hand, as if he is bidding the moon to rise from the horizon. A long length of twisted brass emerges from between the waves, as if tugged on invisible strings. It hangs in the air, dripping and suspended before him.

'Who are you?'

The creature wearing Thyme's face glances back at me, still smiling with a genuine joy that defies the old knight's pointed face. 'There were two brothers,' he says, and he continues talking as he raises his other hand, conjuring pieces of the fallen *Metronome* around in the air as if he is a conductor and they are his orchestra. 'They each owned a modest farm, and were each married to a modest wife, and each had modest children. Every year they struggled by. But both were pious, and worshipped the Lord and His teachings unquestioningly, and in that way, they were happy.

'One day, when they both mounted the hill upon which they had built for themselves a small place of worship, they saw an angel waiting there. The angel was tall, and proud, and had great white wings that seemed to encompass the whole horizon. The angel was also armoured, and battle-scarred, and in one hand he held a broken spear. The two brothers fell to their knees when they saw him, and pressed their hands together in worship.

'"Behold," said the angel. "The Lord has sent me to gift thee both with wealth, for He knows well of thy piety, and wishes to reward it." And standing beside the angel was indeed a heavy-looking chest, which the angel opened to reveal hundreds of gold coins.

'The first brother looked upon the wealth, and said, "This must be a test, surely?"

'And the second brother looked upon the angel, with his battle-worn armour and broken spear, and said, "Are you a tempter, sent to tempt us?"

'And the angel said, "This is no test, and no temptation. This is the generosity of the Lord."

'The first brother stood, bowed and said, "I will not accept this gift, because it must be a test, and I must prove my humility to the Lord." And he turned away, and left the hillside, and the angel, and the chest full of gold.

'Then the second brother stood, and he did not bow, and he said, "I will not accept this gift, because I know of the war in heaven, and I believe that you are one of the fallen, come here to tempt me." He too turned away and left the hillside and the angel and the chest full of gold. When both brothers stopped at the foot of the hill and turned back, the angel was gone and the chest full of gold was gone with him.

'Now, both brothers led good and full and happy lives, but they never prospered. Their farms remained modest, and their families remained modest, and each winter was as much a struggle as the last. And as they both lived, each felt a gnawing of regret. They knew that the gold the angel had offered them would have allowed them to live comfortably for the rest of their days, and even live charitably, able to share their wealth with the less fortunate of the world. Thus ends the tale of the two brothers.'

The air between me and the creature wearing Thyme's face is now full of pieces of the *Metronome*. I watch in awe as the bulk of the wrecked skyship shudders from its resting place and gently falls apart, joining the maelstrom of floating parts, whirling slowly around as if gravity no longer applies to them. I clutch hold of Thyme's sword with both hands.

'Are you telling me that you're an angel?' I ask.

'I'm telling you that you should learn to accept generosity where it is given.'

'Give me a name at least. Something to call you.'

The tangled brass shaft first raised begins to unravel itself as if it is made of string instead of metal. Cogs and coils coalesce around that central piece, unbending and repairing themselves as they do. I am reminded of those books I would read as a child, filled with the cross-sections of various mechanisms.

'Do you know what the word "Satan" means?' asks the creature wearing Thyme's face.

'I know it means "Adversary" in Hebrew.'

'I am a voice of dissent in a universe designed to affirm its creator. As such, you may call me Satan. However, I do have six siblings also named Satan, and if you would like to avoid confusion, then I suggest that you might instead wish to use my title. Solomon and his followers used to call me The Magician because I was the greatest liar they ever met. You may call me The Magician as well, if you like. That name belongs to me and me alone.'

As the *Metronome* begins to come together, reforming in the air before us, I wonder if I really am stood before a piece of God. I wonder if this is one of His nightmares. Perhaps I should be falling to my knees in worship of this absurdly powerful being with his casual God-like powers, just as June would. Instead, I stand my ground and try to avoid the floating pieces of the clockwork skyship as it is repaired.

The creature calling himself The Magician brings his hands together, and so too the skyship comes together. 'Generosity,' he says. 'I will be generous. Your time will come soon. I will see to it that you are well rewarded.' The last pieces of the *Metronome* fall into place, the golden feathers of the phoenix figurehead smoothing themselves over. She looks complete again. With the triumphant flourish of both of his hands, The Magician bids her to tick.

It is such a wonderful sound.

'One more thing...' I say.

The Magician turns to me. 'I do not mean to linger here. Your friends have earned a lot from me, but they have not earned an audience. This privilege is for you alone.'

'Could you remove the storm for them?'

Solomon's Storm rages still in the distance, a great black ring around the sea, brightly flaring where lightning flickers. 'Yes,' says The Magician, still smiling his benevolent smile, and I consider just how genuine that smile really is. Maybe this is some old god of liars. With the wave of his hands, as if he is some parlour magician performing a trick, Solomon's Storm begins to dissipate, revealing an endless blue beyond. 'Fair skies all the way back to the Golden Gate.'

I am still very uncertain about The Magician, but I am glad for Reid and Slint.

'Now,' he says, 'for your reward.'

This time, instead of gesturing at the sea or the *Metronome*, he gestures at me, as if he is casting some conjuration upon me. And the world shifts around me again.

>•<

When I regain my senses I am standing along a cobbled lane.

Before me is the mouth of the Firth of Forth, where it yawns widely and becomes the sea. The buildings around me are tall and close, and the sky seems low, as if at any moment it might rain. I wander along the lane, feeling as if I should abandon the sword I am carrying, because just ahead of me are Leith Docks, and I rather think that the medieval weapon feels a bit out of place this far north of Edinburgh Castle.

Where the lane widens out it becomes clear why everything around me seems so damned familiar, and I feel a welling of excitement within me. Further along the docks, beside a wooden bus stop, a broken-down double-decker bus flounders, grey smoke rising from its exposed engine. Men stand around it, leaning the engine grille against its flank and pressing their hats to their chests as if they are in mourning for the dead vehicle. I was on that bus, barely able to sit still. I remember it breaking down. In fact, I know every detail of this day, close to sixty years ago.

It will rain soon.

Standing at the edge of a jetty, divided from the Firth of Forth by a low chain, stands The Magician. He is still wearing Thyme's pointed face, but instead of armour he has instead donned an ill-fitting brown suit, perhaps one size too large. The Magician beholds the Forth estuary and tugs thoughtfully at his beard.

'How did you…?' I feel breathless with excitement.

'This is your dream,' says The Magician. 'This is my gift to you.'

'But… how…?'

'Sweet dreams for as long as you live. This is your reward.' He turns to me and reaches up to my head. I flinch, startled by the sudden movement, until he reveals that his empty hand is no longer empty. From behind my ear, he has conjured up a small green velvet box, which he holds out to me. 'You're going to need this,' he says. My joyous reaction triggers laughter; his great smile returns.

I give The Magician Thyme's sword, and in return I accept the green box.

'You should get going,' he says, holding the dull blade at his side. 'She's waiting for you.'

I want to run, like I did that day. I want to go and relive every moment of what happens next. I clutch tightly at the small green box, and remember how I held it so tightly that the lid cracked at the corner. I step from foot to foot, ready to dash back up the cobbled lane and through the streets of Leith. But I hesitate.

'What will you do,' I ask The Magician, 'now that you're free?'

'Oh,' he says. 'I need to resume the work that Solomon interrupted. It has been a long time, and I have a lot to do. But don't worry about me. Go on. Go to her. You've earned this.' He nods at the cobbled lane, and the static storm in both of his eyes flickers madly. It is enough to send me on my way.

Helplessly grinning from ear to ear, I hasten back across the road, and up to the first tall buildings there.

At the point where I will lose sight of The Magician, I stop and turn to see him one last time. He has his back to me, observing the river. He brings Thyme's sword up before himself, and in the same manner as a street magician, flicks it through the air, causing it to transform miraculously. Instead of a sword, he now holds a long wooden flute, which he brings up to his mouth.

I hear the song he plays. It is the fourth from the sequence that led us to Solomon's Eye. A pretty, dancing piece, with enough rhythm to make even the most stalwart tap their foot along.

I rush through Leith, running with all the flightiness and swiftness that I can muster, pushed along by my joy. Strangers move aside to let me through, shouting at me to slow down, and friends laugh to see me, so red-faced and determined, and they call at me to run faster, because they know what this day means. Uphill I go, until the lanes become streets and the crowds get thicker. The beating of my heart in my ears is almost enough to drown out the song. But still the song persists, impossibly through Edinburgh, following me. No matter how far from Leith Docks I run, I can still hear The Magician's flute.

At last I reach my destination. Leading off from a highway at the very south end of Leith, where it very well may just be central Edinburgh, is a small side-street. At its entrance I wait for a moment, listening to The Magician's music. The song is long and jolly, and it drifts through Edinburgh and my thoughts, causing me one last moment of doubt. I reach for March's compass, where it is still wrapped up in my pocket. But I change my mind. I know what waits ahead of me, and I will not miss it. I will return March's compass another night. And with that thought, I carry on, catching my breath and strolling down the street.

It begins to rain, at last.

At the end of the street, two storeys up, I can see that Lily has opened the windows of our new living room wide. White curtains billow in the winds as they pick up, and the first of the rains patter against the glass. As I approach the song slowly changes. Instead of a flute, it is being sung, drifting out from that open window. My steps become shorter as I listen, entranced – until the flute is gone altogether, and there is only Lily's voice, singing the song wordlessly as she paints our living room white.

I use my new key to open the stairwell and head up, taking my time now – enjoying Lily's song. Quietly, I open the front door to our flat, and close it behind myself, doing my best not to interrupt her. I slip through the hallway, shaking the rain from my hair, and feeling just as nervous as I did back then, fumbling clumsily at the green box between my fingers as if it is a puzzle I am unable to solve.

Then I see her. She is halfway up a stepladder, wearing overalls coated with just as much paint as the walls, and her hands and fingers, and the brush she is holding, are all white as well. I admire her for as long as it takes her to notice me. When she does, her song fades, and she smiles her sly slip of a smile for me. She steps down from the ladder – perhaps sensing my nerves, wondering what it is that has me so excited.

Strange, how difficult it can be simply to kneel at a time like this, as if I have forgotten how to operate my legs, but somehow I manage. On one knee, I raise the green box and open it towards her, feeling so overwhelmed by nerves and love and joy that I forget that I am dreaming. I forget that this has happened before. I forget everything except for the moment – the wonderful, beautiful, moment – and I live it again.

The dream is long and sweet, and it lasts for as long as it lasts.

ACKNOWLEDGEMENTS

The Author would like to thank:

Rob Dinsdale

Alanah Knibb

George Sandison

Gary Budden

THE ARRIVAL OF MISSIVES

BY ALIYA WHITELEY

From Aliya Whiteley, author of the critically-acclaimed *The Beauty*, comes a genre-defying story of fate, free-will and the choices we make in life.

In the aftermath of the Great War, Shirley Fearn dreams of challenging the conventions of rural England, where life is as predictable as the changing of the seasons.

The scarred veteran Mr. Tiller, left disfigured by an impossible accident on the battlefields of France, brings with him a message: part prophecy, part warning. Will it prevent her mastering her own destiny?

Get a free extract
www.unsungstories.co.uk/trymissives

OR SCAN THE QR CODE

Follow Aliya @AliyaWhiteley

DARK STAR

BY OLIVER LANGMEAD

The city of Vox survives in darkness, under a sun that burns without light. In Vox's permanent night, light bulbs are precious, the rich live in radiance and three Hearts beat light into the city. Aquila. Corvus. Cancer.

Hearts that bring power to the light-deprived citizens of the city of Vox whilst ghosts haunt the streets, clawing at headlights. Prometheus, liquid light, is the drug of choice. The body of young Vivian North, her blood shining brightly with unnatural light, has no place on the streets.

When Cancer is stolen, the weaponisation of its raw power threatens to throw Vox into chaos. Vox needs a hero, and it falls to cop Virgil Yorke to investigate.

But Virgil has had a long cycle and he doesn't feel like a hero. With the ghosts of his last case still haunting his thoughts, he craves justice for the young woman found dead with veins full of glowing. Aided by his partner Dante, Virgil begins to shed light on the dark city's even darker secrets.

Haunted by the ghosts of his past and chased by his addictions, which will crack first, Virgil or the case?

Get a free extract

www.unsungstories.co.uk/trydarkstar

www.oliverlangmead.com

OR SCAN THE QR CODE

THE BEAUTY

BY ALIYA WHITELEY

☆ **2014 SHIRLEY JACKSON AWARD NOMINEE**
☆ **2014 TIPTREE AWARD – HONORS LIST**
☆ **SABOTEUR AWARDS 2015 NOMINEE**

A book for the brave, *The Beauty* is a post-apocalyptic tale straight out of the New Weird.

Somewhere away from the cities and towns, a group of men and boys gather around the fire each night to listen to their stories in the Valley of the Rocks. For when the women are all gone the rest of your life is all there is for everyone. The men are waiting to pass into the night.

Hear the tales, watch a myth be formed. For what can man hope to achieve in a world without women? When the past is only grief how long should you hold on to it? What secrets can the forest offer to change it all?

Discover the Beauty.

Get a free extract
www.unsungstories.co.uk/trybeauty

OR SCAN THE QR CODE

Follow Aliya 🐦 @AliyaWhiteley